ANNO DOMINI

ANNO DOMINI

BY

JOHN OXENHAM

Author of "The Hidden Years," "The Splendour of the Dawn," etc.

"And so let Thy glory, Almighty, impart,
Through Christ in the story, Thy Christ to the heart."
W. Chalmers Smith

WIPF & STOCK · Eugene, Oregon

Resource Publications
A division of Wipf and Stock Publishers
199 W 8th Ave, Suite 3
Eugene, OR 97401

Anno Domini
By Oxenham, John
Softcover ISBN-13: 978-1-7252-9684-8
Hardcover ISBN-13: 978-1-7252-9683-1
eBook ISBN-13: 978-1-7252-9685-5
Publication date 1/7/2021
Previously published by Longmans, Green and Co., 1932

This edition is a scanned facsimile of
the original edition published in 1932.

IN
REMEMBRANCE
OF
HIM
WHOM WE SO CONSTANTLY
FORGET

FOREWORD

THE four Gospel narratives—written between thirty and sixty years after the events of which they tell—give us four unique presentations of The Master's life from four different angles.

As evidence from four different men of facts of which they were, for the most part, actual eye-witnesses, they are invaluable. But to gather from them a plain, connected story of The Master's life is beyond the power of any ordinary man.

Many eminent scholars have devoted years of intensive study to the endeavour to reconstruct that story of The Greatest Adventure of All Time—the story of the most wonderful life ever lived on earth—that epochal life which, in its effects, changed, and is still changing, the whole outlook of mankind—and which, in its ultimate realisation will, in God's good time, redeem man from himself—to Himself.

I make no pretence to such scholarship. Building on wiser men's foundations, I have endeavoured to tell, as simply and clearly as possible, that great story as seen through the eyes of a keen intelligent young follower, whose life, saved by The Master at the very beginning of his ministry, was thenceforward dedicated to his personal service.

He lived with The Master and his chosen ones in terms of most intimate fellowship. He saw and heard most of what happened during those strenuous months and immediately afterwards. In his own convincing way he tells all that he saw and heard.

In studying that life for the purposes of this book, it has unfolded itself to me more clearly and more helpfully than ever before. If it does the same for others it will have done its duty and fulfilled my highest hope.

The correct sequence of the three books is *The Hidden Years—Anno Domini—The Splendour of the Dawn*. *The Splendour of the Dawn* came out of its proper place through the urgent request of a number of American papers for a story dealing with Pentecost, special celebrations of which were being held in 1930. And as that request represented the wishes of one and a quarter million readers in America and Canada, I felt bound to comply with it.

But to get a full and comprehensive story of The Master's life, from boyhood to the end, the books should be taken in the above order.

CONTENTS

BOOK I—THE MASTER

BOOK II—THE CITY

x

BOOK V—THE CROWNING WONDER

ᴬNNO ᴰOMINI

BOOK I — THE MASTER

CHAPTER I

I, THE WRITER of this, am Esli, the son of Maath-ben-Jessai, the net-maker and mender, of Bethsaida on the great lake. And my desire in writing it is to show to you who may never have known him in the flesh, what manner of man was the Great Teacher, Jesus-ben-Joseph, whom some of us with all our hearts believe to be The Christ.

For it was my great, though wholly undeserved, happiness to have known him well. During the short course of his ministry I accompanied him on most of his journeyings. I was with him on the last fateful journey to Jerusalem — and after. What I here set down is, for the most part, what I myself have seen.

I HAD, I suppose, as miserable a childhood as any boy in this world ever had. And the reason for that was that I was, from the day of my birth, possessed of a devil.

My parents were nearing middle age when I came to them. And the devil which was born in me was in such a state of fury at being brought into the world that it cost my mother her life.

A bad beginning ! — for my father never forgot it, nor ceased to impute to me the loss of one whom he had held

A   [1]

very dear, and whose going left his life broken and desolate.

And truly it was a poor exchange — a good wife, as even all the neighbours acknowledged, for a noisy, squalling baby-boy undoubtedly possessed of a devil.

Of my very early years I, of course, remember little — except that they were drearily unhappy. Not one single recollection have I of any bright or comforting thing in them — until little Ruth came.

The first thing I recall at all clearly is of being, for some reason which I do not remember — or quite possibly for no reason at all — in so furious a rage that I wound about my small neck a piece of cord so tightly that I was, they have since told me, black in the face and at the point of death, before a knife could be got below the string.

Many times in the years that followed I wondered if it had not been better for me and for them if the knife had been awanting. Now, I am glad to believe that I was saved for better things.

I have no recollection whatever of any child friendships, though certain names remain in my mind, and many of the men and women I know now must have been my companions in those days.

Companions, do I say ? Well, as you will see, there was not much companionship possible between them and me. And the fault and the loss were entirely mine, though the fault was due to something beyond my control.

From the day I was born I was subject at times to fits of blind, senseless fury which knew no bounds, and as often as not seemed entirely causeless. The neighbours tersely condemned and executed me with, "He has a devil," and that seemed the simple truth.

For I was not naturally, or of my own will, malevolent. The loneliness that was like a blight about me distressed me terribly. Had I been an actual leper I could hardly have been more shunned.

Yet, all the time — save when the devil in me roused himself and would out — I craved companions and friendship as much as any. And these being denied me by the devil within me, he rejoiced greatly and waxed fat by gnawing at my sick heart.

Even as a very small child, being shut out from human companionship, I sought and found some relief from my solitariness among the things of Nature, which bore me no malice for those outbreaks for which I was not responsible. Indeed, among them I found no provocations; they soothed and calmed and never failed me when I fled to them for comfort and help.

All animals were dear to me, especially the small and weak and despised ones. I had a fellow-feeling for them, and they did not fear or scorn me.

I never wilfully hurt bird or beast — except once, about which I will tell in its proper place. And all the trees and flowers and growing things of our beautiful plain between the hills and the lake were my friends. And very helpful also were the hills and the lake.

At school, as far as learning was concerned, I did well. For whatever the power that possessed me might be, it really was a power. And one of the ways in which it manifested itself was in making me keen and clear in my mind and strong in my body.

I have wondered sometimes if it may not in very fact have been moulding and fitting me for some grim purpose of its own, and therefore made me strong in mind and body, in order to be its fit instrument for whatever that purpose might be.

It is difficult to reason the matter out, or to arrive at any comprehension of it. For if I could but have overcome these tempests of rage which suffered no obstacle to stand before them, I might have done as well as any and better than most. But those terrible outbreaks put a blight upon me and set me without the pale of ordinary life.

At school, the old teacher, who drilled into us the Law and the Prophets and taught us to read and write, would have been proud of me as a scholar but that he never knew when

I might break out, and he feared me as much as my fellows did.

I must have been very small indeed the first time he tried to punish me — but it was also the last time. For the devil inside me boiled furiously, and broke out, and I flew at him like a little wild beast, and beat and bit and tore till some of the bigger boys dragged me off.

He would not have me back in the class until I had said I was sorry and promised to behave better in future. I had no hesitation about both matters, for I had not known what I was doing. But thereafter he went very warily with me and always regarded me with apprehension, as did all the others.

I have another similar recollection, but it must have been some years later, for the whole matter and my own feelings are sharp and clear in my mind even yet.

This time it was my father. For some probably very good reason, he was beating me relentlessly with a stick. I think he must have made up his mind to beat the devil out of me. I think now that he ought to have known that you cannot beat devils out, you only beat them deeper in.

I remember, as I struggled in his grasp, how everything inside my head suddenly darkened into a wild confusion — thunders and lightnings and roaring whirlwinds. A blinding red mist fell over my eyes. When I succeeded in tearing loose from him, I saw nothing through that red mist but his figure dim in front of me. I had only one desire in life at that moment, and that was to smash him into pieces. I felt that same mad desire many times afterwards, so I know just how I felt then.

I put down my small head, and with every bit of the devil that was in me, I hurled myself, through the darkness, into my father's bulky body. From the nature of his occupation he was ponderous and slow. He doubled up under the thrust of me like a door-post under a battering-ram. And I disentangled myself from his fallen body and rushed blindly away into the hills.

[4]

I recall the feeling of fierce exultation that possessed me as he went down and lay still. — An overwhelming desire fulfilled to the fullest ! Therein, if the desire be a lofty one, is happiness. In this case, and for the moment, it was the intensest satisfaction life had, up till then, afforded me.

It might well have killed him. As it was, it was some days before he could get back to his work. And often thereafter I saw him fingering his big stick with desire in his eyes as he looked at me. But he never tried to beat the devil out of me again.

CHAPTER II

SUCH being my case, it cannot be wondered at that I had no companions and was thrown entirely back upon myself, and it was not good for me.

I became, I suppose, unnaturally suspicious of words and looks, and altogether too prone to believe the others were ridiculing me. And so, at times, and one never knew when, the whirlings and thunderings and lightnings would turn my brain into a stormy chaos, and I would hurl myself blindly on the transgressors, caring nothing for the consequences to them and still less to myself.

And when the storm had spent itself and me, I was always as sorry as the schoolmaster had made me say I was. For, in very truth, when the storm inside me broke loose like that, I remembered nothing of what I did.

At times, when I came to my right mind again, I would find myself lying face down on the ground, with my fingers ragged and bleeding, and my mouth full of the earth that I had torn and bitten in my frenzy. And at other times I would find myself up in the hills with no knowledge of how I got there.

It was after an outbreak such as that, that I, the utterly friendless, found a friend in one more lonely and outcast than myself.

As I came slowly back out of the storm and darkness of my passion, on that occasion, I became conscious of something unusual and strangely soothing happening to me. And when I lifted my head, my heavy eyes looked into the pathetic brown eyes of a dog which was patiently licking the blood off my hands.

[6]

When I raised my head he stopped and looked wistfully at me for a moment, and then ran off with his tail between his legs, as though he knew that he had been taking liberties.

I called to him and he only ran the faster. But his action had been kindly, and there seemed to me to be more friendliness and fellow-feeling in his frightened brown eyes and shaggy face than I was in the habit of seeing in the faces of my fellows.

Dogs were greatly despised among us. One could hardly offer a man a greater insult than to call him a dog. I had never dared even to think of possessing a dog, but I had always had a feeling for them — a fellow-feeling, because of their forlornness and outcastry and the something that looked out of their eyes. And that dog's patient, appealing face, meeting mine as I came back out of the shadows, was impressed firmly in my mind. I was sure I would know him if I met him again and I felt kindly towards him.

The very next day, as I was going along to the school, I heard a tumult down by the waterside, and saw a little mob of my school-mates evidently bent on some exciting mischief. Then I heard a yelp of pain, and remembering my dog-friend of yesterday, and sure that they were tormenting some poor beast, as they delighted to do, I gave one great bellow of rage and rushed down at them. They fled like sparrows, for none ever willingly faced me when the devil was uppermost in me. And from the shore I saw that they had tied a dog to a heavy piece of wood and pushed it out into the lake and had been stoning it.

The poor beast was struggling hard to get loose, but the knots were well tied, and it came nigh to strangling in its frantic efforts.

I waded out up to my neck and then had to swim, and so managed to reach it. I drew it in and loosed its bonds, but I had to carry it ashore in my arms. And as I did so, spent as it was, it tried to lift its head and lick me.

That settled it. That dog was mine, cost me what it

might. As I came up out of the water, two men stood on the shore watching me.

I knew them because they were often seeing my father about their nets — mending the old or buying new ones. Our little house stood a short way back from the shore of the lake, about halfway between Bethsaida and Kaphar-Nahum, and they had to pass it each time they took their fish into the town.

The brown-faced, bearded one was Simon, and the other was Andrew, and they were the sons of Jona, the old fisherman of Bethsaida. They worked in company with James and John, the sons of Zabdai, and had several boats and were said to be doing well.

As with most others who came to the house, I had had very little to do with them. But I had always liked the looks of these two, even though they held aloof from me like the rest.

But now, as I came ashore, panting with my swim and the excitement of it all, Simon said, "Why, it's Esli, old Maath's boy." And then to me — "What have you got there, Esli ?"

"A dog," I said curtly, half ashamed, and so putting on a bold front as I held him up with the water dripping out of him.

"A dog ! We thought it must be a child. Why risk your life for a dog ? One more or less wouldn't matter."

"They'd tied him to that log and were stoning him. I couldn't stand that. Besides, he's a friend of mine."

"A friend !" and they both laughed out and looked at me with curiosity.

"Yesterday, when my devil had thrown me down, and I was covered with blood, he came and licked my hands," I said sturdily.

"He was hungry, I expect. They are always hungry," said Andrew. "Tell your father we lost half our nets in that squall last night and we'll come round tonight for some new ones."

"I'll tell him," and as they went on towards Kaphar-

Nahum I sat down on the shore and squeezed the water out of the dog and stroked him gently. At first he was frightened and kept looking up at me with quick white gleams from the corners of his eyes. But soon he lay quiet and tried to lick my hand when it came within reach of his clean pink tongue.

I had never been so friendly with a dog before, nor, I suppose, had he with a boy, and we both seemed to like it. It was a new and pleasant feeling to me to have someone who did not look askance at me, and who even seemed to like me a little. And it was certainly new for him to be so near to a boy and not to be kicked or stoned by him.

I had been sure, when I swam out to him and could see his face, that he was the dog that licked my hands the day before. He had been almost mad with terror as the stones whistled about him and he unable to dodge them, but I knew him and I was glad that it was he.

I believe he knew me too; anyway I chose to believe it, and when we had got dry in the sun I took him home to do battle for him with my father.

He, when we went in, glowered blackly at us both, and I glowered back at him, ready, as he well saw, to break out into a fury if he said me nay.

I gave the dog half my dinner which he ate ravenously, and thereafter I always shared my portion with him and felt all the better for it.

I had much difficulty in settling his name, for until he had one our comradeship could not be quite complete.

I thought of Esau, because he was hairy; and Sim, because he was obedient; and Job, because he had been persecuted; but finally decided on Zeke, which very soon became Zick, because he was certainly a great help and comfort to me, and the name seemed to fit him.

I had to stand a great deal on his account — scorn from the neighbours, derision from my school-mates, the disgust of my father. But none of them ventured to express these things to my face lest I should do my best to make an end

[9]

of them, and the only effect of this universal condemnation was to drive Zick and myself into still closer fellowship. Fellow-sufferers, we were very close friends. He was a dog, and I had a devil, and nobody wanted either of us.

The change wrought in Zick by my adoption of him was very marked. For, whereas he used to slink along with his tail between his legs, and apprehension in every hair of him, now he carried his tail on high like the plume of a soldier, and he bristled with pride when other dogs approached him. With the result that he dared not go out alone lest the others should unite to fall upon him and reduce him to less even than themselves.

But in the house, when my father was there, he made himself as small as possible and crept about very quietly. For to my father he was an object of extremest disgust, and a symbol of my defiance and his own impotence to control us.

Maybe this was all very wrong on my part, but, looking back now on all the circumstances and my peculiar position, I cannot feel it so. Zick's love and faithful companionship did great things for me in those days.

I had at last someone to care for, someone who cared for me — one who looked into my eyes without fear or scorn but with deepest love and longing and understanding. Life became more bearable for me, and the devil in me was quieter than ever he had been since I could remember.

It seems to me now that I had never known any happiness until Zick came. He gave me everything I had hitherto lacked, and never one ill-thought passed between us.

We spent days, and sometimes nights, up in the hills. We tramped along the shore, splashing joyously through the shallow streams, and once went right to the head of the lake and forded the Jordan itself.

In the hot summer weather we were in the lake in the sunlight and the moonlight; though Zick, remembering how near he had come to death in it, was at first not very willing to go into the water. But when I went in and stopped there, and he, after running to and fro on the shore for half a morning, barking and whining at me, at last ventured in also, he found it so much to his liking that he would hardly come out again.

Life was better to us both than it ever had been. And then it became still better — when little Ruth came.

CHAPTER III

Now THE coming of Ruth was in this wise.

My father got word by a traveller from the north that his sister had died up in Dan of Naphtali.

She was the widow of one, Joseph-ben-Er, who had done business in timber, and had been reputed to be well off. And as my father was her nearest kin, he thought it advisable to go up there and see how things stood, though he loathed the thought of the journey.

He arranged with a reluctant neighbour to keep an eye on me, and went off on a quiet old ass belonging to Jorim, the inn-keeper, promising to pay him out of the fortune that was waiting for him in Dan.

He was gone for nearly two months, and Zick and I enjoyed them exceedingly. The neighbour provided us with our meals, or the wherewithal to make them for ourselves, and we wandered far and wide — in the loneliest places we could find — round the head of the lake towards the gloomy mountains on the eastern side, and following our own little rivers up to their sources in the hills behind our plain.

For days at a time we scarcely spoke to a soul, and life went quietly and happily with us. I began to hope that my devil was dead. But there was nothing at the moment to provoke him and so he lay quiet.

Then when we came lingeringly back in the sunset one evening, happily tired and hungry, there was my father come home again, and he had brought with him a stranger woman and a girl. The woman was preparing food. The girl sat watching her, and I stood looking at them and wondering who they could be.

They had evidently been told all about me, and in none too favourable a fashion, for they both eyed me apprehensively, as though expecting me to break out into violence at any moment.

"This is my wife, Leah, and her daughter Ruth," said my father briefly.

The woman looked up for a moment from the meal she was preparing. She regarded me coldly, and Zick, at my heels, more coldly still.

The girl, sitting on her feet near the fire, looked up at us timidly and shyly, and then sat gazing into the fire again.

I was so taken aback by this unexpected enlargement of the family that I could only stare at them all in silence, which no doubt they took for ill-temper.

I sat down in a corner, with Zick under my arm for safety, and stared and wondered.

Leah, I decided on the spot, I did not like. She was heavy-faced and tight-lipped, and looked as if she had never smiled in her life.

Ruth was small and slight, and there was nothing about her that made me want to look at her again. But, presently, she turned her head and looked at Zick and me as though she had been making up her mind about us and wanted to see if her ideas were right. I saw then that her face was white and thin and that her eyes were large and dark.

I do not know if she made any sign or sound to Zick. If she did, I did not catch it. But, to my great astonishment, he slipped quietly from under my arm, and crept close along the wall to where she sat, and pushed his nose under her thin arm. Her other hand stole to his head and caressed it, and her little white face suddenly lit up with a smile that made me think how pretty she was, and I wondered how I could ever have thought her anything else.

I wished she would smile like that at me; and, as though she had felt my wish, she looked straight at me and I thought there surely could not be a sweeter little face in the world.

Leah was evidently a good cook, for I had not tasted any-

[13]

thing so good in all my life, and I could have done with more than she gave me. But I shared, as always, with Zick, and Ruth gave him some bits as well.

When her mother noticed that, she looked as though she were about to say something unpleasant. But a word from my father checked her, and she tightened her lips still more and said nothing — which was just as well. I disliked her being there, and it would have needed no more than a show of bad-feeling towards Zick to make me flare up, which I would have been sorry to do, that very first night, before little Ruth.

But I went to bed in a gloomy state of mind and lay long awake, for I did not think it possible to live peaceably with a woman as sour-faced and thin-lipped as Leah. And I thought of Ruth's face when she smiled, and wondered how such a sweet little flower could have grown on such a thorny bush.

I was up very early next morning, but Leah and Ruth were up before me — Leah sweeping and clearing away the results of two months' neglect, and making the house as I had never seen it in my life before.

Ruth was sitting on a mat outside, watching the lake and all its wonderful colours, as the sunlight streamed in long white shafts through the clefts in the eastern hills.

Zick ran up to her at once and she showed herself very friendly with him. As I stood beside them she looked up shyly and said, "It's the first time I've ever made friends with a dog in all my life," and her voice was like herself, small and sweet.

"He's more than just a dog," I said sturdily, "he's the best friend I have, and the only one."

She seemed about to say something but did not.

"Come along down to the water," I suggested. And at that she looked up at me quickly, and her face went all red and had a queer look on it.

"Don't you know?" she said, almost sharply. And then, seeing by my puzzled face that I did not know, she said, in a strange, quiet little voice, "I can't walk . . . I have never walked a step in my life."

And I sat down very suddenly in front of her and stared at her in amazement, while Zick licked her little hand sympathetically, as though he knew something was not as it should be.

"Never walked ?" I gasped. "But why ?"

"I was born so," she said quietly. "It's my ankles. They are wrong and won't bear me."

"But that's terrible for you," I said at last, dimly wondering how I would feel if I had never walked a step in my life.

"I am used to it now, but . . . oh, how I wish sometimes that I could walk, even if it was but a step or two. You are very strong, aren't you ?"

"Yes, I am strong . . . but" — some feeling that telling her of my own weakness might lessen her regret for her own, made me add — "I have a devil and sometimes he's too strong for me."

"I know. Your father told us about him. It must be strange to have a devil," and she looked at me inquisitively, as though she might even catch sight of him.

"It's only at times that he breaks out," I said, so that she should not be frightened — "when people make me angry. Then I don't know what I'm doing."

"I hope I'll never make you angry."

"You couldn't. You're so small and weak. And you're good. It's big bad things that stir up my devil and make him want to smash them."

"I think he must be rather a good devil," she said cheeringly.

"No one else thinks so. Everybody's frightened of me."

"I'm not. I like you — and Zick. I'm glad we've come."

That was little Ruth, and her coming made a great difference in my life.

CHAPTER IV

As to how it came that Ruth and her mother were there, I may as well set down here what I learned only bit by bit later on.

My father's sister up in Dan had been left quite well off when her husband died, and Leah had lived with her and helped her in the house ever since. When my aunt died she left half of all she had to Leah and half to my father. Both would have liked the whole, and sooner than divide it they decided to marry. Neither of them had ever had much, and this sudden and unexpected acquisition awoke in them the desire for more. They both became rather close and saving in all their ways so that they might add coin to coin, simply for the pleasure of seeing them multiply.

We ourselves had always lived very simply, plainest of faring but sufficient. The coming of Leah and Ruth made no difference in that matter, save that Leah was such an excellent cook that she made a little go a long way. She was a very thrifty housekeeper and looked twice at every coin before she spent it, and then saw that she got fullest value for it.

Up there in Dan, Ruth had made baskets and mats. She was skilful with her fingers, and my father very soon had her at work on his nets, making and mending. And she loved it, sitting there in the sun with the lake gleaming and glimmering in front of her.

To me she was a joy which I could not have explained at that time, though I understand it better now. To the others she was just saved from being an encumbrance by the fact that her skilful fingers were a source of profit.

I gathered from her that she had always been a disappointment to her mother from the day she was born.

Leah, like all other women, had ardently desired a son, and the coming of a daughter, and a crippled one, had been a blow which she could not get over. The poor girl's terrible affliction, which might have moved any heart, she seemed to look upon as a personal reproach to herself. She did just what was absolutely necessary for her, and that in her hard forbidding way. The little extra which would have made all the difference to both their lives, she left undone. That Ruth was not embittered by her neglect speaks much for the sweetness of her nature.

But Ruth's coming made all the difference to us two. Both of us had, through our circumstances, been set rather apart from other people. Now that we had come together each of us seemed to supply just what the other had needed.

The time had long passed when I ought to have gone to Jerusalem with my father for the Passover Feast. He had always made a point of going. He disliked the travelling, but enjoyed the change and the meetings with old friends.

Leah had never been — or at all events not for many years. Dan was a very long journey from Jerusalem, and besides, she was a native of the Lebanon and fuller of superstition than of religious observance.

For myself I had no desire to go, and my father feared to take me. Among the crowds and bustle of the great city, my devil might find many causes of provocation and there was no knowing what might happen.

Besides, I would have had to leave Zick at home and he would undoubtedly have been killed, for Ruth could not look after him, and Leah would have rejoiced in his death.

I can remember only one or two outbreaks about this time. Not that my devil was dead or had gone out of me, but simply that people had learned that it was better, for them and for me, that I should be left to myself. And so I suffered no molestation, and little Ruth more than made up for the aloofness of the rest.

B   [17]

I had learned all the old teacher at the school could teach me. That strange force, whatever it was, that filled me at times and made me fierce and powerful beyond my years and my nature, made me, as I have said, strong both in mind and body. The trouble was that it was too big for my body, and so it boiled over when provoked and came out in those blind fits of fury which estranged me from my kind.

You must not suppose that I yielded willingly to the evil thing that held me in thrall. I hated both it and myself after every outbreak. I did my best to keep control of myself. But when the time and the provocation came I could no more hold myself in than I could stop breathing and still live.

No one understood this, nor would if I had tried to tell them. No one believed me anything but evil-possessed and exulting therein. No one except little Ruth.

She was surely sent by God to help me through those evil times. For no small part of my torment of mind was the fact that I really craved companionship, and was very much the worse for being feared and held at arm's-length by everyone, and so being driven in upon myself where my only company was that spirit of evil.

Zick had helped me greatly, Ruth helped me still more. She never feared me, and I would have drowned myself in the lake sooner than harm her in any smallest way. She was one of the helpless and needy things that drew my heart.

She had never seen me in one of my fits of madness; for, so far, nothing had occurred to upset me while I was with her, and her very presence always had a soothing effect on me.

Indeed, I know now that she believed the stories of my evil-possession were just idle tales which had grown with the years, and that I was not really much different from others, except that I was unusually strong and active and keen-witted, and full of some restless spirit which made me always want to be up and doing.

She envied me these things, and more than once said she

wished she also had a devil and a pair of ankles that would carry her.

I did my best for her, for she and Zick were the dearest things in my heart and life.

She loved to sit outside doing her nets, with the lake spread wide before her. But, day after day, and week after week of the same thing grew wearisome to her at times. And when I saw that in her, and how she was feeling it, I would lift her in my arms and carry her away up the hill. She was pitifully light, and when she knitted her hands behind my neck, I could carry her a long way. And always when she found herself moving like that, the smiles would break out on her face and she would say, "It is good to walk about, even though it is on somebody else's feet," and then she would be her own bright self again.

With short rests now and again I could get her far up the hillside, and there I would seek out a proper place and she would sit in great content, gazing out over the whole lake and following with longing eyes the sails of the boats as they flitted to and fro.

And more than once she said, with a sigh of longing, "How I wish I could fly about like that! They have wings and I have not even legs to walk with. Why do you think God made me like this, Esli?"

"I do not know, Ruth. But then there is so much that we don't know. Why have I got a devil?"

"I don't believe you have one. I've never seen him."

"I hope you never will. I think you help me to keep him in."

"Do you really think so? Then I'm glad. I'd sooner help you with your devil than have feet to walk with."

"And if I could make you whole, Ruth, I would give half the strength I have."

More than once we saw the shining lake suddenly overcast, and black whirling storms would come tearing across it from the North, where the river came in, or down the deep clefts of the mountains on the other side.

Her wish to go sailing prompted me to the making of a boat for her.

For thirty days I worked hard, fetching and carrying for one, Jonathan-bar-Jona, in Kaphar-Nahum, who made boats, and I watched keenly all that went on.

He happened to be very busy, and so was glad of even such assistance as I could give. He offered me a regular job at a small wage, but at the moment that was not my object. And though I had been able, with that object in view, to keep myself under control, it had been a fight at times, because of Zick being with me, and I could not have stood it much longer. My father was so accustomed to my fitful ways — to my disappearing for days at a time when the black mood came on me — and so loth to interfere with me, that he asked no questions as to what I was doing, quite satisfied at getting no ill tidings.

Ruth, however, was full of curiosity, and when we were alone she tried in every girlish way to beguile my secret out of me. But to it all I said,

"Just you wait. It's a surprise, and if I tell you now it won't be," and then she would begin on a new tack, but I was proof against her. From the boat-builder I got a few planks and some nails and the other small things I needed. And there, in his yard, I put together something resembling a boat, though more than once it came near to an end before it was finished, by reason of the laughter it provoked, and the ill effect that had on me.

But I thought of Ruth and managed to go stolidly on. And I thought often of the ancient Noah, whose boat-building also provoked the scoffers.

I remember every detail of that curious boat, but there is no need to set it all down here. It was made of two good planks about a cubit in width, nailed to a flat bottom which was the shape of a boat. I caulked it well and painted it white, and when it was dry it carried me buoyantly enough and let in no water. But because of its flat bottom it would only be able to sail in very limited directions.

By the advice of the master I added something like a keel to it. I made also two oars and a rudder and a mast, but the sail was to be made by Ruth herself.

The boat-men prophesied an early death for me, and Jonathan warned me to keep a very open eye for sudden storms, as my boat might be good enough for fair weather but would certainly not stand rough.

And I was glad indeed when the time came that I got cautiously into my boat — with Zick sitting up in the hinder part, very doubtful and not at all happy — and pulled away along the shore, away from the cheers, which sounded to me like jeers, of the boat-builders.

I saw Ruth sitting at her netting, and when I drew near, I shouted and waved to her, and saw her gazing at me and the odd little boat, stiff with amazement.

Then I went ashore, and ran up to her, and picked her up and carried her down into the boat and rowed out onto the lake.

"Esli!" she gasped. "Where did you get it?"

"I made it all myself all for you."

She clasped her little hands and cried,

"Oh, it is beautiful, beautiful . . . I have so wanted to sail on the lake. . . How good you are to me, Esli!"

"The sail I've left for you to make, but it will only need to be a small one. Then we can really go sailing."

"It is beautiful, beautiful," she said again, and let her hands trail happily in the water on each side of her.

And presently she said musingly,

"If I'd had feet like other girls you might never have made this little boat for me."

"I might not," I said, "but you are not like any other girl. And if you'd had feet you would have been like them, and you'd have scoffed at me and feared me." But she only shook her head and smiled at me in a way that somehow did me good.

After that, we three spent many happy hours on the lake. That was, indeed, the happiest part of my life up to that time, and I never can be thankful enough for the coming of Ruth.

In her company I was always tranquil — my true self, and when we were together, the aloofness of others, and the fear and disapproval in which they held me, troubled me not at all.

Sometimes we caught a fish or two with the hook, and that commended itself to Leah, since it contributed to our living without costing anything. For the saving disposition grew steadily both in her and in my father.

CHAPTER V

THE TIME came at last for me to begin earning something to pay for my living. The difficulty was to find anyone willing to employ me.

I had helped Ruth and my father with the nets now and again, but it was too slow and inactive an occupation for me ever to settle down to. After an hour or two of it at a time, the unquiet spirit inside me would chafe at the restraint till it came near to breaking out. Then I would rush down to the lake and swim far out, or make for the hills with Zick, and climb till even the unquiet one was tired out.

It must have been about this time that Leah tried her hand at getting rid of my evil spirit.

I woke one morning in my little room, feeling sick and heavy, and found it full of a most evil smell which came nigh to choking me and had made Zick very sick. And under the bed I found a small dish which was giving off a thick smoke full of that evil odour.

I pulled it out and kicked it out of doors, and wondered who put it there and why. And then I raged so furiously that even Ruth was frightened, though it was not against her.

And when her mother acknowledged that it was her doing — the burning of the heart and liver of a fish with dried herbs being the accepted method of driving out devils among her people — I vowed I would tear her in pieces if ever she tried any of her spells on me again. And I had to have a very long swim in the lake that morning before I could get rid of that deadly smell and the fury it had roused in me.

I tried digging for a neighbour who had a fruit and herb

[23]

garden, and was getting too old to do the hard work himself. But when the digging was done, the regular daily work and the long slow waiting for the harvest did not suffice me.

Simon of Bethsaida offered to try me in his boat at the fishing. I stood it for a month and so came to know his brother Andrew, and James and John-ben-Zabdai who were his partners. And I liked them all, for they were good upright men, and their quiet talks in the boat among themselves were at times of deep and high matters though they were rather beyond me.

But the long slow hours of waiting in the dark were very irksome to me, and often I came near to jumping up and shouting aloud, or leaping into the water, just to break the spell that seemed to grow tighter and tighter about me every minute, and made the restless one within me rage and boil.

Between times I used to take Ruth out in the boat, for its smooth gliding movement without any exertion was like a new sense to her and was the greatest joy of her life.

But that came to an end, and we too within a hand's-breadth of it also.

Immunity from danger had perhaps made me somewhat careless. As a rule we kept within reach of the shore, and at the first sign of a storm were safe on land before it could reach us.

But one golden afternoon we set out under a cloudless sky, with no more wind from the east than barely filled our tiny sail.

We were wafting gently along when Ruth cried suddenly, "Oh, Esli — look — !" and I had no more than time to catch sight of a huge purple-black cloud, which came whirling up over the eastern mountains, and to tear down the sail, when the storm was upon us.

The wind, pouring through the clefts and gullies, had outpaced the warning clouds, and in a moment the lake was like a boiling cauldron.

The vicious white waves leaped and bit at our little boat

like wild beasts. They came tumbling in over the side. The boat filled and, with our weight in it, sank under us, but as I caught at Ruth with one hand it came slowly up again and floated heavily and full of water alongside us.

"Lay hold, Ruth !" I gasped into her ear, and clasped her hands on the side of the boat, while Zick paddled, puffing and snorting, alongside.

She was very brave. Her face was white and pinched and her eyes were full of fear. But she uttered no cry and gripped the side of the boat tightly.

The waves were so sharp and jerky that her small white hands had difficulty in retaining their grip. First one hold was wrenched from her, then the other. And the sight of that, and the thought that she would surely drown, roused in me that blind fury which had so often led to my undoing, but this time made for good.

I raged against the powers of the winds and waves that were bent on ending her. I saw them pluck the boat out of her grasp. I remember seizing her round the body and striking out with my other arm, and the storm in my heart was fiercer than the one outside.

My devil for once served me well. I was conscious of nothing save that one of my arms was round Ruth's slim body, and that with the other I had somehow to make the land, no matter what hideous forces tried to stop me. I fought them with blind fury, as if they had been flesh and blood which I could clutch and rend and tear.

I remembered nothing of reaching the shore, but I came to myself with the feel of a hand on my head.

I was lying face downwards, with my fingers clawed deep into the ground as though for anchorage. When I rolled over and sat up, Ruth, very dazed and bewildered, was sitting beside me, looking down upon me anxiously, and Zick sat shivering beside her. The storm was gone. The sun was shining brightly again.

"God be thanked !" she said fervently, "I feared you were dead."

[25]

"It's a mercy we're not," I growled, as I spat the sand out of my mouth.

"Oh, it was terrible, terrible . . ." she said, squeezing her hands into her eyes, which looked twice as big and black as usual. "But for you I must have drowned, Esli."

"But for me you wouldn't have been there."

And presently she said, "I think you went mad out there, Esli. Or is it that you always swim like that in a storm ? You shouted at the waves as if you would frighten them."

"Did I ? I don't remember. But I was mad with them. I feared they would get you."

"It was terrible . . . terrible. I shall never want to go on the water again as long as I live. We were very near death."

"Perhaps I shall find the boat — at Kaphar-Nahum — or maybe at Tiberias. If not, I can always build you another."

"No — never again ! It was terrible."

And that mind remained in her.

CHAPTER VI

THE CARAVANS from Damascus to the coast and Jerusalem often came down our side of the lake, and as a rule gave us no trouble. They made, indeed, an interesting break in the slow life of the countryside, and introduced a touch of foreign colour into it.

They usually halted for the night near Tiberias, and our village folk would stand at the side of the road to watch the soft-footed swaying camels, and shudder at the angry growlings of wild beasts in their cages.

There came a caravan one day, with half-a-score of patient lumbering elephants, on their way to Rome probably, and, for some reason of his own, the leader chose to camp a little way further along the shore, between us and Kaphar-Nahum.

In the distance we saw the elephants disporting themselves in the lake, and they seemed to be enjoying it mightily. And, presently, some of the people of the caravan came wandering along the shore towards us.

We never liked such to come amongst us. Their ways were not ours. They looked upon us as of no account. They stole anything they could lay hands on as though we had no right to our own, and at times they tried to take liberties which we resented.

These were black men, attendants, perhaps, on the elephants. Ruth was busy at her netting. Zick and I were lying on the ground behind the net and almost hidden by it. But we could see through it, and Zick, at all events, did not like what he saw. He lay under my arm, tense, and rumbling his dislike inside him.

[27]

When the black men saw Ruth they stopped and stared at her. Then they said something in an unknown tongue, and then they came up towards her.

One stooped and made a run at her as though to pick her up in his arms. I jumped up, but Zick was before me. He flew, with a howl, at the black man's legs and received a kick which laid him breathless.

And the devil in me broke out and raged furiously. My understanding darkened. In all heaven and earth I was conscious of only one thing — that there in front of me was something hateful and that I had to smash it.

I hurled myself at the black with a roar of rage, hitting, kicking, gnashing as though I would tear him with my teeth. He went down under the shock. I danced on him. And when the others made as though to come to his help, I turned on them in my fury. And they, seeing, I suppose, that I was possessed, turned and fled back along the shore.

I tore after them for a space, but they got away. When I turned back the first one was limping off, bent double, towards the high road, and Ruth sat staring amazedly at me.

Then the devil went out of me, and I fell to the ground and dug my fingers into the sand for something certain to hold on to.

When in time I came to myself, Zick was licking my cheek and whimpering pitifully for me and for himself; and for days thereafter he liked to lie rather than walk and walked as little as he could help.

I stumbled up onto my feet and went dazedly back to Ruth. She looked at me anxiously. I think she was somewhat afraid of me — lest some of the devil should be still in me.

I dropped down on the ground near to her.

"You went mad, Esli," she said timidly.

"Yes."

"But it was for me . . . What did that hideous man want ?"

But I only shook my head.

"Do you think they'll come back ?"

"If they do I'll tear them in pieces."

It was the first time she had seen me at my worst. I could feel that the sight had shocked her, and I felt shamed and lowered before her.

"When it comes over me like that," I growled, "I cannot help myself, you know. . . It's not really me. It's the devil that comes into me and he's too strong for me."

"You were something like that when you were fighting with the storm in the lake that day," she said musingly. "And each time it has been for me. . . If your devil always helps you to do good things I don't mind him."

"When he comes I don't know what I do. That's the trouble."

We had some fear that the black men might come back in the night to revenge themselves — perhaps to set fire to the house or destroy the nets. And when my father heard about it, he feared the same, and he and I and Zick sat up all night. But they did not come, and next day the caravan went on its way.

CHAPTER VII

My FATHER never ceased to let me feel that it was time I was earning something. But the old difficulty remained. No one cared to take the risk of employing me, for fear that at any time I might break out and destroy them and all their works.

My outbreaks had, indeed, been rarer of late, but that was because people kept out of my way, and so the evil spirit in me had had no reason to show himself. That he was there, ready to flame out at a moment's notice, with reason or without, they knew as well as I did.

At last, however, an opening offered, and one that gave me the chance of work after my own heart and with little opportunity of falling foul of anyone.

Old Symeon-ben-Amon came heavily along one night to see my father. He lived just the other side of Bethsaida, and among other things had a large flock of sheep and a number of goats. He knew more about them than anyone in all the countryside, but he was too old and stiff to tend them himself now.

I wondered what he had come for, but presently my father called me, and as I stood before them, with Zick at my feet, he said, "Symeon has come to offer you work. You had better take it . . . and see you stick to it."

And old Symeon said, "I know, from what they say, Esli, that you have a devil, and that he sometimes gets the better of you. But I've heard say also that you are good to dumb beasts," and he looked at Zick.

I nodded.

"My son, Jorim, has been tending the sheep. But he's

[30]

taken a craze to go to sea — says he wants to see the world. He neglects the sheep, so he'd better go. If he doesn't get drowned he'll come back in time and be glad to tend the sheep again. And seeing that you care for animals, I thought you might make a good shepherd."

"Yes," I said, without hesitation, "I can make a good shepherd," and my father gave a sigh of great relief.

"When can I start ?" I asked.

"Tomorrow morning. At sunrise, Jorim and I will be up at the fold on the hillside. We'll count the sheep together, and we'll tell you their names and all we can about them and their ways. You'll soon pick it up from all I can tell you, for I've been learning them most of my life. And Jorim shall go with you the first few days till they get to know you."

"I'll soon pick it up, for I like beasts and their ways," and I went out, very full of it, to tell Ruth.

"You'll make a good shepherd, Esli, I'm certain of that," she said, but not so joyously as I had looked for. "But I shall miss you. It will be lonely here without you. You have been very good to me."

"But I'm not going to sea, like Jorim. I shall be home every night, or almost every night."

"That will be better than nothing," she sighed. "I shall miss you all day, but I'm glad you're going to be a shepherd."

I was at the sheep-fold before the sun came up like a great ball of gold over the hills of Gadara. Old Symeon's house was close to the fold and he and Jorim came out when they saw me.

Jorim had been at school with me. He was a rather clumsy lump of a boy. I would never have thought him enterprising enough to wish to see foreign lands. But I thought it might do him good.

He greeted me with a broad smile, which suggested to me recollections of the past and desire to be friendly now. He may have been thinking of my encounter with the old

Rabbi, and it was more than likely that he had at some time or other suffered at my hands, as most of them had.

However, he bore me no ill-will. The fact that I was helping him, though without intention, to realise his heart's desire, made him anxious to help me all he could.

They called the sheep by name, one by one, and counted them out of the fold, and then Jorim and I led them away up into the hills.

In a week I had learned enough to set Jorim free. He had been only too eager to teach me all he knew; and the sheep, I think, knew that I liked them, for they followed and obeyed my voice as willingly as they did his.

And Jorim and I had had no troubles. He was on his best behaviour because he wanted to get away. I caught him looking at me cautiously out of the corner of his eye at times, but he gave me no provocation and everything went smoothly.

The sheep were at first rather doubtful about Zick, but they very soon accepted him as a strange wandering part of myself, and I saw that he might become very useful to me.

Jorim had never used a dog. He told me some shepherds had them, in the wilder parts, but mostly to keep away wolves and robbers, and he doubted if I would find him much good for anything else.

When he had gone off to foreign parts I set to work to train Zick. He would do anything I told him within his comprehension; and while he was quite gentle with the sheep, there was nothing he liked better than to be sent off to bring in stragglers on the run, which made him feel himself a very big dog and a person of importance.

I found the simple shepherd life entirely to my liking. Up on the hills I was my own master, responsible for the welfare of the gentle trustful beasts who very soon came to regard me as their leader, and I am sure they liked me as I liked them.

And I had plenty to do — finding out the best pastures,

and when there came a drought, seeking springs where water was always to be had.

Jorim had been very clever with his sling — the shepherd's pastime from long before the days of David. By much practice I became so expert that I felt sure I could have beaten Jorim. But it was just as well he was not there.

And always there was the wonder of the things I saw from those hill-tops — the gleaming white cities in the distance — Safed on its hill; Julias, the new place built by the Tetrarch on the other side of Jordan; Tiberias on the shore of the shining blue lake; away up in the north the white cap of Hermon, and right across the lake, which was always alive with boats, the rugged heights of Decapolis which were always full of mystery to me.

When I had got my work properly in hand I would sometimes carry Ruth up into the nearer hills, and whenever I did so her joy made her a very light and happy burden.

Each morning I ran down to the lake for a cleansing swim, and more often than not saw the sun come climbing up over the opposite hills.

Then when we had eaten, and my wallet was packed with the day's food, I would sometimes take Ruth up in my arms and carry her along to the fold, and she would help me to count out the sheep.

When I laid her down for a moment, to ease my arms and legs, the flock would wander about in search of the sweetest grasses, and Zick would watch them with a fatherly eye to see that none went too far. And then, when I picked Ruth up again, he would be off like an arrow to round them all up, and we would climb on and on till we reached the chosen ground, and Ruth would lie in her niche on my sheepskin coat, completely and radiantly happy.

Her enjoyment of the wonderful wide views from up there grew ever greater. She could never have too much of it all. Her keen questing eyes spied out things I had missed, and we wondered and argued together as to what they could be.

c

And then there were always the sheep. Like most people I had always regarded sheep simply as sheep, and saw little difference between one sheep and another. But now, when each had a name of its own, I found them as different from one another as human beings are — each with a mind of a kind and its own peculiar little ways, and I wondered that I could ever have thought them all just alike.

Ruth got to know them all very quickly, and they accepted her readily and liked her, which was not surprising, for she delighted in them, and they had sense enough to perceive it, though in other things they could be very foolish at times.

Sitting there, she would root in my wallet for the round ball of rock-salt, which Jorim had passed on to me, along with his sheepskin coat and his crook-headed staff. Then she would call her favourites by their names, and her clear sweet voice which sounded like a song would reach them wherever they were, and they would come hurrying up for a few licks of the salt which always rewarded them.

We spent long days up in the hills, eating from my wallet when we were hungry, and drinking of the cool clear water of the springs, and sometimes, leaving Zick on guard, falling asleep in the mid-day heat.

Very happy days those were. And, having nothing whatever to provoke him, I had great relief from my devil. But he was by no means dead, and there came a day, when I had carried Ruth up, and we were as happy as could be, when he broke out again as furiously as ever.

He put me to sore shame before her that day . . . and yet I cannot but think I was in the right.

It was a time of drought, and many flocks further away in the hills were sore put to it to get water enough to keep life in them.

I had no trouble of the kind, because by this time I had traversed the hills in every direction and knew of springs where the water never failed.

We had been sitting by one such all day, and I was watering the sheep before leading them home, when, over the shoulder of a near-by hill, there came a rough-looking shepherd with his flock in search of water.

He broke into a run at sight of our spring, round which my sheep were gathered thickly, taking in their supply for the night.

We were almost ready to go, and I jumped up and called to him that if he could wait two minutes I would draw off my flock and leave the water to him.

Perhaps he was over-wrought with anxiety for his flock. He paid me no heed but urged his sheep into the water, thrusting mine aside, even beating and hauling them out with his crook in his haste.

I shouted angrily and ran to save my sheep. When I drew near he raised his crook and made a fierce blow at my head. I had just time to put up my crook to take the brunt of it, but the weight of his smashed mine to pieces and the rest of his blow came down on my shoulder. Zick was biting at his legs. The sheep had scattered, all mixed together.

He kicked Zick into the water just as the red fury broke out in my head, and I hurled myself at him in my usual Bull-of-Bashan fashion, seeing nothing, caring nothing, except to make an end of him. He had probably never suffered such an assault of the devil before and he had not expected it. He struck at me with his fists, but under my mad rush he fell in a tumbled heap and lay still, with his head cut and bruised on a piece of rock, and I went headlong into the pool.

The cold plunge cooled the evil in me and brought me back to my right mind. I waded out and looked at the fallen one, and saw that he would come to himself all right.

Then I hastily separated my sheep from the others, Ruth helping me by calling shrilly every name she could remember in her upsetting, and at last we got clear. I counted them to make sure, and then picked up Ruth and we went off down the hill.

And, as we went, her little hand would unclasp from round my neck at times and she would gently stroke my head, which was always very soothing to me.

"I'm sorry he broke out again," I said, excusingly. "He gets too strong for me at times."

"If you had not gone mad like that, that man might have killed you. He seemed quite mad, too."

"If he would only have waited just a minute or two — "

"He was mad, and he looked terribly strong and fierce. I'm glad you knocked him down . . . but I'm glad you didn't kill him."

"I always feel like killing them when the devil gets too much for me . . . But oh, Ruth, I wish I could get rid of him !"

"He's not been so bad of late," she said encouragingly.

"It's only because he's had no occasion. He's there as strong as ever, and I can never be a proper man and live like other men till he's gone."

"He'll go sometime, Esli, I'm sure he will, for you are a good man in spite of him. I wish I could take some of him from you."

"Nay, that would never do, Ruth. I can't imagine any devil in you. You have nothing in common with such things."

"Except you," she said softly.

We had to rest oftener than usual on the way home that night, for those outbreaks always left me spent. However, we got there at last, and together counted the sheep into the fold and found none missing — to my great content, for if there had been I would have had to go back to look for it, and I was tired out and my shoulder was aching.

CHAPTER VIII

I LOOK back on the years of my shepherding as the happiest I had had up to that time. I liked my work and became clever at it; and in the solitariness it entailed I sometimes forgot that I had a devil and that he might break out at any moment.

At long intervals — lest I should think I had got the better of him — he did break out, as I have told you, and let me down into the depths. But the neighbours knew me too well, and such of my fellows as I came across in the hills soon learned that I was a difficult man to have any dispute with, and they kept clear of me.

The happiest times of all for Ruth were when the lambs came, in the early part of the year, though for me they were times of constant hard work and much anxiety.

But when they had all safely arrived, and could follow their mothers to the nearer pastures, Ruth's delight in them knew no bounds.

She would sit among them, watching all their antics, their quaint gambols, their freakish friskings and kickings, their rough rejections when they hungrily sought mothers not their own, their anxious wailing searches for the right mothers who had wandered away after food.

And though she would laugh at them till her eyes were abrim, I thought at times I caught in her face something of envy and gentle protest at her own impotence. These senseless little new-born creatures were so prodigal of their powers of motion. They frisked and kicked out of pure joy of the life that was in them — and she, who would have rejoiced in it with so much greater understanding and thankfulness, could not move one step.

Not very often did she say anything about it — she had grown so used to her affliction. But once I remember her saying softly, while the tears ran down her cheeks — "Esli . . . I would give half my life to be able to do as they do . . . ay, or to be able just to walk . . . to walk even very slowly."

What could one say to so natural a longing ? I tried clumsily to console her.

"You have so much that they haven't got, Ruth — the dearest and truest heart in all the world — and a mind that understands. They don't even know why they go on like that."

"No, they are quite happy in just being alive," she said with a sigh.

Naming all the lambs, and teaching them, when they were old enough, to answer to their names, was a great business and taxed us severely. For, though sheep as they grow up develop marked characteristics of their own, lambs have absolutely no minds. It needed much ingenuity and a very keen eye and an unfailing memory. But all these Ruth possessed and she was a great help to me. Those were very happy times.

In winter, when there was little feeding to be had, I always took my flock to the great oak forests beyond our own hills, towards Safed. There one could always find something — tender twigs with young green shoots and small hidden grasses in the undergrowth.

I had a curious encounter up there one day.

My flock was in and about the woods, and I was sitting wrapped up in my sheepskin coat, thinking my own thoughts and with never an idea of danger to the sheep, when, without a warning sound, a shadow swept over me. Zick started up and rushed forward with a howl of anger, as a huge bird fluttered over one of my lambs with grasping claws, and now a stormy beating of powerful wings.

I sprang up with a shout and ran at it, and just as it began to rise with the lamb in its claws, I got my crook round its neck and pulled with all my might. It gave an angry scream, dropped the lamb, and wrenching its neck free flew off, and the lamb ran bleating to its mother.

I had never seen an eagle at such close quarters before. I never wish to see another.

But, in spite of my hatred of him, what remained long in my mind was his proud high bearing, the majestic poise of his head, the fearless courage in his keen unwinking eyes. No wonder they call him the King of Birds! He looked as if he knew well that there was nothing among all the fowls of the air that could rival him.

After that I kept my flock in the woods where the ravening things of the sky could not get at them.

And so I come to the greatest day of my life, though when it came I did not know how great a day it was or what was to come of it.

CHAPTER IX

I HAD started very early on that day of days, for we had a long walk before us. I was striding along in front of my flock, and I remember I was singing aloud for joy of the crisp quickening of the morning air. The sun was shooting through the hills of Gadara, and the lake below was like a basin of milk, so thick lay the white mist upon it.

We were climbing to the broken shoulder of our hill, when suddenly my whole flock rushed past me in a panic and nearly swept me off my feet.

And there, below me, I saw the evil reason for it — a great, long-legged, tawny-grey wolf which came bounding up the slope, his eyes ablaze with hunger, his sharp yellow fangs dripping in anticipation of his meal.

Wolves were rare with us, though there were plenty of them up Lebanon way. This one may have been an old one, turned out of his pack to shift for himself. But he was big enough, and famished enough, to be a dangerous foe.

My brave little Zick, full of courage and devotion, forgot all the natural fear of dog for wolf and flew at him with a howl which was his last. I can hear it yet. In the twinkling of an eye he was flung aside with his throat torn out, and the gaunt beast, spluttering blood, came on at me.

It was a mad business. He was mad with hunger, and at sight of Zick's torn-out throat, I went mad with rage.

The whirling red mist filled my head, and as the thunders and lightnings roared inside it, the great beast leaped upon me and reared himself up to get at my throat.

The devil in me raged furiously and left no room for fear.

Dimly now, I remember the feel of his shaggy skin as my hands caught him by the throat. His hot mad eyes blazed into mine. His still-bloody teeth gnashed and foamed at me. His foul breath got into my panting throat like the taste of death. His ragged claws tore streaks out of my arms and chest as he scrabbled furiously to beat me down.

But I held on and kept his teeth an inch away. I felt the sinews in his throat crumpling under my fingers which felt to me like iron spikes. He began to gasp and choke hot froth into my face, but still struggled furiously.

My fingers tightened. They seemed almost to meet in his neck. His paws ceased their wild scrabbling. He grew limp as I wrung him to and fro, as one wrings a sack to empty it. And in me there was a wild devilish joy as I wrung the last gasping shred of his life out of him. My devil had always longed to kill, and at last its desire was fulfilled to the very uttermost of its craving. It had for once torn an enemy to pieces.

Long after the beast had ceased to breathe I held it and shook it. Then, of a sudden, all the strength went out of me and I fell prone alongside its body.

WHEN I came to myself I felt a soft hand on my head, and vaguely my confused brain thought it must be Ruth's.

But when I turned my head, slowly and heavily, I saw it was a man who was sitting beside me. And as my dull eyes lifted slowly to see who it was, they looked at last into his, and then . . .

There are things one cannot describe, any more than one can understand them. I have tried many times to recall all that I felt at that time, or even a portion of it. But it is all very dim and confused — as things generally were when I was recovering from one of my outbreaks. And besides, I have come to know him so well since then that my first ideas have become overgrown with the later ones.

But I know that as I looked up into his eyes, the remains of the great turmoil within me, which usually left me in a state of deepest shame and depression, were suddenly lifted off me, and in their place there came a great calm — a sense of peace such as I had never before known; and in place of the usual waste and weakness a sense of new strength.

Then he spoke, and his voice was at once strangely strong and gentle. It sounded in my throbbing ears like music.

"Good lad !" he said. "You have done well. A good shepherd is always ready to give his life for his sheep and counts not the cost. You had a tough fight."

"Ay," I said, looking down at the dead wolf, "he was a big one and he was mad with hunger."

And then my eyes lighted on the mangled body of my poor little Zick, and I stumbled hastily up onto my knees and across to him to see if any spark of life was in him. But there was not, and I bowed myself over him in very great grief.

Then I heard again the voice that was like music,

"I too had a dear dog friend, and he died. And I still grieve for him."

Such feeling for a dog was so unusual that it went right home to my heart, and I sat on my heels and gazed up at him in wonder.

"You loved a dog ?" I asked.

"Very dearly. He was my very faithful friend. I miss him sorely. . . What was his name ?" he asked gently, looking down at the poor little torn body.

"Zick."

"Strength ! . . . Well, he did his best, and none can give more than his life. Let us lay him where none will trouble him."

And when I had scooped a large enough hole with the end of my crook and my hands, we laid Zick gently in it. The stranger rested his hand tenderly on the quiet body for a moment, and then we covered him up, and piled rocks high above him so that no wild beast should disturb him. And it has always been a joy and consolation to me to think of his burying.

[42]

My heart warmed to this kindly stranger who had loved a dog as I had, and had helped me to bury my friend.

As we stood beside the pile, he said, "Now the sooner you see to your own wounds the better — "

"I had forgotten them" — but when I looked down at my arms and my breast I saw they were torn and scored with the wolf's foul paws and were bleeding freely, and they immediately began to pain me.

"But — my sheep !" I said, coming suddenly face to my duties.

"They are waiting for you in the valley over there. I passed them and wondered what had become of their shepherd. Wash your arms well in the quick-running water down there. Wash them again and again. A wolf's claws are dirty weapons."

"Who may you be ?" I asked bluntly, for I felt that I would like to meet again this strange but comforting man who had loved a dog even as I had. "I do not know your face."

"We have only just come to live in Kaphar-Nahum," he said — "the black and white house on the shore, the first house on this side of the mound."

I nodded. I knew the house well, for it was where Jonathan-bar-Jona the boat-builder had lived and where I built the boat for Ruth.

"And how do they call you, sir ?" I asked.

"I am Jesus-ben-Joseph. We come from Nazaret, up there among the hills. And you ?"

"I am Esli-ben-Maath. We live just outside Bethsaida. My father is the net-maker."

He nodded cheerfully, and said, "Now, see to those arms without delay. We shall meet again, Esli."

He went off down the hill with a long free stride that showed me he was fond of walking. And, with a last good-bye to my poor Zick, I hurried after my sheep and the cold running water for my torn arms.

The sheep were still much disturbed but were very contented to see me again. I led them along to the stream and plunged into it where it fell, white and cool, over a ledge of rock, and let it run over my arms till they were clear of the blood and dirt and the flesh was clean and firm again.

I think that clear cool water must have had in it some unusual virtue — as I knew some of our streams had. For the pain in the rough red furrows in my arms grew less, and I felt that they would heal quickly.

I bathed them again and again, and then, feeling much the better, went on with my flock to the woods. But I missed Zick at every turn, and my heart was heavy at thought of him and that I should never see him again.

When I got home that night and told my story, Ruth was in great distress about my wounds, though I assured her that they were beginning to heal already. And for Zick she wept quietly and was inconsolable.

To take her mind off Zick, I told her of the stranger who had loved a dog and lost him, just as we had, and had been so friendly and full of understanding. And her interest was roused at once, for I was very full of him, and that was rather unusual with me, since I had no friends among my fellows.

She began to question me at once about him.

"You had never seen him before, Esli?"

"No, he was a stranger. He told me he had just come to live in Kaphar-Nahum — from Nazaret. He has Jonathan's house, where I built the boat."

"I heard some new people had come to live there. I think somebody said they were carpenters."

"My man did not look like a carpenter. He looked more like a Rabbi. But," I said, searching back in my mind, "his hands were not those of a Rabbi. A Rabbi's hands are smooth and soft. . . And his hand was soft enough when I felt it on my head, but when our hands touched, as we laid Zick down, his were firm and strong, not at all like a Rabbi's, and there were marks on them which had been cuts and bruises."

[44]

"Tell me more about him, Esli. He seems a nice kind of man. He must be, since he was sorry about our poor Zick. Is he old or young ?"

"He's a grown man — at the full of his powers, I should say."

"And is he big and tall ?"

"Yes, he is tall. . . At least . . . I don't know. . . He is just about the proper height of a man, but he is so shapely and carries himself so well that he looked tall to me. When he went I wanted to stand and watch him, though my arms were hurting badly — he walked with such a swing, you see, as though he loved walking."

"And his face ? What is he like ?"

"His face is very comely. It was grave and full of pity just then, but it looked as if it could be very glad and happy. But we were on a pitiful business, you see, for he knew what it was to lose a friend like Zick. But it was a very good face, as if he understood men and things more deeply than most . . . and far-seeing. I am sure he understood me better than anyone else has ever cared to do, except, perhaps, you, Ruth. His eyes looked right into me. I could no more tell that man a lie than I could fly."

"You never tell any man lies, Esli. You may have a devil in you, but you don't lie. Tell me more about him ! What colour were his eyes ?"

"I'm not sure — brown, I think; but you don't think about their colour when they look at you. They were large . . . and they were deep. . . They made me think of the dark pools up in the forest yonder. And there was a little spark in each of them — like a star."

"How I wish I could see him !"

"He may come past here someday. I should think, from the way he walks, that he walks a good deal. He must have been up very early to be where I met him at that time of day. . . And I am right glad he was there. It made a great difference. There was something very comforting about him."

I am setting this down here as fully as I can because, comparing these first ideas of mine concerning him — ideas gathered in that few minutes of our first meeting — with all that I came to know of him later, it showed how deeply he impressed any who met him with an open mind.

"I do hope he will come past here someday," Ruth said longingly. "If ever you see him anywhere near, Esli, run after him and try to get him to come. I would so love to see him."

CHAPTER X

THE SHEPHERD'S life is a very exacting one, for sheep must always be fed. But old Symeon was a punctilious observer of the law, and he kept the Sabbath as strictly as necessity would permit. The sheep always remained in the fold that day and we fed them there. But they were always very eager to get up to the hills the next day.

So I rejoiced in the Sabbaths, since they were the only days in which I could spend much time at home with Ruth. I usually carried her down to the edge of the lake, and we would sit there and talk over the doings of the week, and tax our brains to discover names for the new-born lambs.

We were sitting so the next Sabbath afternoon after I had met the stranger in the hills. And Ruth was telling me of the stir a new teacher was making among people. Andrew and Simon had been up seeing my father about some nets the previous night, and had also been speaking about him. They had been down the river to see him and he had impressed them very deeply.

He was, she gathered, a strange, wild-looking man, dressed in skins, who never slept in a house or lived as other men do. His name was John-ben-Zacharias and he preached furiously against the sins of the people, and threatened them with terrible punishments unless they repented of them and publicly renounced them. Andrew and Simon said the people were flocking to him in thousands, and some said he was Elijah come back, and some said he was the messiah we had been so long expecting.

But they said that John himself claimed nothing of the kind. He said plainly that he was only a fore-runner, sent to proclaim a greater one who would follow him, and all the people were agog to know who this could be. For the coming of one who would deliver us from Rome, and restore us to our rightful place in the world, had been the one great hope of our people for generations past — about the only point on which there was no dissension amongst us.

"And," said Ruth, "Simon and Andrew are sure they have found out who it is — "

"The Deliverer ?" I jerked.

"Yes. They found it out through something the Baptiser said. . ."

While she was speaking I had been watching the distant figure of a man who was walking slowly along the shore towards us. He stopped now and again and stood looking out over the lake, like one in deep thought, and then came slowly on again.

"Who is it, Esli ?" asked Ruth. "I don't think it's anyone I know."

"No" . . . and I eyed the coming one more intently still. "Ruth . . . I do believe you are going to get your wish . . . It's my stranger — Jesus-ben-Joseph . . . I'm sure it is," and she leaned forward with eager face and sparkling eyes.

"Oh Esli !" she cried, clasping her hands as if in prayer. "Don't let him pass, or go back ! I do so want to see him."

"If he turns I'll run after him," and we watched his every step lest he should disappoint us.

But he came quietly on, and when he drew near I jumped up and ran up to him, and said, "Oh sir, I am glad you have come. My little sister Ruth is longing to see you since I told her all about you and how you helped me to bury Zick."

His face which had been full of thought lit up with a smile, like the sun coming out on a clouded day.

"And the arms ?" he asked cheerily, as we went along towards Ruth.

"They are healing very quickly . . . and it's wonderful, for they were badly torn, and they say a wolf's claws are always poisonous."

"You bathed them well in that running water ?"

"I bathed them till they were nearly dead with the cold."

"It is always best to get rid of poison as quickly as possible, lest it spread through the whole body." And then we came up to where Ruth was sitting on her mat.

"How is it with you, my daughter ?" he asked gently, as he smiled down at her, and she smiled up at him, with her joy in him in her eyes.

In the natural course of things she would have risen and met the stranger with courteous greeting. And, fearing he might think her wanting in respect, she said hastily, with her face flushed red, "It is well with me, sir, and oh, I am glad, glad, you have come. But I cannot rise to greet you for I cannot stand."

"Cannot stand ?" — and his face was full of concern for her, as it had been for Zick and me that other day.

"I have not been able to stand or walk a step since I was born, sir."

With her face all crimson like that, and her eyes shining like stars in the lake at night, she was, I thought, the sweetest and prettiest thing I had ever seen.

His face was full of tenderest feeling as he stood looking down at her.

"You cannot walk ?" he said softly " — and the power to walk is surely one of God's best gifts."

And as he gazed earnestly down upon her I saw a thrill run through her slight body, and she gazed up into his eyes as though nothing else was possible to her.

Then he said quietly, "If God so wills !" and he reached down his hand to her, and I saw again, as I had seen up on the hill, that it was a firm strong hand with the scars of cuts and bruises on it.

Ruth put her own small hand into it, and then — marvel of marvels, which I shall remember to the day of my death ! — she seemed to draw herself up by clinging to his hand, and she stood upright on her feet — for the first time in all her life.

D

She clung to his hand, with both her own hands now, gazing at him with amazement that was not far from alarm, and her face went white and red in great waves of colour.

His face was very intent upon her as he watched her, but there was in it also a look of great joy and content.

"Now, child — walk!" he said, gently, but with vast depth in his voice, soft as it was.

Very slowly and quietly he drew his hand from hers, and she, in fear of falling, held her arms outstretched to balance herself.

Between laughing aloud for joy, and crying out with fear and wonder at the marvel of it all, she essayed a step or two. He held out his hand just in front of her, as though inviting her to still bolder effort. But she, who had never walked in her life, and was overwhelmed with the wonder of it, found walking a hazard almost too great for her.

"God has given you back the power," he said encouragingly, "now you must use it. You will soon learn to walk. Even the lambs have to learn before they can skip."

I had watched it all agape with astonishment, but when, now, Ruth fell on her knees, I ran to her to help her up again. But she had caught at the edge of his robe and was kissing it passionately.

"Oh, sir," she cried, "all my life will not suffice to thank you. . ."

But he lifted her hastily, saying, "To God your thanks, child! I am but his instrument," and as I caught her arm and placed it securely inside my own, he added with a smile, "Esli has a strong arm. He will soon teach you to walk."

And then, Ruth, thinking past her own marvel, that I too needed help, cried, "Oh, sir, cure Esli too!"

"Esli?" he asked in surprise, with a searching look at me.

"He has a devil, and sometimes it is too much for him."

"Esli has no devil," he said weightily. "Up there in the hills he cast him out with the shedding of his own blood for his sheep. He will trouble him no more," — and even as he said it, I believed it, and I felt a new freedom coursing within me.

"Now I must go," he said. "They will be expecting me at home."

"But you will come again, sir ?" begged Ruth.

"We shall meet again. And next time I shall see you skipping like one of Esli's lambs. . . Now — " with an almost imperceptible lifting of his right hand — "May God's blessing rest upon you both !" and he went.

We stood watching him till he turned into the black and white house on the shore at Kaphar-Nahum, and then, with Ruth's arm clasped tightly inside my own, we went up towards our own home.

And as we went, I could feel the new life in Ruth throbbing tumultuously in her arm against my side, and I felt towards her as I had never felt in my life before.

We went slowly, but I knew that every step was a gain and gave her fresh assurance.

"Esli ! . . . to think of it ! . . . I am really walking," she said, with bated breath, lest too loud assertion should prove it but a dream.

"And my devil has gone out of me. I am as sure of it as you are sure that you are walking, Ruth."

"It is very wonderful ! . . . Who can he be ?"

"I don't know who he is, but I have never met anyone like him, and I have a great desire to see him again."

"He said we should meet him again. I am sure he will come again," she said confidently.

Just as we drew near the house, her mother came to the door, probably to call us to supper. At sight of Ruth walking she clutched hastily at the door-post, drew her other hand across her eyes, and called to my father inside, and they stood there eyeing us with stark amazement.

"Ruth !" gasped Leah "How . . ."

"I am cured, Mother," said Ruth simply.

"But how ?" jerked my father.

"I do not know, except that it is by the goodness of God and that good man whom Esli met up in the hills the day he killed the wolf."

"Who is he then?" and he looked at me as though I ought to know.

"His name is Jesus-ben-Joseph. He comes from Nazaret, and he lives in the nearest house there in Kaphar-Nahum, where Jonathan-bar-Jona used to live. That is all I know, except that he is the most wonderful man I have ever met. For he assures me that my devil has gone forever, since I killed the wolf up there. And I believe him, for I feel like that."

It was a long time before we could settle down to such an ordinary thing as eating, for the world felt turned up-side down for all of us. And we were all very full of our own thoughts, and they were all about the wonderful man who had wrought this wonderful thing in us.

But when at length, and long after the usual time, we got to our supper, Leah, after watching Ruth eating with an appetite very unusual with her, said,

"You'll be able to help me with the housework now, Ruth."

"It will be a joy to me to be able to help, Mother."

"That will take her off the nets," said my father, "and I shall miss her."

"I will try to do both," said Ruth, in great content at the enlargement of her powers and the new possibilities it opened before her.

CHAPTER XI

WHEN I got home from the hills the next night, Ruth told me that they had been overrun with visitors all day. They had come buzzing round like flies about a honey-pot, to see the marvel of her walking, and to ask her endless questions as to how it had come about.

"But all I could tell them was that the man through whom I was cured was Jesus-ben-Joseph, and that he lived in Kaphar-Nahum, and was a very wonderful man," she said.

"They have been going along there in troops," said Leah, "and some have taken their sick folks with them, hoping he will cure them too."

"He'll have his hands full," said my father. "If he can cure like that, and can make them pay for it, he'll be a very rich man."

"If you had seen him you would never imagine him thinking of money. He is not like that. He is not like any man I have ever seen," said Ruth.

"No," I said, "money and he have nothing in common. It's the very last thing in the world you'd think of in connection with him. You'll feel that when you meet him."

"Still, a man must live, and with a gift like that—. They say he's a carpenter. He'd do better with his healings . . ."

"A carpenter ! Well . . . he may be. I don't know. But I do know that he's a great deal more than any carpenter I've ever heard of. He's a wonder-man, if ever there was one—and a great deal more than that too. . . He's my idea of what a great prophet would look like — a man of God."

"They are not too common these days," said my father, dryly.

And now — it was very strange that a week before this we had never heard the name of Jesus-ben-Joseph, and yet before another week had passed we seemed to hear nothing else. The whole countryside seemed to be talking about him, and vying with one another as to who could tell the strangest stories.

And, truly, they had reason. The wonders that he wrought, and the strange wise things he was reported to have said — which seemed so different from the usual teaching of the priests and Rabbis, and from the accepted order of things. And these passed from mouth to mouth and no doubt grew in their passage.

But we learned most, and most reliably, from Andrew and Simon-bar-Jona, the fishermen, who lived just the other side of Bethsaida and were often in seeing my father on business. They heard of Ruth's healing and they came up to see her and to hear all about it.

They were partners in the boats with James and John-ben-Zabdai, and John was often away in Jerusalem attending to their affairs up there.

Andrew told us how he had been up to Jerusalem to see John, and had found him and everyone else more than ever exercised by the vehement preaching of John the Baptiser.

There never had been such a stirring of people's souls. All the world went down to Jordan to hear him, from the highest to the lowest — members of the Sanhedrin, Rabbis, Pharisees, Sadducees, soldiers, taxgatherers, publicans, and all the common folk. And he stormed at the sinfulness of them all alike, and called on them to repent, for he was sent to tell them that the Kingdom was at hand.

No one knew exactly what he meant, but he carried conviction to all hearts that something of overwhelming import was very close upon them, and the people were being baptised in Jordan in thousands as a sign of their desire for a better life.

Now between Andrew and his brother Simon there was a very close bond of feeling. And so Andrew's first thought was to share this great matter with his brother. He sent off a letter by a speedy messenger, urging Simon to come up at once, and Simon, in his usual impetuous fashion, dropped everything and went.

John had been down to the river several times and had even got to know The Baptiser slightly, though most folks stood somewhat in awe of him. John, however, was a very pleasant-looking and attractive man and most people took to him.

Everybody worried The Baptiser with questions as to who he was; and to all he answered that he was nobody — just a Voice sent to proclaim The One who was close at hand.

Then, one day when John and Andrew had gone along with the crowd and were standing by the·Preacher, they saw a new strange look come over his face as he watched one who passed close by them, and they heard him murmur to himself — "The Lamb of God !" which struck them as a very strange saying.

The stranger was not known to them, but as they watched him they felt so greatly attracted by him that there sprang up in them an overwhelming desire to learn more about him.

The Baptiser's puzzling words had seemed to come from the very depths of his soul . . . "The Lamb of God !" — strange, pregnant words which sounded as though they must mean much.

They struck some chords in Andrew and John which would not cease quivering till they found out what they implied. For The Baptiser never wasted words though he used many, and every word went right to the mark.

And their minds were strung to a high pitch of expectancy by all that he had said before — that he himself was but a Voice telling of One who was to come.

Could this be he ? . . . the Promised One, for whom the world had been waiting ?

He was a comely figure, gentle-looking yet commanding, and his face was calm and gracious, and quite free from the pride and craftiness, and keenness and littleness, which had left their marks on so many of the faces about them.

They looked at one another for a moment, and then with one mind set off after the stranger.

He had walked quietly on along the road that led to the desert. Presently they were outside the crowd, none near them save the stranger.

He heard their footsteps and turned and stood waiting for them — "and," said Andrew, as he told us of it, "our hearts beat quicker as we drew near to him, for his eyes seemed to look quietly right through us, and he seemed to know all about us."

He asked gently, "What do you want, my friends ?"

And John said, "Rabbi, where are you staying ?"

And he said gently, "Come and see !" and they went with him to a small shelter made of branches of palm covered with a shawl, of which there were many all over the plain for the use of those who came out to see and hear The Baptiser.

There they sat down on the ground and talked with the stranger. It was late in the afternoon, and they talked — or mostly listened — far into the night.

Andrew did not tell us much of what the stranger said, perhaps he did not quite understand all of it.

"But," he said, "as we listened and watched him we grew more and more certain that he could be no other than the Promised One of whom The Baptiser had spoken. For he spoke as we had never heard any man speak, and he opened to us a new way of life such as no other had ever dreamed of, and our hearts went right out to him and we were filled with joy."

The next morning Andrew set off to see if Simon had

arrived, and presently he found him among the crowd listening to The Baptiser.

"He is a great man," said Simon. "He speaks bravely."

"We have found a greater," Andrew told him — "the messiah — the Promised One ! Come !" and he took him to the little booth where the stranger — whom they now knew as Jesus-ben-Joseph — and John-ben-Zabdai were still talking earnestly together.

And when Jesus saw them coming he eyed Simon very keenly, and then he said,

"You are Simon, son of Jona. But you shall win the name of Kephas — the Rock."

"And," said Simon, as they told us about it, "all I could do was to stand and stare at him. He is a very wonderful man, and he's living here in Kaphar-Nahum, in the house where Jonathan the boat-builder used to live."

"And you really believe he is the Promised One for whom we have waited so long, Simon ?" I asked with bated breath, as I thought of how Ruth and I had spoken with him, and of all he had done for us.

"We are certain of it, and so is John. He will tell you when he comes, tomorrow or next day."

"I knew he was not like any other man," said Ruth, "when he gave me back my ankles with a touch."

"The Promised One !" I said, in great amazement still. "I would I could serve him."

"You have got your sheep to look after," said my father.

It was on my tongue to say that there were greater things in the world than sheep. But I thought of Jesus-ben-Joseph and I said nothing, but wished it all the more.

CHAPTER XII

HOW PHILIP SOUGHT NATHANIEL, AND NATHANIEL SOUGHT
PHILIP, AND I TOOK SERVICE WITH THE MASTER

OUR HEARTS and minds were very full of Jesus-ben-Joseph
and the new joy of life he had brought, not only into our
lives but into the whole countryside.

Every day we heard of some new wonder he had wrought
— of some strange new enlightening thing he had said.
We heard too that many of the priests and Rabbis were
speaking against him, because the new way of life which
he so graciously and joyously lived and taught was so different from their own.

To them the old law was absolute. If a man kept rigidly
to the letter of it, that was all that mattered. But, as most
of us knew by experience, there could be much hardship
and meanness and sharp-dealing under cover of the law,
without actually breaking it.

And so the words of this new Teacher were like new
life to us and we treasured them in our hearts.

I was leading my flock along the ridge of the hills behind our plain one morning, when I saw, like a little white
speck, a man appear over the brow of the western hills and
come striding across the valley towards me.

And, when I chanced to look back over our own plain,
I saw another man coming quickly across it; and it seemed
to me that they too would just about reach the top of the
ridge at the same time. It was like looking on at a race
in which the runners were not aware of one another, and I
watched them to see which would win.

And as they drew nearer I recognised both of them.

The man from the west was Nathaniel-bar-Tholmai of

Cana. I had seen him in Bethsaida but a few days before.

And the other I saw was Philip, the young fisherman who lived, with his wife and two little girls, not far from Andrew and Simon.

I waved my hand and both waved back to me, each thinking I waved to him alone.

But our side of the hill was the easier ascent, and Philip sank down, very short of breath, a few feet below me before Nathaniel was near the top on his side.

"Where are you bound for in such haste, Philip?" I asked.

"I'm going to Cana . . . I seek Nathaniel," he panted.

"Cana! — that's a good stretch" — and I laughed inwardly at the knowledge that Nathaniel was only a few minutes away. "He was here the other day, looking for you."

"I know. That's why I want him now."

"Well, if it's Nathaniel you're after . . ." I waved my hand to the climber on the other side, and hailed him. "Ho — Bar-Tholmai!" and Philip sprang to my side; and at sight of his friend, plodding sturdily up the steep track, he ran down to meet him and they came along together.

"I am on my way to Cana to seek you, Nathaniel," laughed Philip joyously.

"And I . . . am on my way . . . to Bethsaida . . . to seek you," panted Bar-Tholmai. "What did you want with me?"

Philip hesitated half a minute, as though he did not know how to tell all he had to say. There was a look in his face the like of which I had not seen in him before. Then he burst out,

"It's great news, Nathaniel — wonderful news. We have found the messiah — The Promised One, for whom we've all been waiting. He has told me he wants me and I'm going with him. I want you to come too."

Bar-Tholmai stared at him in great amazement. I think he thought he had lost his wits.

"The messiah ? . . . The Promised One ?" he jerked incredulously.

But Philip paid no heed to his doubts. It was too great a matter, and he too full of it, for doubting looks to stop him. It poured out of him like a mountain torrent—

"I was down at Jordan to hear The Baptiser. He is a great man, but he told us, over and over again, that he was only sent to announce the coming of a greater. And then, one day, a man came down to the water to be baptised by him, and The Baptiser was stricken so that he could hardly speak — though in general he is like a thunderstorm. And when the other had gone, he said softly, as if he was just thinking aloud — 'That is he of whom I spoke — The Lamb of God, that taketh away the sin of the world' . . . A strange thing to say ! . . . and the way he said it ! . . . And the next day, when I was on my way home, that man came up to me and told me he had need of me and I was to follow him."

"But — " Nathaniel broke in, through the amazement which still held him — "Who *is* the man, Philip, and why should you follow him ? You cannot. . ."

"His name is Jesus-ben-Joseph, and he comes from Nazaret, but now he is living in Kaphar-Nahum."

"From Nazaret ?" and there was a touch of contempt in his voice. "Can anything good come out of Nazaret ?" — for between Cana and Nazaret there was no good feeling.

"Come and see him for yourself, Nathaniel. He is the most wonderful man I have ever met."

"You haven't met many, my good Philip. It looks to me as if he was making a fool of you. How are you going to follow him ? What are you going to do ?"

"What about Zillah and the little ones, Philip ?" I asked, for this idea of his of going away with the new teacher seemed to me strange, though I knew what a wonderful man Jesus-ben-Joseph was, and what it must feel like to be asked to be one of his followers.

"I asked him that, and he said they would be all right."

"And you really mean to give up your work and go off with this man ?" said Nathaniel.

"Yes. I am going with him," said Philip, and his frank honest face was aglow with the knowledge and the feeling that was in him.

"Well — I can't understand it," said Nathaniel, staring at him as if he hardly knew him. And that, I suppose, was really the case, for this new Philip was very different from the Philip we had known.

"Nathaniel," said Philip, laying his hand persuasively on his friend's arm. "All I ask is — Come and see him for yourself ! Esli here can tell you how wonderful he is. He has cured little Ruth. She can walk now like anyone else — and Esli himself . . . Jesus has cast out his devil from him — and many others has he cured — all who come to him."

Nathaniel looked enquiringly, perhaps a bit doubtfully, at me.

"Yes," I said, "he has done all that, Nathaniel, and much besides. The whole countryside is full of his wonderful doings and wise sayings."

"Well," he said, reluctantly, as one consenting, for the sake of peace, to the whims of his friends, "I'll go with you, Philip, but . . ." and he ended with a dubious shake of the head.

"Put in a word for me, Philip," I cried after them, as they went off down the hill. "I would dearly like to go too."

"You ask him yourself, Esli. You know him," and I stood and watched them with a great desire.

My heart was full of this great new wonderful thing, and the more I thought about him the more I longed to be of some use to Jesus-ben-Joseph.

Here was I, away up on this hill-top tending a flock of sheep, and somewhere down below there was he, teaching the people his New Way of life and curing them of their ills.

[61]

I ached to be with him, and for the first time I was sorry that I was a shepherd of the hills. If any man had come upon me then I would have had to pour out to him all I was feeling, just as Philip had done. It was too great and too wonderful a matter to keep to one's self. I wanted everyone to know of it and to feel about it as I did.

And presently I led my flock down into the further valley, where the stream gathered itself into a good-sized pool. And there, in a spirit of purification — as though to make my body more meet for that which was working in me, as I thought of the Great Teacher and his sayings and doings — I bathed myself many times, and the desire to serve him in some way grew upon me till it possessed me completely.

He had asked Philip to follow him. He would without doubt be asking others. If I could muster courage to ask him to let me be of his company, to do no matter what . . . there was no knowing — perhaps he would take me too; and I began to think who could take charge of old Symeon's sheep.

There would be no difficulty about that. Shepherd boys could be found, though he would never get one who would care for them better than I had done. And it was only to help me, when no one else would, that he had given me the chance.

When I had folded the flock that night, I spoke to him about it.

"Yes, surely, I can find another," he said, "but I thought you liked the work, Esli, and you are good with the sheep and they like you."

"I like the sheep and I like the work," I said, "but this great new teacher draws me. He has done wonderful things for Ruth and me. He is gathering followers and I would serve him if he will have me."

"I see . . ." nodding his white head thoughtfully — and then, wagging it gravely, "They tell marvellous things about him, but we have had so many who thought themselves great men and yet came to nought."

[62]

"I have not heard Jesus-ben-Joseph say much about himself, but I have seen himself and I know what he has done for Ruth and me. And I know that he is the best and most wonderful man I have ever met."

"They say the priests are against him."

"His teaching is very different from theirs."

"Still . . . they should know."

"He knows better. I'm sure of that. And he's not a bit like a priest. It makes you feel better just to sit and look at him and listen to him."

I told Ruth that night of all I was feeling about the matter, and while she felt as deeply about the Teacher as I did, she was rather overcast at the idea of my going away, even with him.

"But," she said, in the end, "he has done so much for us, Esli, that nothing is too much for us to do for him." And that was just what I felt.

I did not speak about it to my father because I knew well what he would say.

The next morning, when I ran down to the lake for my swim, the sun was not yet above the hills, and everything was half-hidden in a soft white haze.

Full of the great new desire that was in me, I swam far out. The first beams of the sun filled the mist with a silvery lightness that went to my head. I felt as if I were alone in the world — the first man or the last.

With my head in that misty brightness, and the soft cool water swirling lightly round my body, I felt as though I floated there between heaven and earth, and like the morning-stars I sang aloud for joy.

But I had to turn at last, and as I drew near the shore I saw, dimly through the mist, a little group of men walking quietly along the white beach towards the head of the lake.

A few more strokes and I saw who they were. There was no mistaking the gracious white figure and graceful carriage of him of whom my heart and thoughts were full.

They were passing out of sight. I stumbled hastily

ashore, picked up my tunic in my hand, and sped after them.

They heard the quick beat of my feet on the hard sand and turned to see who came.

"Master," I panted, as I came up with them, still dripping with water, "may not I come with you too?"

They all stood and stared at me, and I feared that James and John deemed it unseemly on my part. But Andrew and Simon knew me better and understood. And The Master himself welcomed me with a kindly look which showed me that he understood still better.

"We were wondering who the singer in the water was," he said.

"Sir," I said boldly, though my heart was kicking like a week-old lamb, "you will need someone to fetch and carry for you — to wash your feet and clean your sandals. I will do anything you ask — and more, if only I may serve you."

"But I am here to serve, not to be served, Esli."

"But, sir," I said hastily, "if the Master does a servant's work he will have the less time for his own. The High Priest does not sweep the Temple floor," at which boyish argument his eyes twinkled.

"And what about your sheep?" he asked, and the encouraging smile on his face filled my heart with hope — "and Ruth — and your father?"

"Shepherds are plenty, sir, but masters such as you are not easy to find. I have arranged with Symeon about the sheep, and I have spoken to Ruth. My father would only say, 'There is no money in it' . . . I would serve you well, sir."

"And you shall," he said, and I thought I saw in his eyes a little sparkle of pleasure at my forwardness. "Come to me in Kaphar-Nahum as soon as you have found a good shepherd for your sheep."

I fell on my knees in the sand.

He lifted his right hand slightly, and I knew that that was his blessing and the seal of my service.

Then he turned and they went on their way, and I knelt

there, overwhelmed with the joy of this mighty happening.

The greatest and noblest and most gracious and wonderful man I had ever met had taken me into his service!

Then I raced home to tell Ruth, and then on to old Symeon to help him to find a shepherd in my place.

CHAPTER XIII

I HAD no great difficulty in finding one to take my place with the sheep, and I did my best to get them friendly with him, as I knew The Master would wish.

Old Symeon said again how sorry he was that I was going, and showed plainly that he thought me a fool for starting on such a doubtful adventure.

My father said it outright and with much force, but as I had foreseen that it did not trouble me.

Late in the afternoon of the day when I had at last got everything settled, I set off for Kaphar-Nahum, and Ruth insisted on coming with me.

"I want to see him again," she said, "and more than ever now that you are to be of his company . . . I shall miss you sorely, Esli, but it will comfort me to know that you are with him."

And the thought of parting from her had made me realise at last that little Ruth was dearer to me than anything else in my life.

It is difficult for me to explain all that I felt at that time. My feeling for The Master was a greater thing even than my love for Ruth. It was different, and yet somehow, it was of the same texture. Ruth had crept into my heart almost unconsciously in the years of our brotherly-sisterly friendship. The Master had possessed me wholly with a look.

I had known him but a few days, but I looked up to him as one quite beyond my understanding indeed, but worthy of the utmost I could give him. I held him in reverence and awe, for I had never imagined any man like him; but there was nothing of fear in my feeling for him, only of greatest love and devotion and desire to be of service to him.

In time, and when I came to know him better, my love for him — for his very own self — became greater even than my love for Ruth. But at first I think the one helped me to understand the other. I loved The Master more fully because of my love for Ruth, and I loved Ruth more truly and purely because of my love for The Master.

As we passed along the shore, hand-in-hand — sister and brother to the watchful neighbours, but very much more between ourselves — I knew that she felt to me as I did to her. The pulse and throb of her little hand as it nestled in my own told me all I needed, and my heart was glad.

We found the courtyard of the black and white house — where I built my boat — filled with a great gathering; and sitting on a log in the midst was The Master, talking with them, earnestly but very cheerfully, like a wise elder brother.

He was not talking at them or preaching to them, or lay-ing down the law as the priests did, but telling them quietly and persuasively his ideas of the way of living that made most for happiness.

He asked them questions at times about their own diffi-culties, and he told them stories to make clear what he was trying to get into them, and sometimes he made them smile at the aptness of his sayings. But as I listened I saw that his little stories, and his unusual way of putting things, drove home the point he aimed at, as a carpenter drives home his nails. They made his words stick in one's mind till that which he taught became a very part of one's daily thought.

There were sick folk there too, whose friends had carried them to The Master to be cured, and they sat listening with wide, surprised eyes, hardly daring to believe that their troubles had really left them.

We had slipped quietly in at the back of the crowd, but I knew The Master saw us; for more than once, though many were sitting between him and us, I saw his eyes upon us in kindly welcome. And when he had ceased speaking and the people were going, he came straight to us.

"Warmest greetings!" he said, with a hand outstretched to each of us, and a glad light in his eyes. "Little Ruth, you were to skip for me like one of Esli's lambs."

And when she jubilantly danced a few steps before him, he smiled happily upon her and said, "You suffered your long captivity with patience, my daughter. Now you will walk joyously in the way God has set before you."

"Sir," she said very earnestly, "I would I might walk it all my life with Esli and with you."

"You will walk our way, my child, even though you do not walk it with us," he said gently. "And your heart's good wishes and your prayers will be with us, we know."

"Always and always!" she said, with all her heart in her voice and in her eyes.

As the night was falling he bade me see her safely home, and we went back along the shore together with scarce a word between us.

I had no desire to go right to the house, as it would only provoke my father to further remonstrance; so within sight of it we stopped and said farewell. And as she clung to me I kissed her on the lips for the first time, and then, with a sob, she broke from me and sped away home.

I watched her into the house and then turned and went back, feeling that I was indeed giving up my all to follow The Master, but feeling also that nothing else would satisfy the desire of my heart.

CHAPTER XIV

As WAS customary with teachers of note, there gathered about The Master many who were drawn to him by his unusual and enlivening sayings, and still more, perhaps, by his wonderful doings, and by something in himself that captured their minds and their hearts and would not let them go.

Wherever he went he healed all who came to him for help, and so he left behind him everywhere a path set thick with grateful hearts — of the blind who saw — of the lame who walked — of lepers delivered from their death-in-life and restored whole and clean to their families. And these all swelled the numbers of his followers.

Never within the knowledge of man had such things been done before. And, besides possessing such wonderful powers, he was so different even in his looks from any man they had ever seen — so dignified and so gracious, so strong and so gentle, so full of the joy of life, so obviously charged with some power beyond the ordinary run of men, and yet so full of understanding and brotherly-kindness for all, which was very unusual in learned Rabbis.

The multitudes grew as word of him spread. They followed him wherever he went and hung upon his sayings, which were sometimes very simple and understandable, but at other times puzzled them mightily and set them thinking hard to discover his meaning, and arguing and discussing among themselves.

But on one point they for the most part were agreed. This great wonder-worker, to whose wisdom and power there seemed to be no limit, could be none other than the

Promised One of whom the prophets of old had spoken, and for whom they and their fathers had waited so long. With powers like that he could do anything and everything. With powers like that even Rome could not stand against him.

He spoke much of the Kingdom he had come to establish, and their hopes ran high. But in their minds it was as yet all very vague and indefinite, and possibly, I thought, this new and upsetting teaching of his was his way of preparing them for the great change when he saw the time was ripe.

I remember as if it were but yesterday my first meeting with The Master's mother.

He took me to her and said, "Mother, this is Esli whose heart is set on serving me." And I felt that she took to me at once because I desired to serve her son.

"But how can you serve him, Esli ?" she asked, as he left us together. "You are very young."

"Not too young to do everything I can for him. It is his own self I would serve."

"If he will let you. But he has always done everything for himself, ever since he was quite a little boy," she said with a sigh.

"Now he is thinking so much of other people, and doing so much for us all, that he won't have time to think of himself. So I will see to him. I will see that he eats. I will wash his feet. I will see to his clothes. . ."

"It will be a great comfort to me to think of you so, Esli. For, you see, I cannot follow him everywhere now. . . And where it is all to end . . . I wonder . . . and sometimes I hardly dare to think."

She was at that time somewhere about of middle age, and her face was white and sweet and gentle, but there was in it always a look of anxious wonder — bewilderment almost, and apprehension; and that look grew still more marked as time went on.

Her eyes were large and dark, and looked the larger and

darker, because of the soft misty darkness which surrounded them. As she looked at me I thought again of the little pools that lay dark amid the snow when I used to take my sheep up into the woods in winter.

The Master's eyes were deep-set too, but his were like the pools when the sun shone down into them and up out of them, always with that fire of life in them; while his mother's, as I remember them, were always shadowed. Perhaps it was that his were lighted with a great hope, and hers were darkened by her fears.

Her big son had grown beyond her, and her heart and mind were troubled about him. For, you see, though she rejoiced with wonder at the things he did and said, and at the way most of the people acclaimed him, she heard too, of the growing ill-feeling and opposition of the priests and all those in high places, and if she could she would have persuaded him to tread a less perilous path. She longed sorely for a return to the peaceful life in Nazaret, before he had set out to teach the world his better way.

My feeling of love and reverence for him grew with each day that passed. For his own bodily self I felt as I had never felt towards any man before.

It was to me an endless joy just to watch him. His very walk, and indeed his every movement, was so different from other men's.

There was a quiet grace and dignity about him which set him apart and drew men's eyes to him, and, still more — women's; for his manner to them showed them in what high esteem and consideration he held every one of them.

His robes were always white, with just the blue fringe enjoined by the law, and as far as that was possible he liked them to be spotless — which kept me very busy.

His hands were strong and gentle and beautifully shaped. And they were very expressive. I loved to watch them when he was speaking, for they seemed full of life to the very tips of the fingers, and they moved gently and eloquently, even though they were folded in his lap or hanging down by his side, and many might not have noticed them. But I got into the way of watching them, for it seemed to me that they told me, almost as much as his words, of the eagerness of the spirit that was in him to help his fellows; and calm and gentle as he was outwardly, I was sure that inwardly he was all aflame.

Now and again I saw the strong, gentle hands curl tightly, as he strove to keep down the anger and indignation stirred up in him by some of those who came to him. And at such times his eyes could be very terrible to the evil-minded ones. They saw more, I am sure, those deep, calm eyes of his, and understood more of what they saw, than any other man's eyes ever did. They missed nothing, and when they looked at you they seemed not to be looking simply at the outside of you but right through into your mind and heart.

If you really came to him for help you were assured of it in his look, for you felt that here was one who understood and desired above all things to help you, and you felt too that you could trust him wholly.

That was how I had felt myself that first time I looked into his eyes, the day I killed the wolf, so I knew just how other men felt when he looked at them.

Whatever he did you could see that he put his whole heart and mind and strength into it; and very often his work — his talkings with the crowds, and still more his healings, left him very weary. For if he had a mind and spirit beyond most men's, he was still to all of us a man. And the demands made upon him were so heavy and so ceaseless that we marvelled that any man could stand it.

He had, however, a peculiar and very helpful power of going sound asleep at will — at any time, in any place, and that did much for him.

I have seen him, many times, when, after a hard day's work, we others had at last, for his sake, succeeded in turning away the multitudes, go into his inner room and stretch himself on his bed and be fast asleep in an instant. And, no matter how short a time he slept, he always awoke fresh and vigorous.

And I have known him fall asleep in a boat on the lake, even when it was so rough that the waves came tumbling in over the sides.

But very often, instead of going to his bed of a night, he would go quietly away into the hills all by himself. And whether he slept there or not — and the others thought he went there to pray — he always came back in the morning like a new-made man.

BOOK II — THE CITY

CHAPTER XV

THE WAY the people flocked to hear and see The Master was very wonderful.

All our lives, of course, every one of us had been brought up to expect the coming, sooner or later, of The Deliverer, who would help us to throw off the yoke of Rome and become once more a nation. Many Deliverers had come, and gone, and only plunged us deeper in the mire, but yet we went on hoping.

But never yet had one appeared possessed of such wonderful powers as those displayed by The Master, Jesus-ben-Joseph of Nazaret, and used by him so unstintingly. No sick person ever appealed to him in vain, no matter what his trouble. There seemed indeed no limit to his powers, which were obviously more than any ordinary man's; and if he could do such things, what was there that he could not do ?

It was the fame of his wonderful healings, which ran through the country like the coming of the Spring, that drew crowds to meet him wherever he went. For there were many sick folk among us, and the like of this had never been heard.

When his healings had gathered them, his wise and kindly — and for the most part, simple — talk gave them much that was new and startling to think about. But it was himself, his comely grace and goodness, his perfect loving-kindness to all who sought him, that won their hearts and made them want to kiss even the hem of his robe as he passed.

I have said his talk was simple. But it was not always so.

[74]

Now and again he said things which even his closest followers could not understand. And at other times, when his opponents — few as yet, but venomous and active — tried to trap him with awkward questions, his sayings to them were anything but gentle or simple. They were like the clever defence of a skilful fighter which turned the shrewdest blows back upon the giver. And sometimes they were cast in the form of joke or banter which hugely pleased the crowd but left the others speechless.

When the time for the Passover drew near, and I heard from the others that we were to go up to Jerusalem for it, I was filled with excitement, for, because of my ailment, my father had always feared to take me.

But that was a thing of the past. Never once since I met The Master up in the hills that day had my evil spirit troubled me.

We started very early one morning and it was to me one of the greatest mornings that ever had been.

I had gone the night before to say good-bye to Ruth. But she had danced with excitement before me, crying, "But I am going too ! I am going, Esli ! We are both going for the first time in our lives — and we are going together ! Isn't it wonderful ?" So it was indeed one of the greatest days we had ever seen.

Our little plain of Gennesaret was at its best and brightest, with its great stretches of growing wheat and barley, and flowers everywhere.

I walked with The Master and the men. Ruth was with the women, some of whom were mounted on mules or asses. But we were often all mixed up and I would find myself alongside her, and we would walk together, marvelling thankfully at the wonder of it all. No one, I am sure, ever had such joy in that journey as we, who were doing it for the first time in our lives, and were old enough to savour it with understanding.

As we crossed the great plain we could see streams of other travellers coming along every path and down all the hillsides, all bound for Jerusalem. And on all sides were meetings of old friends and joyous greetings and much eager talk.

Greatest joy of all to us was the reverent welcome everywhere accorded to The Master. We were proud indeed to be of his company.

For the word that he was coming flew on ahead of us, and in every village we came to there would be waiting for us by the side of the road every sick or maimed or blind person that could be got there. And he healed them all, and that so lovingly, and with such tender understanding, and such wise and simple words, that his passage was like the sun breaking through and chasing away the shadows on a stormy day. Everywhere, he left behind him comfort and hope and fresh cheer, and the white seed of his New Way.

The people did not understand him any more than we who followed him did. But we all saw the wonders he wrought on the bodies and minds of those who sought him; and, even without understanding him, we all felt that here was a new power for good come into the world, and we were filled with hope of what might be to follow.

At the places where we stopped for the nights, the people gathered about him in such numbers that it was with the greatest difficulty that we were able to get him any time to himself, even to eat and to sleep. They would have kept him talking and healing all night long, had we not insisted on them leaving him for a space.

For, wonderful as he was, and in such perfect health and strength that it was a joy to watch his every movement, he was still a man, and there is a limit to the endurance of even the greatest of men. Later on, we came to know that he was very much more than any man who ever had been. But at this time our eyes were not yet opened to that great wonder, and I am trying to live over again those days just as they were.

We crossed the great plain, splashing joyously through the many little streams which went to feed the river Kishon — past Nain and Shunem and Jezreel, and the bold bare mountain of Gilboa, where Gideon lay before he fell upon the hosts of Midian in the night; and where King Saul and his son Jonathan were killed; and past Megiddo, where Deborah and Barak defeated Sisera, the great captain of the hosts of the King of Hazor: and where King Josiah was wounded to the death by the archers of the King of Egypt.

That great plain, full of flowers and flowing streams, was full too of the memories of the past, great memories but mostly of turmoils and fightings. And we could not but recall them as we passed.

But I remember, as we followed close behind The Master and the others, how Ruth said one time, with a knowing little nod towards him, "Maybe if he had come earlier all those terrible things would not have happened." And truly he seemed the very opposite of all such doings.

We were drawing near to the end of our first day's march when we saw a small crowd gathered in front, growing greater as everyone who came along stopped to see what was the matter.

Supposing that someone was needing help, The Master pushed gently through and we followed him.

And there we found Simon, who worked for old Peleg of Kaphar-Nahum, and one of his little asses which had fallen to the ground and could not get up. It was laden with fish, a very heavy load. We had noticed it on the road, and Ruth had remarked pitifully on the thinness of its legs compared with the burden on its back.

Simon, who was usually easy-going with his beasts, seemed to have lost his head and his temper. We heard afterwards that it was the first time he had been sent on this new venture to Jerusalem, and it was rather much for him, for he was not any too bright in his wits.

He was distraught and angry, and his only idea seemed to be that if he kicked the little ass hard enough it would get up.

As a race our people are callous towards animals, and never seem to think that they have feelings and can suffer.

[77]

Some of the onlookers were jeering and offering provoking suggestions, which only made Simon the more angry; and the angrier he grew, the harder he kicked.

Then, just as he delivered a lustier kick than ever, and the little ass winced and made a desperate effort to get up but only sank back with a groan, I heard, "Simon!" — and looking up quickly saw The Master's face, sad and reproachful, as was his voice.

And whether it was that Simon overkicked himself that time, or what did it I know not, but he fell suddenly flat on his back beside the little ass, which turned its head and looked at him as though saying, "What, you too, master?"

"My leg! my leg!" cried Simon, in great pain and fright. And we saw that his right leg was fixed stiff and straight so that he could not bend it.

"Serves you right!" said an old woman, looking down at him, and Simon howled the louder.

I do not think he had heard The Master's voice. But now, as his frightened eyes roved about him, he caught sight of his face, and shouted, "Ah there — you — Jesus! . . . Help me! . . . my leg's broken."

They were cousins, you know, and had lived in the same house at Nazaret, but they had never been great companions, for Simon had less understanding of Jesus even than the others, and they had not much.

"It is your own doing, Simon," The Master said gently. "You overload your little beast till it sinks and then you maltreat it."

"My leg! my leg! . . . Help me, Jesus!"

"Let it be a lesson to you then!" said The Master, as he stooped over him and ran his strong sensitive fingers up and down the useless leg. And I watched them with delight, for I could almost see the new life passing out of them.

"Remember always," he said, "that even little asses have their feelings just as you have!"

Presently the leg grew supple again and Simon found he

could bend it, so he got up onto his feet but he still shook as he stood.

"Now take off that load and give away half of it — " said The Master.

"But my fish ! — Old Peleg — "

"Better get to Jerusalem with half a load than never get there at all. Do as I tell you, and never ill-treat a dumb beast again lest worse befall you !"

And as Simon, with hands that still shook, cast off the load, The Master, with his face full of pity, bent and stroked the little ass's rough forehead encouragingly, and it got up onto its feet, and its great gentle eyes seemed to me to look back at him gratefully.

CHAPTER XVI

WE STOPPED the night at En-Gannîm, setting up our little shelters in a grove of beautiful trees, with flowers and streams all about us. And the next day we climbed the mountains of Manasseh and came down among groves of figs and olives as good almost as those of our own plain. We camped that night near to Jacob's Well, not far from Shechem, between mounts Ebal and Gerizim, from which the curses and the blessings were ordered to be delivered by Moses, and some hold that it was on Gerizim that our father, Abraham, was about to sacrifice his son Isaac when God stayed him.

And everywhere, even in Samaria, which was never friendly towards us Galileans, the sick and the maimed were brought out for The Master to cure. And as we walked, he talked quietly with those nearest to him of this New Way of his, of which his mind and heart were full, giving them much to think about, and sometimes to puzzle over, and to argue about among themselves.

But even when he was speaking most earnestly to them, I could see that those searching eyes of his missed nothing of what we passed on the road. He saw everything, especially every chance that offered of helping anyone in need.

The next day our road wound round the feet of the mountains of Ephraim, by Shiloh and Gilgal, and Beth-el and Ai and Ramah — names full of meaning to us — and we spent that night at Gibeah.

Very early next morning, away in the distance, we got our first sight of Jerusalem. . . Jerusalem ! — for the first time in our lives ! . . . — The holy city, the city of David and Solomon, with its great shadowy walls and dark gateways; and

up above, the white houses without number; and over all —
the Temple, with its great rounded dome shining like gold
in the morning sun. A wonderful sight, to us who had never
seen anything like it, and to whom Tiberias on the lake had
seemed a great city. . .

And our thoughts were full of all the things that had happened there . . . though this indeed was not the actual city
that David knew, nor that the Temple Solomon built. Time
and many wars had destroyed them, and this Temple was of
Herod's building. Still it was all so very wonderful that
Ruth and I fell over our own feet as we walked on towards
it, with bated breath and eager eyes, lest it should vanish like
a dream before we reached it.

When I glanced round one time I saw that many of our
company felt it much as we did. Most of them must have
seen it many times before, but that first sight of it as we left
Gibeah was very overpowering, no matter how often they
had seen it.

But when my eyes sought The Master's face the look upon
it surprised me — it was so different from his usual high
sweet calm.

There was in it something of that look which he turned on
the priests and Pharisees when they came trying to trip or to
trap him with their artful questions.

And I thought there was something too of the look I had
seen at times in his mother's face when she was speaking
about him — very difficult to say exactly what . . . intense
yearning, eager expectation, and something, it seemed to me,
of doubt — not doubt of himself but of that on which his
gaze was fixed with such eagle-like directness and penetra-
tion.

I had never seen just that look on his face before. It
startled and astonished me more even than the sight of
Jerusalem. For he seemed to be looking through and
through the great city and reading its heart, as he read the
hearts of all whom he met.

Afterwards . . . ah well — afterwards, Jerusalem came to

have a very different meaning for us, but at this time we saw only the wonder and the glory of it, shining there in the distance, all fair and white in the morning sun.

I have wondered since if, even then, he may not have had a feeling of the menace of the great city to him. For it was the home and centre of the upholders of the Old Ways, and they had already shown him clearly that he and his New Way were hateful to them.

Later on, I grew in understanding of him just as he himself grew at last into the full comprehension of all that lay before him. But at this time I am sure he was full of hope that his work would be successful in the end, though he could not but see also the difficulties and perils that lay before him. And that, I think, was what I saw in his face that morning as he gazed at Jerusalem.

If we had been amazed at the streams of people we had everywhere seen making their way towards the city, now, as we drew near to it, we were appalled by the multitudes gathered all about it. The whole countryside seemed to me like a nightmare colony of ants, all in motion, all busy with their own little affairs, flitting hither and thither, and setting up their little shelters for the night, for the city itself could not contain a tenth of them.

As we threaded our way quietly through the wandering crowds, my heart swelled again with pride at the way they regarded The Master.

In his white robes he was truly good to look upon — tall and shapely, and of a comeliness that was all his own, and the like of which I have never seen in any other man. Not that he was really any taller than the average of men, but that he always seemed so because of the exceeding grace and dignity of his carriage.

He looked, indeed, like a messenger from some other land or some other world, an envoy of some great king, and all turned to look as he came, and then turned to ask who this was.

But many already knew him, and there were few that had

not at all events heard of him; and so, as the word flew round that this was the wonderful prophet from Galilee — the Great Healer — the New Teacher — they gathered so thickly about us that we could scarce get through.

We came at last, by the dark Damascus Gate, into the city, and found the narrow streets choked with people from, it seemed to me, every land under the sun, all jostling and shouting at one another as they sought for lodgings for the night or friends from whom they had become parted.

The Master made his way at once to the Temple, and there again I saw a new and, to me, very unexpected side of him.

I had always seen him so quiet and calm and dignified. For, even when the wily ones set themselves against him, and tried to catch him with their tricky questions, he was never upset by them.

But as we entered the outer court of the Temple — called the Court of the Gentiles — I, close beside him, saw him suddenly stop and stiffen as though he had been struck. I saw his hands clench tight, and his face was, as I had never seen it before, filled with distress and with growing anger and indignation.

And no wonder. For that Temple Court was packed with sheep and oxen and those who sold and bought them, and with baskets containing doves. The filth and stench and flies made it an abomination. The loud chafferings and bargainings of the buyers and sellers, and the cries of the troubled animals, made an uproar that was deafening.

Under the arcades of the great Corinthian columns sat rows of money-changers, each at his little table piled with coins. And there the noise was worst of all. For all the various moneys of the country-folk and strangers had to be changed into the only coins the priests would accept for the Temple dues, and the money-changers drove hard bargains and grew fat on them. And so there were endless wranglings and disputings, and shameless greed provoked bitter recrimination, and all was most unseemly noise and clamour.

For one moment only The Master looked round with eyes that missed nothing of it all. Then the distress in his face gave place to the anger and indignation.

He snatched up a piece of rope and began driving the sheep and oxen out into the street in a tumultuous torrent. The sellers of doves he ordered out after them. And the owners of all these were so astounded, and so anxious to recover their property, that they made no resistance but sped after their vanishing beasts.

But for the greedy money-changers he had no consideration. He knocked over their tables, sending their money flying, and they went sprawling all over the place in search of it.

It was truly a most amazing sight — one man alone putting to rout such a rude and angry mob. Yet, even to me, as I watched breathless, it was dimly understandable. For he was like a flaming white fire, a blaze of righteous indignation against a crying wrong. He was in the right — and they knew it. They were in the wrong — and they knew it. Their evil consciences made them cowards and they could not face him.

Nevertheless, some, even as they groped about the filthy floor after their coins, turned to curse him and threaten him with the anger of the priests. But his only reply to them was — "Away with you! My Father's house is not to be turned into a shop!"

And later, when some of those in authority came to him and asked him to show them proof of his right to do such things, he looked right through them and then said quietly, "Destroy this temple and in three days I will raise it up" — which was quite beyond their understanding or ours. We puzzled much over it, as we had to do over many of his sayings. But, after their first amazement, it filled them with fury.

"You will build it in three days!" they foamed. "Forty-six years it took to build and you will build it in three days!"

And had they dared they would have laid hands on him

then and there and held him to account. But the people were for him because of his wonderful doings and sayings, and the rulers went off full of wonder and hatred.

Long afterwards some of us recalled that strange saying of his, and we came to understand what he meant by it, because of all that befell him, and by that time we had grown into a better knowledge of him. And some of the rulers recalled it also and turned it to evil purpose.

But the people approved of what he had done, for the state the Temple had got into had become a scandal; and especially were they pleased at the discomfiture of the money-changers who had robbed them without reproof all their lives.

And so, for a time — as long indeed as he was there — the Temple remained clean.

CHAPTER XVII

THE MASTER knew perfectly well the violent opposition his new teaching was rousing among the priests and Pharisees. But I think he hoped to overcome it in time and perhaps even to win them to his way, as he was winning the hearts of the people.

He knew men too well, however, to take any risk that would interfere with his work. And so he would not spend a night in the city, but went out before the gates were closed and walked quietly across a little valley and up a steep foot-path that led to a hill covered with olive and cedar trees.

And before he went down the other side of the hill, he turned and stood and looked back at the great city, penned inside its dark walls like some great threatening monster. The noises of its teeming multitudes came up to us in a low ceaseless growl, though it lay there looking so fair and stately with the gold of the evening sunlight on its white buildings and colonnades and shining Temple.

His face, as he stood and gazed, had on it that same look which I had seen in the morning, when we first came in sight of the city as we left Gibeah — expectation, longing, and something of questioning and doubt. But the expectation and the longing were greater than the doubt.

As he stood there, in his white robes turned to gold like everything else by the setting sun, there seemed to me something of a challenge in the way he looked back on the city, — almost as though he were thinking, "I know you — I know you, and all your ways. And my heart is sore for you. But I will win you yet, for I want you — I want you!"

It is possible that my later understanding of him creeps

[86]

into my thoughts of him as he was then. But I do not think so, for in my heart and mind I can recall his face just as it was as he stood there that first evening among the grey olive trees.

When he turned and went on over the hill his face soon became as calm and high and hopeful as it usually was.

Far away in front of us was a great range of mountains, purple in the distance, which made me think of the mountains on the other side of our lake.

We came down over the shoulder of the hill towards a little village almost hidden among its olive and palm trees. After Jerusalem it looked very peaceful and homely.

The Master had evidently been expected, for long before we got there some of its people came running to meet us — two very comely young women, and behind them, more slowly, a man of about thirty, tall and somewhat thin, with a pleasant thoughtful face.

His name was Lazarus and he was a Rabbi, learned in the Law and the writings of the prophets. His sisters were Martha and Mary, and I saw that The Master was very dear to them all, and they to him.

They greeted him joyously. The younger, Mary, reached him first and clasped his hand in both hers, her face beaming with happiness. Martha, the elder, took his other hand in hers, saying breathlessly, "Her feet are younger than mine, Jesus, but my heart was in front of them," and the eyes of both dwelt lovingly on his face which was now as glad as theirs.

Then their brother came up, and he and The Master stood for a moment looking quietly and deeply into one another's eyes and hearts. And then we went along to their simple but very comfortable home.

The others told me all about them, and that The Master never would stop a night in the city because of the noise and the crowds. But he loved this little village of Bethany, which was always sweet and clean and peaceful. And however worn and troubled he might be with the perversity and opposition of the priests and rulers in the city, a night at Bethany always recovered him.

The Master stayed, as he always did, with his friends, and the rest of us were made welcome by their neighbours, but each morning we all walked back over the little hill into the city, and The Master spent the day in the Temple, telling the people of his New Way and healing any who came to him with their ills or were brought to him by their friends.

So each day I was able to see and comfort Ruth, who was stopping with her mother and my father at the house of her mother's cousin.

For, now that the first wonder of the great city had worn off, Ruth found it not at all to her liking.

"Oh, I long to be back at our own clean lake, Esli," she said, on the third morning. "I cannot breathe here, there are so many people. — And the smells and the sights and the ceaseless turmoil ! How can people live here ?"

"I suppose they get used to it. They would probably find our lake very dull."

"It will be like heaven after this," she sighed — and then, more cheerfully, "But we have only four more days of it. . . I shall never want to come to Jerusalem again as long as I live. The people all seem strangers, even those who live here."

I knew just how she felt, for I was feeling just the same.

There was no friendliness towards one another such as we were used to at home. It was, of course, an unusual time, and there were people there from many lands, with strange faces and garments, and uncouth tongues, and mostly with quick, suspicious eyes, as though they thought every man they met was going to take advantage of their ignorance. And no doubt they had good reason, for it was a great harvest-time for all the city-dwellers who had any service to render, and they made the most of it.

The crowds to whom The Master spoke each day in the Temple listened to him with lively interest. It was all so

different from what they were accustomed to. Never before had they heard such strange wise words delivered in so
kind and homely a way, nor seen such wonderful deeds.
But I could see from his face that he was disappointed that
so few of them really accepted his teaching to the point of
making it their way of life.

They listened and they wondered. They said among
themselves that it was good. But they passed on, and
whether any more came of it we could not tell. There was,
however, this in it — his hearers came from all over the
world, and if his words took any root in their hearts the
harvest might be found later on in places far away from
Jerusalem. And I think now that perhaps that was why
he went on speaking so earnestly to them although so little
seemed to come of it at the time.

The priests and rulers set themselves stonily against him.
They hovered about the listening crowds with venomous
faces, as though they would have liked to take him and
work their will on him. But for fear of the people they
dared not — even when the people said openly among themselves — "We have never heard any man like this man, or
heard of any man doing the things this man does. Can he
really be messiah — the Promised One ?"

The priests were furious when they heard that, for if that
belief grew, and the people should try to make him King,
the Romans would be down upon them and the whole
country would suffer.

The clearing out of the traders from the Temple hit them
hard too, for they had reaped a goodly harvest from that
business, and so they hated The Master the more.

His nearest followers knew well all that the priests and
rulers were thinking and hoping. They saw that there was
not room in the world for the New Way and the Old. And
the Old Way was deep and wide-rooted, and its upholders
were many and powerful, while we were as yet but few, and
not without our fears.

They urged The Master to turn his back on these perverse

ones and go again to the country-folk who everywhere welcomed him. But he went on with his work quietly and calmly, and without a sign that he knew that the rulers would make an end of him the first chance they got.

But even those in high places were not all of one mind concerning him, and one at least, if not more, came to him by night, all the way to Bethany, to learn more of his teaching, and they talked long together.

When the last of the people began to leave for their homes, we also went and were glad to go. For myself, I never could get away from the feeling that the great city, with its grim high walls and gloomy gates, and its proud Temple and haughty columns, and its grasping people, was like a fierce beast of prey waiting its chance to devour any it could lay hold of.

And so my heart rejoiced greatly when, one morning, instead of setting off to cross the Hill of Olives, we said goodbye to the friends at Bethany and went off the other way — towards the river Jordan, which came right out of our own lake, and the bold bare mountains which always made me think of our own mountains of Gadara.

Ruth and the others had already gone and would now be at home where she had longed to be, and I was sure she would never wish to come to Jerusalem again.

CHAPTER XVIII

OF THE WOMAN AT THE WELL

WE SET up our little shelters on the bank of the river, and when the word spread that The Master was there the people came flocking to him again from all the neighbouring parts and some even from the city.

Day after day he spoke to them of his New Way, and urged them to turn from their old evil ways and repent, "for," he never ceased telling them, "the Kingdom of heaven is at hand." And though none of us knew exactly what he meant by that, and many even among ourselves believed that he would in due time set up a new Kingdom for our own people, it was evident that the first step was to repent. And many came asking him to baptise them in the river, as John the Baptiser did, as a sign that they really did mean to live better lives.

He would not, however, baptise any himself, but let his nearest followers do it. And I often wondered why, but could only suppose it was because he knew that if he did it himself some would boast that they had been baptised by The Master, and so would lord it over those who had not been so fortunate. You see, he knew men's hearts all through, and he would do nothing that might give them occasion to stumble.

His cousin John — the Baptiser — was still carrying on his own work further up the river, but so many more came to The Master that John's followers felt sore about it, and that troubled The Master greatly.

Then, suddenly, word came that John had been seized by Herod the Tetrarch and shut up in the Castle of Machaerus, on the other side of the river close by the desert, and The

Master decided to return to our own country, Galilee, at which we all rejoiced.

We passed by Jericho, and through the hills, till we came upon the road by which we had come down; and as before, the village-folk everywhere came out to meet us, for word of The Master's wonderful works had spread all over the country.

The weather was very hot, and at times we all grew weary. Even The Master himself showed it, and that was very unusual with him.

As a rule he paced steadily on, with that firm light step which had so gladdened my eyes that first morning when I met him up in the hills. And he would talk happily to us as we went, sometimes about the things we saw — or would not have seen but for him — and often explaining things he had said previously and which we had not properly understood.

For at times in his talks with the people there were puzzling things — odd sayings, and stories which sometimes did not seem to us to fit in — which we could not make anything of till he made them clear to us. We were some of us very dull, I fear.

But on this journey he was more silent than usual, and his mind seemed burdened.

Perhaps it was the bad news about his cousin; or it might be that the ever-growing opposition of those who ought to have been the first to welcome anything that might make for the general good, lay heavy upon him.

When we came to Jacob's Well, this side of Sychar, between the hills Ebal and Gerizim, which seemed to shut out the air and make it hotter than ever, The Master dropped onto the stone wall of the well which was shaded by a wooden roof, and said quietly that he would fain rest there for a time.

We knew his liking to be alone when he was over-tired, so, when I had loosed his sandals and dusted his feet, the rest of us went slowly on to the town to buy some food.

This, in the ordinary course of things, might not have been possible, for the Samaritans and the Jews hate one another and there is no intercourse between them.

Even as we went we passed a woman with a pitcher on her shoulder going towards the well, and she looked at us sourly, knowing we were strangers.

But The Master's wonderful works were known even in Samaria, and when they heard who the food was for we had no difficulty.

When we got back to the well we found him in deep converse with the woman we had met before, and as we approached she sped past us with her face strangely excited, leaving her pitcher on the wall of the well.

The Master sat there, full of thought, but showing no signs of the weariness in which we had left him. We tendered him what we had brought — bread, and fruit and Jericho dates. But though he thanked us for them he did not eat. And when we pressed him, he said quietly, "I have food of which you know nothing," — which surprised us greatly, and we wondered if the woman could have brought him anything.

And when he saw that that puzzled us, he added, "My food is to do the will of Him who sent me, and to accomplish His work." And, indeed, he seemed completely himself again, full of life and strength and the joy of living.

It seemed very strange to us, but there was so much concerning him that we could not comprehend that all we could do was to sit and eat and wonder.

And as we did so, he went on talking quietly to us about sowing and reaping, and fields white for harvesting — which I supposed had some reference to the bread we were eating, but what it meant was beyond me.

Then we saw a crowd coming running towards us from the town, with that same woman in front of them. They crowded round him full of excitement.

"She says you are messiah". . . "She says you told her all the doings of her life". . . "She says you can give us water which will last us forever". . . "She says it is neither on Gerizim nor at Jerusalem that we ought to worship". . . "Rabbi, stop with us and tell us more of these things !" . . . and much more of the like.

And when he looked round at their eager faces he said quietly, "Yes, I will stop with you and tell you more of these things. Truly the harvest is ripe."

We went back into the town with them and stopped there for two days in much comfort, for we were well entertained by them. They listened eagerly and gladly to The Master's teaching, and very many of them promised faithfully to follow it.

CHAPTER XIX

OF A PROPHET IN HIS OWN COUNTRY

THE PEOPLE of Sychar would have had us stay longer with them. It was very surprising how friendly we all became, seeing that we were, by custom and tradition, enemies. But that was The Master's doing. With him there, the old ill-feelings and prejudices seemed of no account. We were all alike seekers after his New Way.

They found us all lodgings and did all they could for us. The Master was in the house of their oldest and most esteemed Rabbi, and of a night they spoke much together. John-ben-Zabdai — at his own request, I know, for I saw him asking her and her husband — was in the house of the woman who had first met The Master at the well. And that was how he drew from her, bit by bit, all that The Master had said to her there. And some of this he imparted to us as we walked.

We spent a night at En-Gannîm again, and from there went on over the plain of Esdraelon to Nazaret, where The Master had passed most of his life and where he had some very dear friends.

It was good to see the great joy of their meeting. For he had scarce set foot on a path that ran along the side of the hill above the village, when, from a house higher up, there came running a man of somewhere near his own age, and so like him in many respects that I thought they must be at least cousins.

With him came a tall slim boy whom, or one very like him, I thought I had seen in Jerusalem; and close behind them two very comely young women, the foremost of whom fairly took my breath by her beauty when she drew near enough for me to see her properly.

She was tall, dark of hair and eye, of a very noble grace and carriage, and her face was so radiantly beautiful that I could not take my eyes off it. Behind these came some others, but I hardly saw them because of the wonder of the tall dark one.

Her name, I heard, was Zerah, and the man's name was Azor, and even I could see that the friendship between them and The Master was something quite beyond the usual. Their eyes, as they gazed into one another's faces, had lights in them and deeps in them which spoke louder than any words could have done.

The Master bade us find lodgings in the village below, as he must stop with his friends on the hillside — in the house, the others told me, in which he had lived as a boy, and until a year or so ago had worked at the carpenter's bench with Azor as his partner.

I stood and watched them all as they went slowly up the path, he and Zerah and Azor talking earnestly together, and the others close about them. And they were very good to look upon, fine upstanding graceful figures all of them, but also something very much more. There was something about them all — it was not easy to say what, but I felt it strongly — a sense of outstanding goodness and gladness that seemed to clothe them with beauty and set them above and apart from any company I had ever met.

"His dearest friends! And they have lived all their lives with him! — that is why," I said to myself, as they all went into the house up above. And I turned and ran after Simon and the rest, lest I should get no lodging for the night.

We did not see him the next day, for he went up into the hills with his friends, Azor and Zerah and the boy I had seen with them the day before. And it was then that he did one of the most wonderful things that ever man did, though we did not know of it till afterwards — he called back to life a young man who had died and was being buried. His name was Arni, and he was his mother's only son and she was a widow, and he and The Master had been playfellows when they were boys.

The next day was the Sabbath, and The Master came down with his friends and we all went to the synagogue together.

And there a strange thing happened, but it did not surprise me as much as it might have done. For, while we were waiting The Master's pleasure the day before, we could not be among the people of Nazaret without becoming aware that they were a strange and difficult lot. I remembered Nathaniel-bar-Tholmai's saying, when Philip told him where The Master came from — "Can any good thing come out of Nazaret ?" — and that was a common saying in those parts and tells its own story.

We heard them talking of The Master in a way that surprised us. . . "He's a great Rabbi now, they say". . . "Ay — sets himself up as a teacher". . . "They say folks crowd after him as though they'd never seen the like of him". . . "They say he's done some strange things. There was that story of the wine up at Cana". . . "Oh — Cana ! they'd say anything in Cana". . . "After all, he's only old Joseph's boy and our carpenter. He made that door for me."

"Seems a good door," said Simon, who overheard this.

"Oh, it's a good door. I will say that for him. His work was always sound. But that doesn't say he's any right to set up as a Rabbi and go teaching things that are against the law."

"He doesn't," said Simon sturdily.

"Ay, but he does. The priests say so anyway."

"Oh, the priests ! His law is a better law than the priests' law — or it's a better way of looking at it, and the people know it."

"The priests' law was good enough for our fathers and

G   [97]

it's good enough for us. You mark my words — he'll get himself into trouble if he goes against the priests, and you too, and you're old enough to know that."

And they had hot argument which only left them both convinced that the other was a fool and absolutely stiff-necked.

There was evidently a good deal of feeling like that about, and we were all rather anxious when, after the reading of the lesson, The Master rose and stepped up to the preacher's seat and the clerk handed him the sacred roll.

Everyone stood while he read some verses of the prophet Isaiah. And, knowing the strange feelings of these people about him, they made me more anxious still.

For these were the words he read —

> *"The spirit of the Lord is upon me,*
> *For he has consecrated me to preach His good news to*
> *the poor.*
> *He has sent me to proclaim release for captives,*
> *And recovery of sight to the blind,*
> *To set free the oppressed,*
> *To proclaim the Lord's year of favour."*

Knowing, as I am sure he did — for he read men's hearts at a glance and he had lived all his life among these — knowing then the feelings with which many of them regarded him, these words seemed to me likely to provoke them.

When he handed back the roll to its keeper and sat down to speak to them, every eye was fixed on him, some in expectation, more perhaps in a spirit of carping criticism.

Quietly but impressively he declared to them that it was he himself of whom the prophet had written seven hundred years before — that he himself was indeed the promised messiah for whom the world had waited so long.

They listened at first in a kind of stunned silence. Then a rustle of discomfort and dislike of it went through them, and there were murmurs of disagreement with his extraordinary claims. . . "Joseph's boy !" . . . "The carpenter !" . . .

"He the messiah ! Why we've known him all our lives !"
. . . "We know all his people."

"Yes," he said quietly, "It is hard for you to accept this truth. You would have me prove it to you by some great sign, as in other places. I tell you truly, no prophet is ever welcome in his native place. It always has been so. There were many widows in Israel in the time of the great famine, but Elijah was sent, not to one of them but to the Phœnician widow of Sarepta in Sidon. And there were many lepers in Israel in the time of Elisha, but none of them were cleansed — only Naaman the Syrian."

At that their anger boiled over. Did he think them of smaller account then than Gentiles and lepers ?

"The   carpenter !" . . . "The   messiah !" . . . "What next ?"

They jumped up, foaming and shouting, and the whole place was in a turmoil. Some of them made a rush at him, but we were before them and gathered round him.

But we were all swept out into the street and they surged and frothed about us, shaking their fists and crying, "To the cliff with him !" . . . "Make an end of him !" . . . "See if he's clever enough to save himself !" . . .

And then — and I shall never forget that sight — as we were thrusting them aside and forcing our way through them with a violence equal to their own, The Master raised his hand to restrain us and passed on in front of us.

I could not see his face but I knew what it was like by the effect it had on the angry mob, and I had seen it when he swept the traders out of the Temple. The weakness of Wrong went down again before the power and majesty of Right, just as it had done then.

They fell back upon one another as he looked on them, and he passed quietly through the midst of them, and we close behind him.

It was a wonderful thing to see, and for myself, and I am sure for the others, my heart was filled with joy and pride in him.

[99]

But when we were clear of the place his face was very sad, and I saw that this rejection by his own people had hurt him sorely. But all that he said was, "Truly, as I said to you, a prophet is never welcomed in his own country."

As it was the Sabbath we could not go far that day. For, though The Master's teaching was often very different from that of the priests, he never, as far as I remember, offended against the accepted laws and customs of the people, unless for good reason and to teach them some new and better way.

There was no village within the permitted two thousand paces of Nazaret, and so we camped that night beneath some palm trees by the side of a stream, and were none the worse for the enforced fasting. For we had left Nazaret too hurriedly to think of taking any food with us.

The Master talked quietly with us for a time, but the perversity of Nazaret was still heavy on his heart, and as the evening drew on he went apart by himself and sat, with his back against a tree, full of thought, and, I am sure, of prayer.

CHAPTER XX

IN THE morning we were early afoot and took the road over the hills to Cana, which considers itself a much more important place than Nazaret. It was here that Nathaniel-bar-Tholmai had his home, and here that The Master had done a very wonderful thing just before I first met him.

For, at a wedding, to which he and his mother had been asked, and to which he had taken with him some of his friends, there were so many more guests than had been expected that the wine ran short. And when he heard this — and perhaps considered that it was the number of his friends that had caused it — The Master in some marvellous way turned some great jars of water into excellent wine, so that the giver of the feast should not be put to confusion before his guests.

It was just the kindly, thoughtful thing one could well imagine him doing. But it was the first sign he had given of the extraordinary power that was in him, and it was much talked about in those parts.

Nathaniel's father and the people of Cana gave him very warm welcome, which cheered us all much after that discomforting time at Nazaret.

When the men of Cana heard of that they expressed no surprise, except that The Master had chosen to live there so long when he might have lived at Cana, and also that, having left the disreputable place, he should ever have gone back to it.

"They are always like that, those Nazarenes," they said, " — rough and uncouth in all their ways and over-satisfied with themselves."

[101]

Here, the people were eager to hear all The Master's new way of interpreting the old laws. They listened to him gladly, and many came in from the surrounding country. And at Cana he did another of his wonderful works.

For one day there came up from Kaphar-Nahum, in haste and great distress, a Roman officer of high standing at the court of Herod, in Tiberias.

The story of the recalling of Arni of Nain from the dead had by this time spread over all the country. The Roman officer's only son lay at the point of death with the fever, at Kaphar-Nahum, whither he had been carried from Tiberias for the quiet and the fresher air. But nothing availed and he was dying.

His father heard the amazing story about Arni and set off instantly in search of The Master. For one who could defeat Death when he had struck could surely fend off his blow before it actually fell.

He found The Master speaking to a great crowd who were listening eagerly to every word.

The Roman pushed his way through.

"Sir," he said, with all his fear and his hope in his voice, "Come down with me to Kaphar-Nahum, I beseech you, and cure my son. He is my only one and is at the point of death."

The Master looked at him quietly and sympathetically — looked right into his heart and mind, as he always did. I think he must have seen that, though the desire to save his son's life was the father's strongest feeling, there was in him also the profound belief that The Master could do it if he would, or he would never have come so far and in such haste to make his request.

Nevertheless he did not accede to it at once. He quietly weighed the man up and said, "Unless you see signs and wonders you never will believe."

"Sir," said the Roman urgently, "I believe you can save my boy if you will. Come down with me, I beg of you, before he is dead," and he and The Master looked deep into one another's eyes.

"Go yourself," said The Master at last. "Your son will live," and, with a salute of deepest thankfulness, the Roman turned and went without another word. Whatever his belief it was strong enough for that.

Two days later we left Cana and walked over the hills and came down to Kaphar-Nahum, and I rejoiced greatly at sight of our peaceful blue lake and the prospect of seeing Ruth again.

But our company had been seen, and before we were clear of the hill we were met by that same Roman and some of his attendants.

He saluted The Master with a face full of joy.

"Sir," he said, "my son is well again. The fever left him at the very time you said the word. I thank you with my whole heart. Henceforth I and all my household follow your Way."

From that time he became a power for good at Herod's vicious court, and nowhere was there greater need.

Those gracious and benevolent deeds were spoken of everywhere, so that wherever The Master went, the people flocked to see and hear him. And all that he said and did was so truly just what he himself was, that the people held him in most loving reverence, and many gave their hearts to him and strove to follow his Way.

But the priests and those in authority for the most part held themselves aloof, for his Way was not their way, and they clung to their own.

CHAPTER XXI

WHEN we came into Kaphar-Nahum The Master went to his own people and we all went to ours.

I raced along the shore, full of joy at the thought of seeing Ruth again. From a long way off she saw me coming and came running to meet me. Ruth — running! How my heart leaped at the sight!

"Oh, but I am glad to see you, Esli. I have watched for you every day," she cried, as she flung her arms round my neck, and I could feel her heart beating against my own.

I had much to tell her and she listened eagerly.

"He is very wonderful, Esli. I am glad you are with him. Every day I am glad, though I miss you much."

"He is the most wonderful that ever was. He is as brave as a lion, and he is so gentle and lovable that it is a joy to serve him. I kiss his sandals every time I clean them."

"Kiss them for me too," she said. "He has made new things of you and me, Esli."

"He would do that for everyone if they would let him . . . But some — " and I told her what happened at Nazaret, which pained and shocked her sorely.

"How could they?" she asked, with bated breath. "And they had known him all their lives."

"He says that is why. — 'A prophet has no welcome in his own country.'" And I was soon to have another proof of that.

"I have always heard that the men of Nazaret were difficult to get on with. I wonder why he chose to live there," Ruth said thoughtfully.

"He's left them now anyway and I shouldn't think he'll

ever go back. Other people want him — " and I told her
how the crowds everywhere flocked to meet him, which
gladdened her greatly.

She had not much to tell me — except of her own feelings
and the wonderful joy of walking like any other. My
father and her mother rarely spoke of me, except disapprov-
ingly. To them I was simply wasting my time in unprofit-
able wanderings with one whom they deemed a dangerous
teacher of doctrines which were bound to get him, and all
who followed him, into trouble with the authorities.

But in spite of their coldness, I stopped there two days
for the joy of being with Ruth again. And on the third
day, which was the Sabbath, we went into Kaphar-Nahum
together. The Master, I knew, would go to the synagogue,
and Ruth was very eager to see and hear him again.

But when we reached the black and white house I was
startled to find it apparently empty. Of course, I bethought
me, they had probably all gone to the synagogue with The
Master, and we turned to go.

Then, in the dark doorway of the house, appeared The
Master's mother, looking enquiringly out at us.

"It is Esli," she said softly. "You are seeking my son ?"

"He has gone to the synagogue ?" I asked. And then
as I saw her eyeing Ruth, I said, "This is Ruth. She had
never walked a step in her life till The Master cured her
with a word."

"I am glad, little Ruth. It was hard to be young and not
to be able to walk. . . But, Esli, he is not living here now.
The others would not have it. . . The crowds, you know,
and all the sick they brought with them . . . I do not know
what to think" — and I saw now, as she came out into the
sunlight, that her sweet face was sorely troubled and full of
care, and her eyes in their misty depths seemed even more
full of anxious questioning than the last time I saw her.

"They cannot understand him," she went on plaintively.
"Nor do I, indeed. I am sure he is not mad, as they think
he must be. But I fear for him. . . I fear for him. . . I

have had such great hopes for him. . . But now I have only
fears. . . You heard about Nazaret? They would have
killed him there — his own people! . . . *You* do not think
he is mad, Esli?"

"Mad!" I said with vehemence. "He is the most wonderful man the world has ever seen, and the bravest, and the
most gracious and the most loving. The mad ones are those
who deem him mad. I would we had more mad men like
him. They said The Baptiser was mad, but The Master is
greater even than The Baptiser, and the people know it."

"Not all," she said, with her fears in her voice. "The
rulers are all against him, and they are powerful and crafty.
They will bring him to his death. I know it. Oh, why
can't he be like other men!"

"Because he is not like other men, Mother, and you know
it. There never was another like him."

"Woe's me!" she said, with her hand pressed tight to her
heart. "They will do him to death, I know. . . They have
put his cousin John in prison, they say — him you call The
Baptiser. And my son they will kill too."

"Do not fear for him, Mother," I said, as weightily as I
knew how. "You know yourself that he has that in him
which can do more than all of them put together. Think of
the things he has done. He has even called a man back to
life when he was dead. One who can do that can do anything."

"I know. I know. And yet I am full of fears for him. . .
Bring me word of him as you come back, Esli, for the others
are too vexed about him to tell me all I would know."

"It is just as The Master said," I said to Ruth as we went
on — "A prophet has no welcome among his own. And
one would have thought that those who knew him best
would be the first to do him honour."

"What a sweet face she has," said Ruth, "but so sad and
full of fears. She must have been very lovely once."

When we reached the synagogue we found it so crowded

[106]

that we could hardly squeeze in, Ruth at her side and I at mine.

Our talk with The Master's mother had made us late. The prayers and the reading of the Law were over, but it was The Master himself we wanted to hear, and he had just sat down in the preacher's seat when we got in.

He spoke to us in the most wonderful way — not in the stiff, superior manner of the priests, whose only idea was to lay down the law, but as a wise elder brother might speak with his own — telling them of some new joyous thing he had discovered, and desired above all things to share with them.

His talk was always most captivating — bright and winning, and at times it seemed quite simple, but when one came to think it over one found in it depths and heights beyond one's complete understanding, and full of profoundest meaning.

He told us quaint little stories and pointed his teaching with sayings so odd that they stuck in one's mind and brought it all back whenever we thought of them; and often he made us smile and sometimes even laugh. — All so very different from what we had been accustomed to.

We were all hanging upon his words, fearing to miss a single one. The perfect silence and tense expectancy were strangely impressive. I felt that if anyone near me said a word or made a sound I would want to smite him.

And, suddenly, that exciting stillness was rent by a wild shriek that made my blood turn cold for a moment, and everyone sprang up to learn what it was.

The shrieks formed themselves into words, wild words, and we saw that they came from old Joanan-ben-Joseph, who, all his life, had been possessed of a devil which kept in perpetual terror all who came across him. For no one ever knew what he would do or how he would break out.

My devil had not been like that. It only broke out on occasion and when provoked. But I could feel for Joanan.

Now he was leaping and foaming and shaking his fists at The Master.

"Ho — You there ! — You — Jesus of Nazaret, what business have you with us ?" . . . he raved, "Have you come to destroy us ? . . . I know who you are. You are God's Holy One !"

The Master had risen from the seat. He stood quietly, a tall white figure, full of grace and dignity; and his face had in it something of that look with which he drove the dealers out of the Temple, but there was in it also a great pity for Joanan.

"Hold !" * he said sternly, and his voice cut like a sword through the possessed one's ravings. "Curb yourself and come out of him !"

The man fell to the ground, screaming and writhing in horrible convulsions.

Then he lay quiet, and presently he sat up and stared vacantly about him, and there was no sign whatever of the devil that had held him.

The Master came down and put his hand in a brotherly way on his shoulder, and looked quietly into his face, and said, "He is gone. He will trouble you no more."

And Joanan drew his still-trembling hand across his eyes, which were tired and blood-shot, and looked back at him.

"I am a man again," he said, in a voice full of amazement yet strong and assured; and all the people poured out into the street marvelling.

I found Ruth at last, very white-faced and shaken with it all, and we went after the crowd which was so thick round The Master that he could hardly make his way through it.

Simon and Andrew were with him and they went to the house where the mother of Simon's wife lived. We could not get near because of the crowd, but we heard afterwards that he had found her lying sick almost to death of the fever, and with a word he had healed her completely.

* Literally — "Be thou muzzled !"

It is not to be wondered at that with such marvels going on in their midst the people crowded to the house where he who did them was stopping.

And no sooner was the sun set, and the Sabbath ended, than all among them who had any sick folk sped away home, and hurried back with them to be cured while the wonder-worker was still there.

I had to take Ruth home, but we heard next day that until late into the night The Master was busy among them, healing and teaching, and bidding them give their thanks to God and strive to follow His Way.

We stopped for a moment on our way home to tell his mother about it all and where he was staying.

"It was just like that when he was here," she sighed. " — Sick folk everywhere — even lepers ! . . . You cannot wonder — . . . And where it is all to end — . . . But I would that I could have him here with me again, as he used to be."

"The sick folk he has cured are full of joy in him, Mother. It is wonderful work he is doing."

But she only shook her head doubtfully and we went on our way.

NEXT morning I went along to Kaphar-Nahum very early, lest he should be starting off again and I should miss him.

And presently I came upon Andrew and John and James, with their boats drawn up on the beach. They were busy cleaning their nets and did not seem cheerful. From their gloomy faces, and the fact that there were no more than half-a-dozen fishes lying about, I saw the fishing had been poor, but I knew better than to say anything about it.

"Where is The Master, Andrew ?" I asked.

"Don't know. He went up the hill yonder, last night, and we've not seen him since. Simon's out looking for him. He's afraid he'll slip away without our knowing The folk do crowd him so."

"Yes, yesterday was wonderful."

"They're greedy for all they can get."

"He gives so much . . . There's Simon — " and I ran along to meet him.

"Have you found him, Simon ?"

"Met him coming down the hill. But the folk are after him already. They won't let him out of their sight. He's gone to the house to get a bite, if he can. They don't seem to think that he needs to eat like themselves."

"I'll go and see if I can be of any use," and I ran on.

But I had gone but a little way when I saw The Master coming slowly along, with a great crowd buzzing about him like bees on a comb.

I could see by his hands that he was talking earnestly to them, but there were so many that I was sure those behind could not hear him.

He saw me and smiled welcomingly, and I turned and followed with the rest.

He came to the place where Simon and Andrew were, and the crowd, in its desire to see and hear him, tightened up till it nearly pushed him into the water.

"Simon," he said quietly, "will you lend me your boat ?" — and as he stepped in, Simon pushed it off an oar's length from the shore. The Master sat down in the boat and from there spoke to the people, spread out along the beach, some of them standing in the water. And he spoke, as always, of his new way of interpreting the Law.

When he had done speaking he turned to Simon and said, "Push out, Simon, and drop in your nets."

"But . . . Master . . . We've been at it all night and got nothing," grumbled Simon, tired and disappointed. "There are no fish left."

"Try just once more, Simon !"

And Simon gave a shrug of his burly shoulders, as much as to say — "Oh, well — to please you, but I know it's no use" — at which The Master smiled understandingly.

Simon, with his warm heart and bluff, at times uncouth, ways was, I am sure, a perpetual joy to him. For I often saw that smile on his lips, as he watched or listened to the impulsive one blundering along towards his goal, and getting there in time though by roundabout ways.

So now, Simon, having shown what he thought of the matter by his shrug, growled a word to Andrew, and they set their shoulders to the boat and pushed it off and scrambled in.

They lowered again the net they had just so carefully cleaned. And then, we on the shore heard an astonished exclamation from Andrew and a shout from Simon, as they and The Master peered over the side of the boat.

"Ho! — John, James, all of you — here quick! We've got all the fish in the lake in the net!" — and when the other boat came hastily up and they hauled in the net, the two boats were filled to the gunwales, and they had difficulty in using their oars to get back to land. Never in all our lives had any of us seen such a take, and all who were watching broke into shouts at the sight.

After his first cry for help, Simon had not said a word. But he had evidently been thinking the more, and now he burst out — "Master — I am in fear! . . . I am but a simple and sinful man. . . You are too wonderful for me. . . Better leave me!"

And The Master, with that same understanding smile on his lips, laid his arm confidingly over Simon's shoulder, and said gently, "Put away your fear, Simon! From now on you shall catch men, not fish."

From that day, those four, Simon and Andrew, James and John, cast in their lot with The Master and gave up everything to follow him.

CHAPTER XXII

IT WAS usual with teachers of repute amongst us to gather round them a few chosen followers, whom they instructed more fully in their special ideas, so that they in turn could pass on the teaching to the outside many. And this The Master now proceeded to do.

Until now, those he had had were, like myself, voluntary followers drawn to him by the attractiveness of his person, and the wonder of his doings and sayings, and the hopes aroused in us concerning the wonderful new Kingdom of which he spoke so much. He was the greatest we knew and so we followed him.

So far the friends he had chosen had still, when time permitted, followed their own various callings. But now the time had come when more active work was necessary. For though we did not know it, I see it now, his time was short for all that he had to do. He needed the whole-hearted help of such as would devote themselves, body and soul, to his service and would give their lives to it if need be.

So to this one and that he sounded his great call "Follow me!" And so wonderful was his power over the hearts of men that every man he called dropped all his other concerns at once and left home and kin and followed him. None of us understood the vastness of the great adventure on which we were bound. We knew only that The Master wanted us, and we went because we loved and trusted him.

Other Rabbis usually chose their disciples because of their learning, which made them able to comprehend their master's teaching and to argue about it with the many who always questioned any new thing.

And so the followers whom The Master chose rather surprised me — as it surprised many others.

I think that, during these weeks of their travelling together, he had been quietly observing his company, and making up his mind as to the ones he specially wanted. One could not doubt his judgement, but his choice of some seemed strange.

For, though they were good men, some of whom I had known all my life, you could not call them learned or even very well-educated men.

They had been through their village schools, just as I had; but several of them were only fishermen from our lake — Philip, and Andrew, and Simon, and James and John-ben-Zabdai, though these last had perhaps been taught rather more, for their father was well off, and they were often in Jerusalem mixing with the clever ones there.

Levi, the tax-gatherer, also had some learning, and he was naturally good at figures and at writing.

Nathaniel-bar-Tholmai had well-to-do parents, and he had had a less toilsome life than some of the others and so had had more time for thought.

The others I never came to know quite so well. And sometimes I wondered . . . But I never doubted that The Master had his reasons for choosing them, for he was too wise and deep-seeing to be deceived by the outward appearance of any man.

There was Thomas, whom they called the Twin. He came from Antioch, and they said that was why he was so loth to accept anything that was told him until he had satisfied himself that it was fact. He seemed to be always arguing with the others, and to be seeing difficulties and taking the least hopeful view of things. But when he was satisfied then he stuck firmly to his belief and nothing could move him.

And then there was James, the son of Alphaeus; and

Thaddaeus, who was also sometimes called Jude, and sometimes Lebbaeus; and Simon, one of the Zealots. I wondered at times how he got on with Levi for the Zealots were red-hot patriots and Levi had been a servant of Rome.

And there was Judas of Kerioth, a dark, eager man from the south country. He had been a follower of The Baptiser, whom he had believed to be the messiah. But when he met The Master he judged him more likely to be the Promised One, and so he became his follower and then was chosen as one of the special disciples.

He was, perhaps, keener than any of the others on the setting up of The Kingdom of which The Master was always speaking. But he understood no more than the rest of us what that Kingdom really was to be.

At first, and for long, we all hoped and looked for a complete upsetting of Rome and the restoring of our people to their rightful place in the world. It was only very slowly and with much soreness of heart that we came in time — and perhaps it was not until we were really prepared for it — to a true understanding of The Master's teaching and mission.

Judas seemed to me always as one somewhat apart from the others. Both they and he, as I have said, looked for the founding of a Kingdom here on earth, and that within a very short time. But with him that hope was like a consuming fire, always burning fiercely. And I think he rather despised the others for what he deemed their lukewarmness.

If he could have had his way, he would have proclaimed The Master at once as the Promised Deliverer, and would have roused the whole country to drive out Rome. For, from what he had seen of The Master's powers, he believed there was nothing he could not do, if only he set himself to do it. But as the time passed, and his hopes came no nearer to being realised, he seemed to me to grow more and more discontented, and sourer and more aloof.

CHAPTER XXIII

DAY AFTER day The Master carried on his great work, healing and teaching, and each day the crowds wanting to be healed and taught grew greater. People came even from far away places like Tyre and Sidon on the coast of the Great Sea, and from all over the south country and Jerusalem, for the fame of his doings had spread everywhere.

It was amazing to us who were with him every day, that any man could stand the strain of it. For, just even speaking to such multitudes, and speaking, as he always did, in that new and bright and most attractive way of his, the like of which none had ever heard before — putting his New Way before them in such winning and attractive words, and driving them into their minds and hearts by such strange striking sayings and stories that they could not possibly forget them — that work alone would have been too much for most men. But when in addition he, in some marvellous way, healed all the sick who were brought to him — well, it was beyond man's understanding, and we watched him anxiously and feared for him.

But each night now, when the crowds at last left him to seek their food and lodging where they could, he went away by himself up the hill, and would have none of us with him. And every morning when he came back he was like a new man and showed no sign of the last night's weariness.

The people came to know of this retreat of his and streamed out each morning to the hill to wait for him.

There was there, just below one of the higher summits where he spent the night, a great flat space covered with short grass, and it was there that he often sat on a little mound and spoke to them for hours at a time, and they never wearied of listening.

I cannot attempt, in this little record, to set down much of what he said in his talks. For that would fill many books, and others more capable will do it.

Levi, from the nature of his previous calling, was a quick and able writer, and he was always taking notes of The Master's sayings. Someday, no doubt, he will write it all out in full, and it should make a roll which might become as valuable as those of the prophets of old. For The Master's sayings were very wonderful and they will surely not be allowed to die and be forgotten.

But some of his great words remain with me. They were so different from the Law we had been taught at school and the way we had come to look at things. In fact, at first hearing, some of them seemed the very opposite of all that. But, coming from him, and put as he put it, it seemed right and good.

And when you thought over it afterwards, you saw that it was not really upsetting the old Law but was just interpreting it in a new and wider way — a way which would make life very much brighter and happier if one could follow it. That was his New Way.

The Law, as we knew it, was full of the things we must not do if we would not be accursed.

The Master's teaching was full of the blessings which his way offered to those who walked in it.

The poor in spirit were to be blessed, and those who mourned, and the meek and humble, and those who were persecuted.

If one's eye was a hindrance to one's good living — pluck it out ! If one's hand was a hindrance — cut it off !

If a man strikes you on the cheek, turn the other cheek for him to strike again if he would. If a man demands your shirt, give him your coat also.

If a man makes you carry his burden a mile, go two miles with him to prove your good will.

Don't hate your enemies — love them !

Such, and many other, strange things he said to us, and pinned them in our minds with quaint and unforgettable references to the birds, and the lilies, and ill-built houses — of which all of us had known some, and cities set on hills — several of which we could see from where we sat, and the foolishness of trying to take a splinter out of another man's eye if you had a plank in your own.

I wish I could remember all that he said. But even if I could I could not set it all down here.

As we came down from the hill one day when he had finished speaking, and were nearing the town, we came suddenly upon Old Jabez, the leper.

Never had man more suitable name than Old Jabez, for he was the most sorrowful object one could possibly imagine — leprous from head to foot, rotten all through, altogether loathsome and pitiable.

I think he had waylaid The Master of set purpose. He had without doubt heard of the marvellous cures he was effecting, and in his desperate misery thought — "if others, why not me ?"

As he knelt there in the way, crying "Unclean ! Unclean !" all who saw him scattered lest even his foul breath should contaminate them, and ordinarily we would have done the same.

But The Master went straight to him while we, I must confess, kept to one side to be out of danger, and the crowd stood round at a safe distance and watched.

That meeting between The Master and Old Jabez is a thing I shall never forget — the contrast between them was so very striking. — The Master, in his white robes, all that was pure and clean and wholesome and good to look upon; Old Jabez, a mass of corruption and filthy rags, first kneeling in the dust, with his remnant of a hand over his mouth; then, as The Master approached him, flat on the ground with his face in the dust.

No need for The Master to ask what he desired. Out of

the dust Old Jabez moaned, "Sir, if you only choose, you can cleanse me," — and even I could feel the longing of his heart in his harsh husky voice.

The Master's face was sad with the pitifulness of it, and yet lighted with a great tenderness, and perhaps with the knowledge of what he could do.

He stooped and put his hand on Old Jabez's patchy white head — the first clean hand that had touched him in all these years — and said, "I do choose ! Be cleansed !" — and Jabez scrambled to his feet and stood up a new man, full of amazement and gratitude.

"Go, show yourself to the priest," said The Master, "and do all that is necessary to notify men that you are clean," and Jabez went quickly.

As we drew near to the town, some priests who had been of the crowd on the hill, after talking excitedly together, came up to The Master, and one said, "Rabbi, you have done a great wonder, if the man is really cleansed; but you have touched a leper and you are unclean. It is not right for you to go into the town."

The Master looked quietly into their faces, flushed and triumphant with what they evidently considered a clever stroke against him, and said gently, "I will go elsewhere," and turned and went toward the open country, while those who had witnessed the whole matter gave the priests black looks and mutterings which did not seem much in keeping with The Master's teaching up above. We felt the same, however, so I will say no more about that.

Out there, for the first few days The Master got time for a little much-needed rest. He spent most of it apart, in thought and prayer. But before long the people, considering more the wonderful things he did and said than that small breaking of the Law, found out where he was and began flocking to him again.

When sufficient time had elapsed to prove even to the priests that he had suffered no ill-effects from his cleansing of Old Jabez, we went back to Kaphar-Nahum.

But, while we were still on the way there, a number of the elders from the synagogue met us, begging The Master's help on behalf of the Roman Centurion who was in charge of the town.

He was a good man and had always been very friendly and helpful, very different from most of the Roman officials. He had even built the finest synagogue in the place for them. Now, one of his old servants, of whom he thought very highly, had been stricken suddenly with paralysis and he feared he would die.

And so he had asked the elders to beg The Master's help, and The Master said at once, "I will go and heal him."

But, before he got to the house, there met him another messenger who said,

"Sir, my master says that he does not feel himself worthy to come to you, nor even to ask you into his house. He says that if you will only say the word his servant will be cured. For he understands what it is to have authority — to order this one to come and that one to go, and to bid his slave do this and he does it. And he knows that you have still greater powers."

The Master turned to us who were following him and said, "I have not met faith like this anywhere, not even in Israel." — And to the Centurion's messenger — "The man is recovered. To God be your master's thanks!" And we heard afterwards that the sick man was better from the moment that word was spoken.

In Kaphar-Nahum The Master went at once to the house where he was always welcome, where Simon's wife's mother lived, but so great a crowd followed him and thronged about the door, and even inside, that some of us could not get in.

And while I was still trying to work my way through, to be of any service I could to him, a curious thing happened of which I have often thought since.

Several stalwart men were trying to force their way in also, but with no better result than my own. For those in the doorway resented their efforts and only bunched the tighter the more the others pushed.

Someone near me said, "Those are his own people and that is his mother," and looking round I saw that it was indeed The Master's mother.

She was not trying to get in but was anxiously watching the others. Her face was partly veiled, but her eyes wore the strained, puzzled look I had seen in them before. I could not help thinking that she was there against her will, brought by the urgency of the others.

Their faces were set and determined, but they could not get through.

"What's your wish?" growled one in front, humping his shoulders at their persistence. "What do you want with him?"

"He's mad. He'll get himself into trouble — and us too," panted one of them.

And another — "We would save him from himself."

"Don't you trouble yourselves about him," said the burly one in front. "If he can't take care of himself we'll take care of him for you."

"As some of you tried to do at Nazaret."

"Oh — Nazaret! This is not Nazaret. We know a good man when we see him."

Then someone further in cried to The Master,

"Sir, your own people and your mother are outside and want you."

And between the heads of those in the doorway I heard The Master's clear quiet voice,

"Who are my mother and my own people? . . . Whoever does the will of God — that is my brother, my sister, my mother;" — and many besides myself, I am sure, felt a new sense of his nearness and dearness to us at that saying.

As for his people and his poor sorrowful mother, they saw that if they tried further the people might turn upon them. So, between their fears for him, and perhaps their greater fears for themselves, they gave up their attempt to get hold of him and went away.

But I was very sorry for his mother, for I knew that all her fears were for her son. And that word that he had said may have been hard for her to hear, for it seemed like cutting loose the family ties. But I never doubted the wisdom of anything he said or did; and he knew men's hearts so well that if he deemed it right I was sure it was so.

I heard afterwards that his people really were terrified as to what would come of his strange teaching and the things he was doing, especially after the outbreak against him at Nazaret. They had all lived very happily together up there, and worked together at their trade of carpenters. But when The Master gave that up, and took to wandering all over the country, teaching things the priests objected to, and doing strange wonders, they gave up trying to understand him and believed him to be possessed, and if they could they would have taken him and shut him up, before further harm came to him and them.

I saw his face a little sad at times after this. I knew that he loved his mother as dearly as ever. But — I know it now — his whole heart and soul and life were given to a work so mighty that this was only one more of the things he had to give up for that work's sake. And he had given up other things that cost him still more.

CHAPTER XXIV

THE CROWDS that gathered to him, and the demands they made upon him at this time were so great that often of a night, in spite of the high spirit that was in him, and the longing to give them all their desire and more, he was utterly weary and worn out.

Often now, to avoid the pressure, he would sit in a boat and speak to them spread out all along the shore. It was one such time, when the weariness came upon him, that he asked Simon, in whose boat he was, to carry him across the lake to the lone bare hills of Gergesa, where he might perchance get a little rest.

There were four or five of the others in the boat, and as I had been curled up under the bit of deck in the fore part, listening to all he said and watching the faces of the crowd as they took his points, or tried to take them and failed, I was presently witness of one of the greatest wonders ever man saw.

As soon as we pushed out and hoisted the sail, The Master stretched himself wearily in the stern, with his head on Simon's leather cushion, and instantly fell into deep sleep.

When they saw where we were going many of the crowd climbed into other boats and came after us.

We had not got halfway across, however, when one of those storms we all knew so well came tearing down from the head of the lake and all was clamour and confusion.

I helped to drop our sail. The other boats turned and put back to land. But the waves grew bigger every minute and more and more threatening. They came roaring down upon us, and their vicious white caps came thrashing in over the sides of the boat.

The others would have had Simon put back to the shore. But he said sturdily, "He asked us to put him across there, and across we'll go."

And The Master slept on as quietly as if on his bed.

We tried to bale the water out, but it came in faster than we could bale; and at last Simon, fearing we must go down, plunged over to The Master and shook him by the shoulder, crying, "Master! Master! we are drowning!"

The Master came full awake·in a moment, and leaned upon his elbow and saw what was toward. Then he gripped the rope that held the mast and stood up, though the boat was plunging and tumbling beneath him like a stricken beast.

For a moment he stood gazing out into the fury of the storm. Then he said — and his voice was just like it was when he bade devils come out of men — "Peace! . . . Be still!" . . . and the wind ceased, the waves fell to a sulky calm, and the boat lay idly rocking, half full of water.

The Master turned to us and said quietly, "Why were you so fearful? Have you no faith?" and then he laid his head on the cushion and fell asleep again, while we baled out the boat, filled with amazement at the endless wonder of him.

"All things obey him," said Simon, in a hoarse whisper, " — winds and waves and devils." Then we got out the big oars and pulled on towards the land.

We had barely got ashore on the strip of rough unfriendly beach, and were walking up a narrow place that led in-land, with many tombs hollowed in the rock on each side, when there came running and leaping to meet us a wild repulsive-looking man. He was stark naked, and all tangled and stained with blood, and very filthy; and as he came he howled and shrieked and whirled his arms as though he would make an end of us for landing on his shore.

My heart went sick at sight of him, for I saw that he was

possessed of a devil; and I knew that, if I had not met The Master up in the hills that day, I might perchance in time have become such as he was.

He was so terrifying in his madness that we others drew close together for protection. But The Master walked on, eyeing him calmly, and quite unmoved by his ravings and leapings.

"Be quiet! Come out of him!" he said, more sternly even than when he quieted the waves, as the madman came threateningly at him.

The man fell in a heap as if he had been thrust through with a sword, and from the ground where he lay that which was in him cried, "You — Jesus, son of The Highest, what business have you with me? I pray you, by God, do not torture me!"

"What is your name?" asked The Master.

"Legion — for there is a host of us."

"Come out of him!" commanded The Master once more, and with a shriek so appalling that I can hear it yet, the devil threw the man into a violent convulsion and then he lay still as though he were dead.

Then a strange thing happened. We had noticed, as we came up from the boat, the number of swine there were about there — more than I had ever seen in my life, for they are not esteemed among us, and their flesh is forbidden.

They were rooting and poking, with uncouth noises, among the rocks on both sides of the hollow where we were. At that terrifying scream from the possessed one, ten times the louder for the narrowness of the place we were in, the nearer beasts took fright and rushed past us towards the lake, squealing with terror; the rest followed in wild panic, and they all plunged into the water and were drowned.

In the silence that befell, the madman sat up, no longer mad, and looked wonderingly about him.

Then he looked up at The Master, who was watching him with a welcoming smile.

"Is he gone ?" he gasped, in doubt and great amazement. "He is gone forever."

"My Lord and my God ! . . . Master, I would follow you."

"Nay — go to your home and your people, and tell them all that God has done for you, so shall you serve God best."

And the new-made one sped away to spread his good news, just as the narrow way was filled suddenly with an excited crowd from the country beyond. For the men who had been tending the swine, when they saw what had happened, had run off to tell their masters, and the whole countryside had come back with them.

They saw their Terror — who had dwelt among the tombs till his whole life had become tainted with rottenness and corruption, and whom they had in vain tried to keep in restraint with chains, which he broke as though they were threads — standing before The Master in reverent awe. They saw him talking quietly and sensibly, and then they saw him, at The Master's word, speed away to tell his people what had happened.

And the one who had wrought the wonder, The Master, in his white robes, calm and dignified, stood quietly awaiting them.

They whirled about him with shouts and cries.

"What is all this ?" . . . "Where are our swine ?" . . . "What have you done with them ?" . . . "Give them all back to us !"

"Think rather that that poor soul is saved," said The Master.

"What is his soul to us ? . . . we want our swine," they shouted.

But when he looked round upon them, with that look which went right through to men's hearts, and saw what poor shrivelled hearts these were that thought more of swine than of souls, they quailed and shrank away from him.

"Leave us, Rabbi !" said one who seemed a headman

among them. "Get out of our coasts! You are too much for us!"

And The Master's face was sad as he turned from them and we went back to our boat.

CHAPTER XXV

THE FOLK on the other side spied our sail at a distance, and
by the time we reached the shore a very great number had
gathered there to welcome The Master back. For they had
feared he might go on to some other place and they would
lose him.

We went up the path into the town, to the house of
Simon's wife's mother, and the crowd filled all the court and
the approach to it.

There were certain doctors of the Law, Scribes and
Pharisees and others, who came long distances to hear him.
But they found his new teaching very unacceptable, and they
missed no opportunity of arguing little points which were
really of no importance, except to their self-righteous con-
ceit and their tightly closed hearts. It seemed to me that
it was not enlightenment they sought but just the opportunity of showing their own cleverness, and perhaps of
catching him in some saying which they could turn to his
discredit.

At such times his face was a delight to me to watch. It
was always perfectly calm and composed, but I, who knew
him better than they did, could see about his lips and eyes
the little movements which told me how clearly he saw
through them and their tricky ways. And then, when they
had carefully made their point against him, with a spark in
his eye and a wise word or two he would upset them completely and leave them on their backs as it were.

There were a number of such sitting round him that day,
anxious only to find something against him.

And, as it happened, the friends of one, Reuben-ben-

Menna, who had been paralysed and quite helpless for years, had made up their minds to ask The Master's help for him that very day.

So they brought him along on his bed and tried to get him inside. But, as even the street leading to the house was packed tight with people, they could not get near it.

They were determined, however, that Reuben should not miss his chance. And by going along the upper way, which passed close to the roof of the house, they had no difficulty in getting right onto the roof itself; and quietly drawing aside some of the rafters, they lowered Reuben on his bed down into the room.

We, down below, wondered what was coming, but when we saw Reuben's straining face, we understood.

And The Master understood more than we did, though even we could see that Reuben and his friends had felt quite certain that if they could only get him there The Master would heal him.

He lay looking up at The Master with all his hope in his tired eyes. And The Master, looking down at him with his face full of pity, and yet somehow full of cheer also, said quietly, "Be of good courage, my son! Your sins are forgiven you."

Reuben lay looking up at him steadfastly and still hope-fully. It was good to have his sins forgiven, but his friends had led him to hope for something more.

But from all the learned strangers there broke out mur-murs and mutterings.

"The blasphemer!" said one. . . "Who is this fellow that forgives sins?" said another. . . "Who can forgive sins but God?" and many like things.

The Master looked quietly at them and then said, "Well? . . . what is troubling you? . . . which is easier? — to say, 'Your sins are forgiven'; or to say, 'Rise and walk!' . . . But to let you see that the Son of Man *has* power on earth to forgive sins" — he bent down to Reuben and said gently, "Get up, my son!"

And Reuben rose instantly and stood on his feet, his face all alight with joy and gratitude. He fell on his knees to kiss the hem of The Master's robe, but The Master took him by the hand and lifted him up, and said, "To God your thanks, my son ! Pick up your mattress and go home !" and he and his friends went away rejoicing.

But the scribes and doctors were filled with amazement and had not a word to say.

That same day Levi made a great feast for all his friends. It was a kind of farewell feast, for he was giving up his post in order to follow The Master, and I had heard them saying that before long his picked ones were to go off by themselves to spread his teaching in the outer districts.

Simon and James and John went in with The Master. Andrew had gone home to attend to some family matter. I waited in the crowd outside to see if I could be of any service.

Those inside were mostly Levi's old friends of his own class, and among those outside were a number of those same Pharisees who were always on the watch to find fault with The Master's doings and sayings.

They were talking so scornfully now of his eating with people like that, that had I not been delivered from my devil I would certainly have flown out at them.

Just before the feast came to an end, a man, who seemed in great distress, came pushing hastily through the crowd, and the word went round that it was Jairus, the chief elder of the synagogue.

He spoke urgently to The Master who got up at once and came out with him. Simon and the others came too, and they all set off towards Jairus's house at the other end of the town, and we heard that Jairus's little daughter had been taken suddenly ill and was dying.

We were all pressing on quickly after them when The Master stopped suddenly and stood looking keenly about him. Then he asked, "Who touched my clothes ?"

And Simon said, what we were all thinking, "Why,

I

Master — the crowd is thick all about you. And you ask who touched your clothes ?"

But The Master continued to look searchingly through, the crowd, while Jairus plucked at his sleeve to get him to go on.

And suddenly a weeping woman pushed through and faced him. She was evidently frightened and yet there was a strange look of joy in her face. She fell on her knees in front of him and cried, "Oh, sir, it was I that touched your robe. For twelve years I have had a hæmorrhage that none could cure. I have spent all that I had on the doctors and they have only made me worse. . . And now . . . I did but touch your robe and I am healed !"

The Master looked kindly down at her and said gently, "Daughter, your faith has made you well. Go in peace !"

Before she could even thank him a messenger came running and said to Jairus, "She is dead. Do not trouble The Master any further."

Jairus clasped his hands and bowed his head in his grief. But The Master, in his calm convincing way, said quietly, "Have no fear — only believe !" and pressed on towards the house.

I could not get near because of the crowd, but I saw him go inside, and the wailing of the mourners stopped suddenly.

Then, after a time, the word ran round that the child was alive, and all those near me talked and talked, wondering what had really taken place inside there.

It was drawing towards evening. It had been a day packed full of great happenings, and I knew that, as soon as he could get free of the crowd, The Master would go up into the hills, for the renewing he always found there. So, as I could be of no use to him, I went down to the shore and set off home to see Ruth.

I think she must always have been on the look-out for me, for while I was yet a long way off she came running to meet me, as she always did. And we sat down there on the hard white sand, with the mountains on the other side of the lake glowing like gold in the last of the sun, and I told her of the strange and wonderful doings of the last two days.

She was still listening in amazement too great for words, when I saw a man coming towards us along the shore.

"It is Simon," I said, and we hastened to meet him.

He waved his hand in greeting. His hearty grizzled face was full of the wonder of it all, mixed with no little puzzlement, which showed in the pugnacious blinking of his ordinarily steady dark eyes as he talked.

"Let us sit awhile," he said. "It is not like the fishing," and he sat down between us on the sand.

"What happened to Jairus's little girl, Simon ?" I asked.

"Happened ? . . . She was dead, and now she's alive and quite all right. . . It's beyond me. It beats everything one's ever heard of."

"Tell us, Simon !" said Ruth eagerly. "She was really dead ?"

"Yes, she was dead. . . The Master took me in with him, and James and John-ben-Zabdai. He turned the wailers out. Then he bent over the little one and looked steadfastly down on her and took her by the hand and said, "Little girl, I am telling you to rise." And she sat up, staring at him, and then she got off the bed and was quite all right. . . I saw it with my own eyes or I wouldn't believe it."

"He is very wonderful," said Ruth softly. "I don't see how anyone can speak against him when he does such things."

"Those Pharisees !" said Simon, with a shrug of disgust. "They find fault with everything that is not their way of thinking. They were growling at him because he went to Levi's feast, and so were some of The Baptiser's people. But he spoke very straight to them."

"Simon," I said, for the thing had been puzzling me, "when he cured Reuben-ben-Menna this morning, he said a word that was new to me. He spoke of himself as 'The

Son of Man.' What did he mean ? The devils, when he casts them out, call him 'Son of God' ! Wherefore 'Son of Man' ?"

He nodded his bushy head several times. "Yes. That word is a puzzle to us all. . . 'Son of Man' ! . . . a Son of God he surely must be, for he is more than any man one has ever heard of. No man who was just a man could do all these wonders and teach the way he does. . . But — 'Son of Man' ! . . . John and Bar-Tholmai say it has something to do with the old prophet Ezekiel. They say he is always 'Son of Man' in the roll. . . I don't know. You see, for myself, I've never had time to read Ezekiel since I was of the age for it. I've heard parts of it read at times, of course, and I remembered that word. But why The Master should call himself that . . . unless," he said musingly, "he means that he is the son of all men everywhere — of all mankind . . . and truly he serves all as a son . . . when they'll let him ! . . . Some won't."

" 'Son of Man' !" Ruth said softly, as we went on along the shore. "I shall always think of him now as both Son of God and Son of Man. That makes him all complete. He is very wonderful."

"He would be going up into the hills tonight, Simon ?" I asked.

"Yes, surely. He was looking weary — and no wonder. . . And very soon we others are to go off into the country to spread his teaching. I'm rather fearing it, for I've never done much speaking."

"But anyone who has been with him as you have could tell people about him, Simon," said Ruth confidently. "Even I would love to tell what he's done for Esli and me."

"I can tell about him and all the wonderful things he has done, and his new way of looking at things," said Simon stoutly. "It's the lawyers and the like, with their tricky questions, that scare me. He's wonderful — the way he twists them up in their own coils. But I'm not clever like that."

"The people don't want fine words and tricky puzzles, Simon — I'm sure they don't. For I watch them when he's talking to them, and it's the simple homely things that tell most with them. . . Though it's true," I said, remembering some of The Master's sayings, "that at times I can't quite make out what he means. . ."

"Ay, I'm often like that myself, and sometimes we have to ask him what he does mean. And when he tells us, I'm not sure but what it's these things that stick in our minds the best."

BOOK III — FROM THE CITY TO THE GREAT SEA

CHAPTER XXVI

OF THE HIGH PRIEST'S FURY

It was a few days after this that The Master called his specially chosen ones together and told them just what he wanted them to do, and then sent them off in twos to the distant villages where he had not yet been.

His instructions, some of which I heard them talking about before they started, were quite clear and to the point, as one would have expected.

Many of them were, like Simon, very doubtful of their own fitness for work so different from what they had been accustomed to — doubtful if they could do what he expected of them. They were to be tested, and one could see from their faces that it was a trying time for them.

He told them plainly that it was no easy road he called on them to travel — that they must be ready for trouble with the authorities, just as he was.

But they felt, as even Ruth and I felt, that nothing he could ask of us would be too much. If he had asked us to do something which we were sure would lead us to our deaths, we would certainly have done it. That was how we felt towards him, and that was how the others felt.

From all that I heard, they were to start off just as they were — without money, without food, change of clothing, extra sandals, or even a staff, unless they happened to have one in their hand. Wherever they found themselves of a night, there they were to ask for food and lodging.

They were to carry the message of his New Way and the nearness of his promised Kingdom, and they were to look to those to whom they delivered the message for everything they needed. Any who rejected them were to be left to their fate. But they were to be gentle and courteous to all, and were to strive to serve them in every possible way.

Wherever they stayed they were to become as the people of that place, and so to win their hearts and their confidence as The Master himself always strove to do.

But he also promised them one thing which more than made up for anything they might feel they lacked. And that was the power to heal all kinds of disease and even to cast out devils. That heartened them greatly, and they set out bravely and full of hope.

When they were all gone, The Master set off with a few of his friends and by slow stages made his way to Jerusalem, and I went with him to serve him in any way that offered.

We journeyed very early in the mornings, and in the evenings as long as it was light, resting during the day.

The Master had been working, these many months, beyond the powers of any ordinary man, and giving of himself without stint to all who asked his help.

We had all been in perpetual amazement that he could keep on day after day, and week after week. For though we felt that he was not as other men, and was possessed of powers such as no man had ever had, yet in the body — this body of him which we knew and loved — he was still a man, and a man's body cannot go beyond the limit of his strength, no matter how great the spirit that is in him.

Night after night, it is true, he would go up into the hills, and come back in the morning refreshed and recharged with that which was given him, and then at once to work again giving it out all round. But still in time it told upon his body, and I think at this time he was very tired.

All this is, of course, only my own idea of the matter as I saw it then. But, even in the light of what I have come to know since, I believe I was right.

It was on this journey that I took to carrying with me for
The Master's use in case of need, a small supply of food —
a few rolls of bread, a bunch or two of grapes or figs, a
gourd of water. For we were off the usual track and at
times villages were far between. And when I could offer
him unexpected food, his enjoyment of it and his smile of
thanks were my very full reward.

More than once, when we happened upon no village, our
little company slept under the stars, with the earth for
our beds and a folded robe or a stone for a pillow, and were
none of us any the worse.

And so in time we turned our backs on the great bare
mountains of Moab, and came up out of the river valley
and over the hills to the little town of Bethany, where dwelt
The Master's friend Lazarus and his sisters.

No better place could he have chosen for a thorough
rest. The little village was almost hidden in its groves of
palm and olive and almond and fig trees; there were grapes
and pomegranates in plenty, and many spreading oaks for
welcome shade.

The house of Lazarus was ample and very comfortable,
for the family was well off. Martha and Mary were excellent managers, and the love of all three for The Master,
and his for them, was good to witness.

There the rancorous opposition of the authorities to his
teaching lost its power to wound him, and his weary body
recovered itself.

In the shady groves of oak and palm, he and the learned
young Rabbi would walk for hours in quiet converse. And
often of an evening the sisters would join them on the flat
roof and they would sit and talk as the sun sank below
the shoulder of the Hill of Olives.

It was a peaceful happy time, and I could see in The
Master's face how much he was enjoying it.

At times he would walk quietly up the hill-road, alone
or with Lazarus, as far as the shoulder of Olivet from
which one caught the first sight of Jerusalem. And there

he would stand long, gazing at the great city, deep in thought, perhaps high in hope — I do not know.

On the Sabbath he told us he was going into the City to the Temple worship, and we set off with him, discomforted with fears. For the great beautiful city was the headquarters and stronghold of all who opposed him and hated his New Way, and they were very powerful and would assuredly work him ill if they could.

Not far from the Sheep Gate is a pool surrounded by arches, where sick folk used to come to be healed. For every now and again, sometimes several times in the day, the water would begin to rise up and bubble, and when it did so it possessed a great virtue of healing, and those who could get down into it then were often cured.

We had several such pools up in our own country, and our own sick folk were sometimes helped by them. What it was that came bubbling up through the water, or why, no one knew — except that whatever it was it was good.

As we passed the pool The Master stopped to watch. For the water had just begun to bubble, and the crowd of sick and lame folk was crawling, and falling over itself, and even fighting, in its anxiety to get into the pool before the bubbling ceased. Every man strove for himself, and some had friends at hand to help them.

The Master's eyes were full of pity. They lighted on one man who had struggled to move with the rest but sank back again in despair.

He went down, and bending over him asked, "Would you like to be made well?"

The man stared up at him dully and in great astonishment. All his days had been passed at the side of the pool, so he had never seen The Master.

He said, "Sir, I have been sick these eight-and-thirty years. But I have nobody to put me in the water when it is bubbling. While I am trying, someone else always gets in before me."

And looking on him with great compassion, The Master said gently, "Get up! Lift your mat, and walk!"

And instantly the man got up and picked up his mat and found he could walk. He was still mazed with the wonder of it as we went on towards the Temple.

We heard afterwards that as the man was walking away he met some of the priests, and they stopped him and said, "What do you mean by carrying your mat on the Sabbath?"

And the man said to them, "But the man who healed me told me to take it up and walk."

"Who was it told you that?" they demanded.

"I do not know. I had never seen the man before. But he healed me so I did what he told me." And they could get no more out of him.

But later on, he went up into the Temple, to give thanks perhaps for his healing, and possibly to see for the first time the inside of the wonderful place he had heard so much about but had never been able to see for himself.

We met him there as he was wandering about, and The Master went up to him and said, "See now — you have been made whole. You are well and strong. Sin no more, lest worse befall you!"

Then we passed on, but when I chanced to look back I saw the man talking eagerly to one of the priests, as though he were asking who the man was that had healed him.

Whether that had anything to do with what happened next, I do not know, but I have since thought so.

For before long some priests and officers of the Temple came up to The Master and told him to come with them to the Council room.

There a number of priests who, by their robes, must have been men of consequence, were sitting waiting, and one who seemed to be their leader — a dark-browed, domineering man, was just what I thought the High Priest would be like; and, from the talk of two men alongside me, I found that it was he — Joseph Caiaphas.

These all sat gazing venomously and slightingly upon The Master, as though to abash him with their looks. And he stood facing them, calm and upright and quite untroubled, and looked back at them gravely and quietly, as though he were trying in his mind to discover what it was in them that made them so opposed to his teaching.

"Why do you break the law of the Sabbath and cause others to do so too ?" asked Caiaphas angrily.

"Nay," said The Master quietly, in that voice that went right to most men's hearts. "I do but carry on my Father's work as he would have me do."

"Your father ? . . . Who is your father ?" bellowed Caiaphas.

"My Father is God — The High and Holy One, whose voice you have never heard, whose word you have not kept. . . You search the scriptures imagining you possess eternal life in them. And they do testify to me, but you refuse to come to me for life. . . There is no love to God in you. Here am I, come in the name of my Father, and you will not accept me. . . None of you honestly obeys the Law. Else why do you want to kill me ?"

Very much more he said, in spite of their growing anger. But that was the gist of it and what remains with me, for my head and my heart were in a whirl with all that his words stirred up in me.

I had seen some of the wonderful things he had done. I had heard much of his teaching of his new and gracious Way of Life. I knew there never had been a man like him. And now, with a rush of feeling that overwhelmed me, I heard this dear and wonderful friend, whom I had tried to be of service to as a man, himself claim to be, verily and truly, the son of the Most High God — whose very name one hardly dared to utter.

No wonder I was overwhelmed.

But Caiaphas was speaking again.

"You are mad," he cried. "Who wants to kill you ?"

But, from the bitter and venomous looks with which they

all regarded The Master, I was sure that if looks could have killed they would have slain him where he stood.

And thereafter I went always with that fear for him in my heart. And I knew now how his mother felt whenever he was away from her.

CHAPTER XXVII

I WAS thankful when we got back safely to the quiet home in Bethany. I did not hear The Master say anything about the matter as we went, but he seemed burdened with thought, and his face, though it was as calm and high as ever, had a touch of sadness on it.

As I followed him on the road I regarded him with new feelings of awe and reverence; for, though it was quite beyond my understanding, I felt that he was all that he claimed to be — so much more than just a man, and yet it was as the man that I knew that I loved him, and there was no room in me for fear — except for his own safety.

It was a day or two after this that a dreadful rumour reached us — that Herod had murdered the great teacher, John the Baptiser, in his castle of Machaerus, which stood among the mountains on the other side of the river and the Salt Sea.

The rumour was confirmed, and we heard all the terrible story of the sacrifice of the great teacher and prophet to the caprice of a wanton.

Perhaps it was this, and the bitterness against him in Jerusalem, that made The Master feel that his time would be better spent in the North country, where the people were glad to hear of his New Way, and where he had many followers. So we bade farewell to the friends in the quiet home at Bethany and journeyed back to Galilee.

There we met again the twelve whom The Master had sent out to teach in the distant villages, and they were all very full of their experiences. For in most places the people had listened to them gladly, especially when they found that

[141]

these followers of the great Teacher possessed also his wonderful powers of healing the sick.

The Master wanted to hear all about it, and they were eager to tell; but such great crowds gathered everywhere to meet him that they could not get a minute to themselves.

"Let us go away by ourselves to some desert place," The Master said. "A rest and a quiet talk will be good for all of us."

So they set off in Simon's boat to cross to the other side of the lake. But the wind was adverse and squally and they made but slow progress. And, seeing this, and that they would have to make the head of the lake, many of those who had gathered to see and hear him set off to walk thither by the shore.

I had heard him say that he wanted to be alone with his followers so I did not go, but instead went home to see Ruth.

She came running to meet me as she always did.

"My heart is never quite at rest when you are away, Esli," she said, as we walked along together. "I am always afraid of what may be happening to you — especially in Jerusalem. . . I do not like Jerusalem. It is so big and heartless. I think of it as a giant living on the lives of men. . . Now tell me everything!" And as I had much to tell we sought the shelter of a boat that was drawn up on the shore and sat down there in the sun.

And I told her of the restful days at Bethany and The Master's friends there, and then — in whispers, for one could not speak of such matters as one spoke of ordinary things — of his being haled before Caiaphas, and of all he had said to him and the rulers.

She stared at me with wide amazed eyes, and then, with bated breath and a catch in the throat, whispered, "Esli! . . . You mean . . . that he is the son of — ?" and she bowed her head rather than utter THE NAME.

"Yes, Ruth. With my own ears I heard him say that he is the son of the High and Holy One."

"But . . ." she murmured bewilderedly, and then shook

her head. . . "No, it is beyond me. Do you understand it yourself, Esli ?"

"No, I don't understand it. It's too big for us to understand. But I heard him say it, and I know him, and so I know it must be true."

"It is very wonderful," she said deeply . . . "and to think what he has done for you and me . . . and that we know him as such a dear friend !"

When, presently, we went on to the house, my father greeted me with a mocking,

"Well, what of your wonder-worker ? — Still at it ?"

"He is doing many wonderful things," I said quietly, for his manner clashed sorely with the talk Ruth and I had been having.

"He will get himself into trouble — and you too. The priests are growing hot against him."

"He is greater than the priests."

"Maybe, but he is only one, and they are many. And he'll have Rome against him too."

"It's not Rome he's against, or the priests. . ."

"What then ?"

"He's against Wrong wherever he finds it, whether in Rome, or the priests, or the rest of us. His New Way would make all things right and all the world happier than it ever has been."

At that he only grunted derisively, and said,

"His New Way would make an end of the Old, and the priests will never stand that. They live by it. . . They say he makes no bones of breaking the Sabbath, and that's one of the first of the laws."

"He does his good works on the Sabbath, as on any other day."

"And he's friends with all the scum of the earth — tax-gatherers and such like."

"He's friends with all who need him. Perhaps they need him more than most."

"It's a surprise to me that men like Simon and Andrew,

[143]

and James and John-ben-Zabdai should have gone after him. They're not fools, at least I never thought them so."

"No, they're not fools," I said.

Next day, as we were sitting at the nets, our neighbour, Philip, came past, and when he saw us he came down to speak to us and I could see that he was very full of some new thing.

"Has The Master got back, Philip? When did you come?"

"We came in the night," — he glanced at my father, for he knew he was not one of us, but what he had to tell was too much for him. — "The most wonderful thing man ever heard of, Esli. We went across there for a quiet time with him alone. But the wind was against us and we had to put in at the head of the lake. And when the folk saw that, they came flocking after him as usual. There were a lot of Passover folk gathered there too — a huge crowd — thousands!

"So he sat and talked to them till it got towards evening, and there they all were, miles away from everywhere, and they had nothing to eat.

"We begged him to send them away to get food where they could. But he told us to feed them ourselves. We said it was impossible — all the money we had would not buy enough for a tenth of them. . . And now — listen, Esli, Ruth, for you'll hardly believe it! But, mind you, I saw it with my own eyes, as everybody else did.

"He asked what food we had, and all we could find was five loaves and two fishes — not much use among all those thousands!

"He told us to make the people sit down in rows. Then he took the loaves and the fishes, and he looked up and prayed over them as he broke them, and then he gave them to us to hand round.

"And, Esli . . . they *went* round! I know it sounds impossible, and I don't know at all how it came about. But it did. Every one of those thousands — and they say there were at least five thousand — every one had all he could eat. . . And, more than that — he bade us gather up what was left and we each picked up a whole wickerbasket full !"

Our eyes were wide with amazement as he told of that most astounding thing, which he had seen with his own eyes, and assisted in with his own hands.

"You saw that, Philip ?" asked my father, incredulous, yet unwilling to doubt a man whom he had known as an honest man all his life.

"I saw it all, Maath — just as I have told you. And everyone else saw it too."

"Then, truly, your wonder-worker is a wonder-worker indeed. If he can do things like that he can overcome the priests and Rome itself," and he sat pondering heavily. . . "If we made him King what couldn't we do ?" And presently he got up and went into the house, to tell Leah all about it no doubt.

"I'm glad he's gone," said Philip softly, "for there is something else I wanted to tell you. But not before him. He would only scoff at it. And yet I saw it also with my own eyes, Esli. If I had not seen it I would hardly believe it."

"Tell us, Philip !" whispered Ruth eagerly.

"Well — it was this. When the crowd had been fed in that wonderful way, its first thought was, just like your father's, that the man who could do such a marvel could do anything. He could overthrow Rome and set us in our right place again.

"Thinking as we all have been about the coming of the Deliverer, it was natural enough, I suppose. But he would not listen to them. He told them to get back to their homes, and bade us take the boat and come across here. And when we asked what he himself was going to do, he said he wished to be alone and would go up into the hills behind there.

"Well — we had a bad time in the boat. The wind was very strong and never two minutes the same way. We had

K

to haul down the sail and row, and we could make no head against it. Truly it looked as if we were to be drowned, and Simon growled that if The Master had only come with us it would have been all right — as it was that other time.

"And then, when it was almost morning and we were quite spent . . ." he leaned down towards us and spoke in a whisper . . . "Esli, we saw something coming over the water towards us — right out there, in the middle of the lake, and we were frightened.

"It came nearer, and it looked like someone walking quietly on the tops of the white waves as though on dry land.

"We were terrified. We were sure it was a spirit, for nothing of flesh and blood could walk on the water like that.

"We cried out in our fear. Then we heard The Master's voice, 'Courage! It is I. Don't be afraid!'

"But we were afraid, and Simon called out, 'If it is really you, Master, bid me come to you on the water!' And The Master said, 'Come!' And Simon scrambled over the side and began to walk on the water to him, and we all watched with amazement.

"While he kept his eyes fixed on The Master and saw nothing else, Simon went securely. But of a sudden he looked down at the waves tumbling about below him, and he began to sink. He gave a great shout, 'Master, save me!' And The Master stretched out his hand to him and lifted him up, saying, 'How little you trust me! Why did you doubt?' and they came into the boat together. And the moment they got in it was calm and we were able to get ashore. . . Now — what do you make of all that?"

Ruth shook her head bewilderedly.

And after a minute's thinking, I said, "When we were in Jerusalem, while you were all away teaching, Philip, the High Priest haled The Master up before the Council in the Temple, because he had healed a man on the Sabbath. And he stood boldly before them and spoke to them as I have never heard him speak before.

"Philip . . . he said that he was . . . *The — Son — of — God*. . . The High and Holy One. . ."

My voice had fallen to a whisper, for that was too high and great a thing to tell in any other way.

But Philip heard and understood — what I had said, at all events.

He looked at me for a full minute with wide startled eyes, and then sat up straight with a deep breath, as though for a moment his life had stood still within him and then came back.

He sat quite still, his eyes fixed unseeingly on the lake, as though his mind was at work rearranging and fitting together the pieces of a great puzzle.

He turned to me at last and said, "That is very wonderful, Esli. It is too much for me to understand at present. Do you understand it yourself?"

"I don't think anyone can understand it, Philip. But if you had heard him say it, as I did, you would believe it, as I do. You have known him even better than I have."

He sat in silence again, and presently I heard him say, very softly to himself, "Jesus-ben-Joseph. . . The Very Son of God!" — as though his mind was labouring over it and trying to see its way through.

And, after a long time, he said, "You are right, Esli. . . It is beyond any man's understanding . . . but we know him and so we must believe. . . And it explains so much that was beyond us. . . I must see Simon and John and the rest," and he went off to find them.

CHAPTER XXVIII

THAT marvel of the feeding of the multitude with a bare handful of bread caused an immense sensation, and the folk all over that district never ceased to talk about it. And, indeed, not in that district only, for there had been many strangers there that day and they carried the word of it far and wide.

For you see it was the kind of wonder that appealed to the imagination of a people who were mostly poor and downtrodden, and it fired them with new hopes and encouraged them with new possibilities.

A man who could do a thing like that — why, there was nothing he could not do — absolutely nothing. He was without doubt the very leader they had been so long expecting.

On the Sabbath, our shore was like a stream of flowers with the coloured robes of the multitudes going to Kaphar-Nahum in hopes of seeing The Great Teacher — to most of them simply The Great Wonder-Worker.

Seeing the crowds, Ruth and I went along very early. The synagogue was filled as soon as the doors were opened and there was a great throng outside.

And as I sat there waiting, I was struck by the number of faces that were strange to me among the many that I knew. From far distant places they had been drawn by the reports of the extraordinary doings in our little corner of the land. And I was rather proud to think of it, for they seemed men of understanding and eager to hear for themselves.

Now The Master knew well what had brought them together in such multitudes, and when he spoke it was on that point.

He said something like this, and his face was sad as he spoke — "I know well why you come seeking me. It is not for the leading of the New Way which I would give you, but because you ate those loaves and were filled. Why will you work for the bread that perishes? Strive rather for the real bread from heaven. The bread of God is that which comes down from heaven and gives life to the world. He who eats of that bread will never be hungry again. He who eats of that bread will never die. . ."

And a murmur went round among them — "Ah, sir, give us that bread!"

He looked round upon us all in silence for a space. He saw every one of us I am sure.

Then, very quietly, but in a voice that went right through to every heart there, he said, "I myself am that Bread of Life which has come down from heaven. If anyone eats of this bread he will live forever. . . The bread that I will give is my flesh which I give for the life of the world. Except you eat the flesh of the Son of Man and drink his blood you have no life in you. It is the will of my Father that everyone who believes in me should have eternal life, and that I should raise him up at the last day."

Very dimly, remembering what he had said before the Council at Jerusalem, I thought I knew, somewhat at all events, of what he meant.

But all about me there arose murmurs of dislike and objection to that strange word of his.

I heard — "What is this? — he came down from heaven?" . . . "Isn't he the son of the carpenter of Nazaret?" . . . "Why, we knew his father and his mother; — came down from heaven, indeed!" . . . "How can he give us his flesh to eat? What kind of talk is that?" . . .

There was very much more that he said, but that is what has remained in my mind.

I have thought many times since of that Sabbath, and the

strange upsetting things he said that day, and the way his hearers took them.

For it *was* a hard saying and difficult to understand, especially to those who had no clue to his meaning.

In spite of all he had done for them, and the wonders they had witnessed, many resented those words of his. Some even of his special followers were staggered and doubtful.

Philip told me afterwards that The Master had perceived that in them, and when they were by themselves he had taken them to task for it. And one thing which he said to them I have never forgotten, for in time I came to see that it was the key to many of his difficult sayings.

This is what he said, "That which gives life is The Spirit. The flesh does not count. The words I have spoken to you they are Spirit and they are Life."

And then, Philip said, he looked at them sadly and anxiously and asked, "You do not want to leave me too ?"

And Simon burst out, "Lord, who should we go to ? You have the words of eternal life, and we believe, nay we are certain, that you are indeed The Holy One of God."

And at that The Master's heart was cheered somewhat.

I went back home with Ruth, and I was not much surprised at my father's greeting when we went in.

"Well !" he said, with a scornful sniff, "You and your Wonder-Worker ! Why, he's as mad as Old Joanan used to be. . . I thought he was the one who was to deliver us from Rome. . ."

"It was The Master cured Joanan," I said, rather aptly I thought. And I followed that up with, "Madness does not cast out madness."

"And we're to eat his flesh !" he scoffed. "What next ? . . . After all's said and done he's nothing more than a carpenter from Nazaret."

I could have said much as to that, but I knew it was useless. It would need more than anything I could say to change such a mind as my father's.

Though from this time some withdrew themselves, there

were still great numbers who followed The Master wherever he went, and always I noticed many strangers. And now and again, and more and more often as the days passed, one or other of them would break in on his talk to put some question to him which generally seemed to me of a carping, fault-finding kind, and in his place I would have resented such.

But he did not — as a rule. He would answer them quietly, often with a wise word or a little story which made his view of the matter clear to everyone and in a way that none could forget.

But more than once he would turn on a questioner a keen searching look that went through and through him, and would quench him with a word or, very often, with another question which ended the matter.

"Who are these strangers ?" I asked Simon, one night as we were walking home.

"They are from Jerusalem," he said resentfully. "And they are here to make trouble if they can. . . Scribes, Pharisees, sent by the Temple folk to find cause against The Master. . . I fear them, Esli, for they are powerful down there, and The Master's Way and theirs cannot live together. They would end him if they could. They will if they can."

"He is greater than them all, Simon."

"Yes, he is greater than them all. But we are few and they are many, and if he prevails and the people acclaim him King, as they would do tomorrow if he would let them, those others are done for, and they know it. There is not room for them and him."

"There never has been anyone like him."

"No . . . I know . . . But . . . I sometimes wonder. . ." and he wagged his grizzled head doubtfully. And I knew well enough what was in his mind, for he and the others were constantly discussing the future and how they hoped things would go.

"He *can* do anything he will . . . everything," he said presently. "But . . . Esli" — dropping his voice almost to a whisper, "I wonder sometimes if what we want is what he wants, and I'm not at all sure."

I too had wondered much about that, and since that day at Jerusalem I had had glimmerings of something more, and those strange words of his in the synagogue the other day had stirred them up afresh. But they were too shadowy for me even to put into words. They were as yet only feelings, not even ideas.

You see, at that time we were all of us hardly even half awake to him and the meaning of him, and what I want to show you is how in time the awakening came.

CHAPTER XXIX

IT SOON became apparent to me, and no doubt to many others, that, as Simon had said, the priests, and those well-dressed strangers who came to listen to The Master, were there of set purpose. And that purpose was to make trouble between him and the people, and, if they could, to trap him into saying things which would make him a breaker of the Law. And the Law was terribly strict, and cruel and ruthless to those who broke it.

Time and again the priests had found fault with him for healing some sick man on the Sabbath — just as they had done at Jerusalem. His forgiving men their sins at the same time that he healed them was another great offence to them.

They spread reports, and made much of them, about his mixing and eating with the lowest classes — tax-gatherers and sinners, harlots and the like. He had even chosen a tax-gatherer to be one of his special followers.

They said that he and his people did not keep the prescribed fasts.

They said he was a glutton and drank too much. And they made a great outcry when, one Sabbath, as he and the others were walking through a cornfield, some of them plucked some ears and ate them because they were hungry.

There was no wrong in their plucking and eating the corn, but to do it on the Sabbath was a crime.

Anything and everything they could possibly lay hold of to lower him in the minds of the simple common-folk, that they did. And yet the people still crowded to hear him, and they reverenced him for the wonderful things he did, and hoped for still greater things through him. And the more the people followed him the more bitter the priests became.

But when they brought these things against him he was, as I have said, never for a moment abashed or at a loss to answer them. He would look calmly round at their eager unfriendly faces, with that keen all-seeing look of his, which showed them how well he understood them, and then he would silence them in a way that even the common-folk could appreciate.

But every such encounter left them the more bitter against him, and it was a very trying time for us all, and still more for him.

His only desire was for their and all men's good. It was like a burning white fire within him. He gave himself to it body and soul, without a thought for himself. Any other would surely have been worn to death with a month of it.

And the sole desire of these others was to thwart him in every way they could.

Day after day he went bravely on in spite of them — calm and quiet and unflinching. But often of a night, when the crowds had at last gone home, there would come a sadness over his face as he sat thoughtful, and he would go quietly away up the hillside by himself and would not allow any of us to follow him.

I recall very clearly that Sabbath afternoon when we went into the synagogue and found Justus-ben-Amon, the stone-mason, sitting there waiting for The Master to come in, and all those priests and Pharisees came crowding in after us, hoping, I suppose, for a further chance of making trouble.

Justus had had a bad accident in his quarry some time before. A rock had rolled down on his arm and crushed all the life out of it. It was withered and useless. He could not work and was faced with beggary, and he had become bitter and hopeless.

Now, at last, he had brought himself to ask The Master to cure him, and that was what he was there for. Perhaps those crafty strangers had, for their own purposes, urged him to ask The Master on the Sabbath. I do not know, but it seemed to me likely, for he could have come just as well any other day.

When he saw Justus sitting there, and all those others eagerly watching what he would do, The Master understood.

He looked gravely round upon them, and then said quietly, "Justus, come here !" and Justus went forward and stood before him.

Then The Master, looking slowly round the ring of hard, expectant faces, asked, "I ask you — is it right to do good on the Sabbath ? — to help and to heal ?"

They made no answer.

He asked again, "Is there a man among you who will not lift his sheep out of a pit if it fall into it on the Sabbath ? . . . How much more is a man worth than a sheep ? . . ."

They remained stonily silent. Only one answer was possible and that would have left them with no grievance against him.

"So — it is right to do a kindness on the Sabbath ? . . . Justus, stretch out your arm !"

And stretching it out, Justus found his arm strong and well again. He fell on his knees and would have kissed the hem of The Master's robe, but he said gently, "To God, your thanks, Justus ! — let it serve Him !"

The crafty ones had not a word to say, for not even the priests could claim that, in speaking that healing word, he had broken the Sabbath. They went out full of bitterness and hung about in groups talking vehemently.

And many, I am sure, besides myself and Simon, would have liked to fall upon them and show them what we felt.

But the common-folk were bewildered by it all and did not know what to think.

They esteemed The Master for his kindliness, and his gracious teaching, and all the wonderful things he was always doing. They could not understand the bitterness against him of the priests and rulers, whose guidance they had been brought up to follow, and whom they had always looked up to as the wisest and best in the land.

This New Way which The Master taught seemed to them, as far as they could understand it, an improvement on the old narrow way taught by the priests.

It seemed a brighter and more wholesome way, and yet the priests asserted that it was an evil way and would lead to their undoing.

They talked and wondered. They were like a flock of sheep without a shepherd.

But we, to whom The Master was the dearest of friends and comrades, as well as something more which was beyond our understanding, saw that this ceaseless and bitter opposition was telling upon him.

His work alone — the teaching and the healings — would have worn out any man. When, every day, he had also to fight these black-brows who gathered about him like birds of prey, it was beyond any man's bearing, and we wondered how it would end.

It was the day after the healing of Justus that matters came to a head.

The Master had been up into the hills, and Simon and John and several of the others, being in these days always anxious about him, had gone up to seek him.

As they came into the town there was brought to him the most distressful object one could imagine — a man from a near-by village who was blind and dumb and possessed of a devil, and had been so all his life. It had surely been better for him — and still better for his people — had he never been born or had died at his birth. For he was held in horror by all, and by his own people most of all since they suffered most by him.

They dragged him by force right in front of The Master, foaming and making hideous noises like a wild beast, and flinging himself about; for the devil within him knew, I suppose — as they always did — what he might expect at The Master's hands.

The Master looked on him pityingly and then sternly bade the devil leave him; and after a final struggle the man lay spent on the ground like one dead.

The Master bent over him, and took him by the hand, which was more like a beast's paw, and lifted him so that he stood shaking before him. Then he touched his eyes, and they opened, staring wildly, and the first thing he had ever seen in his life was The Master's eyes looking lovingly into his. Then he touched his lips, and his tongue was loosed, and in some marvellous way, he spoke, who had never spoken a word in his life.

The folks had crowded close to see, and they were filled with amazement, and then they burst out — "Who can he be that can do such things ?". . . "Surely he *must* be The Promised One, The Deliverer !" . . . "*Can* he really be the Son of David ?" and they gazed wonderingly at The Master as if they were seeing him in a new light.

But the priests and those with them, seeing how stirred the people were, scoffed at it all and said loudly — "It is very simple. This fellow is possessed himself by Beelzebul. It is only by the power of the prince of the devils that he is able to cast out devils." And some heeded them.

Then there came again into The Master's face something of that which I had seen in it at Jerusalem. He stood there, tall and straight and masterful, and looked at them for a space, and then he said, so that all could hear him —

"A realm divided against itself cannot stand. If Satan is divided against himself how can his realm stand ? If I cast out devils by Beelzebul, by whom do your sons cast them out ?"

For the priests themselves claimed to have the power to cast out devils, and used various methods which, in mild cases, seemed at times to have some effect.

"So," said The Master, "Your sons will be your judges. But if it is by the finger of God that I cast them out, then the Reign of God has come nigh you. . ." Then, lifting his hand with a threatening forefinger, he said,

"Who is not with me is against me — who does not gather with me, scatters!"

As he turned to go, a woman in the crowd, in spite of the angry faces of the priests and strangers — perhaps, indeed, because of them — shouted out a blessing on The Master's head, and he looked kindly round at her and said,

"Nay, rather — blessed are they that hear God's word and keep it," and so went on into the town.

There he was met by one who, by his dress, was a man of good position and a Pharisee. He begged The Master to enter his house and partake of food. It was just the time for the mid-day meal. So, regarding him thoughtfully for a moment, The Master turned in and lay down at once on the couch by the ready table, and the crowd outside sat down and waited, impatient that he had been taken from them.

At the time I wondered why he chose to go in with that Pharisee and his friends, who were so evidently bitter against him. But I have since thought that he may have seen in it a chance to tell them to their faces all that was in his mind about them, and he would not let the opportunity pass.

And while we waited I saw again in the distance the white anxious face of his mother, and I was sure she had come with the rest of his family to try once more to take him away from his dangerous work. They were sure to have heard that he was in bitter dispute with the priests and they feared for his safety. But they could not get into the house and he paid no heed to the messages they sent to him. He had his work to do, and even his mother's fears for him could not turn him from it.

But we had not very long to wait for him. Within a very short time he came out, and his eyes were very bright and there was a warm colour in his face.

What had happened inside we did not know till afterwards. Then we learned that the company, and even his host himself, had rudely taken him to task for omitting the ceremonial washing-before-eating in which they themselves were indulging.

And at first The Master had tried to banter them out of their assumption of superiority — their outward show and inward neglect. He laughingly told them that they strained at gnats and swallowed camels, humps and all. And then, finding them impervious, he had flamed out at them, and told them to their faces that they were foul and full of rottenness inside in spite of all their washings — that God saw through their show of respectability and would hold them to account for all their shortcomings. He said they were like unsuspected tombs over which men walked, knowing nothing of the corruption within, and much more to the point.

When he came out to us the anger against them was still hot within him, and facing the crowd he cried —

"Be on your guard against the leaven of the Pharisees ! It is hypocrisy. Have no fear of man. Fear only Him who has power to cast your souls into Gehenna."

That was plain speaking and we understood it. But he said much more that was beyond our understanding at that time, and the people were much bewildered by it all and by this open breach between him and their leaders.

CHAPTER XXX

ALL OUR hearts were relieved and gladdened the following day when we heard that The Master had decided to leave Galilee for a time and travel through the remoter districts, where the people had not yet seen or heard him, though there could be few who had not heard of him.

He wanted a rest from the ceaseless cavillings of the priests, and we soon found out that this journey was to be turned to account in the deeper and fuller instruction of his special followers in the spirit and meaning of his New Way. For there was much that they did not as yet understand, and we all of us still had within us the great hope that, with the amazing powers he possessed, he would in some way prove himself the Deliverer we had been brought up to look for.

"Where will you be going, Esli ?" Ruth asked anxiously when I told her.

But all I could say was, "I do not know. We follow The Master." And I knew she would be full of fears for me till I got back.

I paid another visit also to The Master's mother before starting, and found her still full of anxiety on his account.

"You are going with him, Esli ? I am glad of that. You will carry with you my love for him, and all the care I would I could give him, wherever he goes. . . They are very angry with him. They will surely kill him in the end, as they have done his cousin John. . . Yes, I know he is wonderful, and doing wonderful work, but the cost will be heavier than I can bear. . . My heart is full of dread for what the future holds."

"He is very much greater than them all, Mother," I urged. "But their constant cavilling wearies him. It will be good for him to go away for a time."

But her fears for him were not to be stilled by any words of mine.

We set off in the very early morning, by a path that led up the course of one of our little rivers and wound between the hills towards Safed, where I used to take my sheep in the winter.

In the higher country up there it was cooler, for the early summer in our plain by the lake is hotter than in most places. It was very pleasant journeying. We made but short stages, and generally managed to find some village where we could spend the night.

We climbed higher and higher, till we left Safed and its oak-trees on our right and passed the place where our river began, and came on another stream running the other way.

From the high land between the hills we had a wonderful view of Hermon's great white crown, and all this new country was full of delight to me.

For the most part The Master walked slowly, with his special followers close about him as he talked quietly and earnestly with them, and often he would stop and stand while he impressed some special point upon them. And always all their faces were grave and intent, and I knew that they were hearing great and weighty matters.

At times they seemed to argue or remonstrate with him — and Simon's voice I often heard like that. But always, gravely and patiently, The Master would make it all clear to them; and sometimes they went along joyously and buoyantly, but at other times they went heavily and depressedly, and I wondered.

But that the journey was good for The Master was plain to us all. The weariness of those fault-finding Pharisees fell from him. He seemed to me to get stronger and braver and more wonderful to look at each day.

There was not much he would let me do for him. But

now and again I could render him some small service, and that was always a joy to me.

I still always carried a small provision of food in case of need and a small skin bottle of water; and more than once, when we had not come upon a village at mid-day, they were useful. For if it was not much among our company it always sufficed.

Then at last we climbed a range of hills, and there before us lay the sea, its great waves dancing in the sunshine and curling over and rushing up the shore in long white tongues.

The Master threw up his arms with a rapturous gesture of delight and stood gazing at the limitless beauty of it. And we others all lay down there on the hill-top and sat staring at it, for none of us had ever set eyes on it before, and we seemed to be looking right out to the end of the world.

When we had gazed our fill we went quickly down, and when at last we came to it we walked in the water as it swirled up the sandy shore, and rejoiced in the crisp tingle of it which was so different from our own soft lake water.

Simon was the first to fling off his clothes and rush into it as if he could not have enough of it, and most of us followed him.

Then for days we walked along the shore, often in the water, with mighty enjoyment. It was a time of great rest and refreshment to The Master, I am sure. But even here word of the wonderful new Teacher had been carried, and when the people learned that this was he they welcomed him, though he was not of their race.

I remember one woman coming boldly to ask his help for her daughter, who was possessed of a devil. And I remember her well, even to this day, because she was a very striking-looking woman.

She was tall and comely, with very black hair, and eyes that looked you straight in the face.

She begged The Master to heal her child, but he went quietly on as though he had not heard her. She followed unabashed, and begged and begged, until John-ben-Zabdai and some of the others said, "Master, turn her away. She is becoming an annoyance."

He said quietly, "It was to the lost sheep of Israel that I was sent," and still went on his way without paying any heed to her.

But that woman was not one to be easily rebuffed. She came and fell at his feet crying, "Lord, do help me!"

Then at last he turned to her and said, not unkindly but still it sounded somewhat strange from his lips, "It is not fair to take the children's bread and throw it to the dogs."

And she, as she looked bravely and eagerly up into his face, perhaps saw something in it that gave her fresh courage. For her black eyes twinkled as she said, "No sir, but even the puppies eat the crumbs that fall from their master's table. Let me be one of the little dogs!"

His face broke into a smile, and I remembered how he had once had a little dog of his own and had loved it dearly, and he said, "O woman, you have great faith. Your prayer is granted."

She flung up her arms in a rapture of joy and ran away home, and when we drew near to her house she came running out and her daughter with her. They fell on their knees and would have kissed his robe. But he restrained her with his usual — "To God your thanks, Mother!" and went on his way.

Yes, I liked that woman. She was a good mother, I am sure. I wished I had had a mother like her.

For many days we journeyed slowly along that wonderful shore of the Great Sea, and it was a time of great refreshment and renewal to us all.

Now and again we passed the dwellings of fisher-folk, and Simon and Andrew, and James and John were mightily interested in them and their great stout boats and all their doings. But that is a bad coast and we saw the bones of many dead ships half buried in the sand.

And so we came in time to where all that remained of a

mighty city lay on an island, which was joined to the land by a long stone causeway.

Inside the causeway was a great smooth harbour shut off from the sea, and in it there were many ships with blue and red and purple sails, coming and going and lying at anchor.

This was Tyre, at one time one of the greatest cities in the world, and we all sat down in the sand over against it and gazed our fill.

Tyrus! . . . Hiram, its King, the friend of David and Solomon, who helped to build our first great Temple in Jerusalem. . . Tyrus! whose trade covered the whole world, till her riches and her vanity brought her to ruin.

Nebuchadnezzar of Babylon besieged her for thirteen years, but could not take her, though he left her crippled. Alexander, the Greek, razed that part of her which stood on the mainland, and with the ruins built that mighty causeway and so took her in a short seven months.

They spoke of these things as we sat looking at what was left of her, and watching the ships with their bright-coloured sails passing in and out of the harbour.

It was Nathaniel-bar-Tholmai who knew most about it all, for he had read and studied much. Possibly he had been up there before.

The Master's face was very grave and full of thought as he sat there — brooding, one might almost have said, over the city that had once been so great.

Once only I heard him speak, as though to himself — " 'Because thine heart is lifted up and thou hast said, I am a god. I sit in the seat of God, in the midst of the seas. . . Behold, I am against thee, O Tyrus!' " . . .

"That was Ezekiel, the Son of Man" — began Nathaniel, and then stopped short — remembering perhaps, as it made me remember, that The Master had called himself by that strange name, that other day in the synagogue. But The Master's mind was full of other things.

One day our journeying brought us to the little town of Sarepta, where, close upon a thousand years before, our great prophet Elijah had lived for three years in the house of a heathen widow woman, during the great famine, and had, in some marvellous way, been fed, along with her and her son, by the miraculous renewal of a handful of flour and a few drops of oil.

We all knew the story, of course, and also how the prophet had restored the boy to life when he had sickened and died, and all these things were talked about as we walked.

All that was long ago when our people were free and great and strong. And now ! . . . Now we were under the heel of Rome, after being under many other heels as heavy and painful. And our history and the old prophets left us in no doubt as to why that had come about.

But there, walking quietly in our midst, was one who had done greater things even than Elijah, and many more than Elijah did.

A greater than Elijah then ! Though many had asserted that he was without doubt Elijah himself returned from the dead.

What could he not do if he chose ? And our hearts beat high at the thought that here indeed might be the Promised Deliverer for whom our forefathers had waited these hundreds of years, and the hope of whose coming had kept our nation alive in spite of all the conquerors' heels that had trampled over it.

Always as he walked, closely surrounded by his chosen ones, The Master was talking quietly and earnestly with them, and at times I could hear something of what he said. But much of it was beyond my understanding.

And at times I would hear them discussing among themselves, and it seemed to me that they also found in his teaching much that surprised them, and even at times bewildered them.

I think that at that time they were assured in their own minds that The Master was in very truth, though they did not understand how, the son of Jehovah — the High and Holy — the One and Only God, the worship of whom distinguished us from all other nations who all had many gods.

He was a mysterious, all-powerful Being, who had done great things for us in the past, but whose harsh laws were very irksome to us and were enforced by the priests with bitter penalties.

But the God of whom The Master spoke was quite different from that — not a harsh judge, living aloof, but a loving father, knowing each one of us, and wanting us all as his children.

It was this new idea of God, which was so very opposite to all they had always taught, that made the priests so bitter against him.

We had seen that The Master had powers such as none other had ever possessed — powers apparently without any limit, and we hoped that he had come to use those powers in the redemption of our race from Rome, and our establishment again as a great and mighty nation.

He was constantly speaking of the building of a great New Kingdom. What Kingdom could he mean but the Kingdom of the Jews — God's chosen people ? We could not imagine anything else. That, I think, states as clearly as I can put it what was in our minds at that time.

We journeyed on along the shore as far as Sidon, and then with regret turned our backs on the sea and took a path along the bank of a good-sized river and were among the hills again.

That day we passed very close to the great mountains of Lebanon, dark and beautiful with their forests of cedar-trees; and when we had climbed the outlying hills, right in front of us stood old Father Hermon, crowned with shining white snow, a very wonderful sight.

We had none of us ever been so near to him before, and we sat long, gazing our fill, for we might none of us ever be there again.

CHAPTER XXXI

I SHALL ever remember that day when Father Hermon seemed to watch us wherever we went. For it set him in my memory alongside something Simon told me as we were going down the hill, side by side, towards the great river.

The Master was walking on ahead by himself. He had signified to them that he wanted to be alone for a time.

"Why is he sad, Simon ?" I asked, for that was what his face suggested to me.

"I don't know . . . unless it's at thought of going back among those snakes that are always trying to turn the people against him. . . I wish they had one head and I could set my heel on it," he said angrily. Simon never disguised his feelings or thought much before expressing them.

Then he laughed to himself rather shamefacedly and said, "I'm a poor scholar, Esh, and very slow to learn. . . That is not what he is trying to teach us."

And presently, after thinking it over, he said, "The other day we went up the hill to seek The Master, and we saw him standing there praying. And when he came down to us we asked him to teach us to pray as he did. And he taught us this prayer, which now we all use.

"He said, 'When you pray, say — Our Father in heaven, Thy name be revered, Thy Reign begin, Thy will be done on earth as in heaven. Give us today our bread for the morrow. And forgive us our sins as we do forgive everyone who has offended us. Lead us out of temptation, and deliver us from evil.' "

"I must learn that, Simon. Say it once again, please," I said eagerly.

And when I had got it safely in my mind and heart, I said to him, "That seems to me to cover everything one needs — everything."

"So it does, but that bit about forgiving our enemies sticks in my throat at times. He may be able to do it but I can't — yet. Sometime, maybe !"

Thereafter I said that prayer every morning and every night; and always, in my mind's eye, there was old Father Hermon, with his snowy crown towering up to the sky in front of us, and watching us as we came down his side of the dividing hills, when I heard those words for the first time.

We crossed a great river by a bridge the Romans had built for the passage of their soldiers. It was a massive little bridge with only one arch, but that one arch spanned a chasm so deep and narrow that one could hardly see the torrent at the bottom, though the sound of it came up to us in a roar like thunder. Then across a plain, and more hills from which we looked out over the great marsh lands, and we were in the country of Dan, where Ruth was born.

She had often told me about those mighty marshes, through which numberless streams ran and lost themselves, but all found their way in time to the little lake of Merom and so helped to feed our own great river Jordan.

We went on into Decapolis, the country of the Ten Free Cities, whose people were not of our race. But they had heard of The Master and the wonders he had done, and at once they began coming to him to beg his help for their sick and afflicted ones, and his heart of pity could not refuse them.

It was down in the desolate neighbourhood on the eastern side of our own lake that the greatest crowds flocked to meet him from their far-away villages.

He healed their sick, and Gentiles though they were, they gave thanks to the God of whom he spoke as the real doer of these wonders, but of whom they knew next to nothing. He told them of his New Way and they listened with wondering faces and open mouths, understanding less.

And, as had happened once before, they hung about him so long that they were nigh starving.

But this was a man the like of whom they had never seen before and might never see again, and as long as he was there they would not leave him and go home, and some had followed him for many miles.

His heart was troubled about them.

"What food have you?" he asked, looking round at us. "They will die of hunger before they can reach their homes."

"I have seven small loaves, Master," I said, "and some bits of fish."

And then, in some marvellous fashion, he did again that great wonder about which Philip had told us some months before. But this time I saw it all with my own eyes.

He made that great crowd sit down in rows on the bare ground. Then taking the loaves and the fishes he gazed up into heaven as though asking for help and blessing.

Then he broke the loaves and fishes into pieces and bade his followers distribute them; and — how I know not, yet it was so — they went from row to row and everyone ate and was satisfied. An amazing thing and quite beyond any man's understanding.

And, as before, when all had eaten he told us to gather up anything that was left, and we filled seven baskets full.

Then he blessed the people and bade them go to their homes, and they went, but lingeringly, and very loth to leave him, because of the wonders he did and the gracious words he spoke.

We found a boatman on the shore, and at The Master's request he took us across to the other side of the lake, and put us ashore near Magdala, the town of Mary, who had at one time been a woman of evil life but had been delivered from it by The Master and had become one of his most devoted followers.

She was a very beautiful woman and very well off. She worshipped The Master for what he had done for her, and she would have given him everything she had. She gave, I know, very generously to the common purse; and abundantly to the needy as well.

We wondered why he did not go to our own country, but maybe it was because he knew the minds of the leading men there, and that nothing would turn them from their violent opposition to his teaching and his hopes.

But as soon as we set foot ashore at Magdala he found it was the same there. The priests and Pharisees had been evilly busy, undoing his good work as far as they could, and sowing the seeds of mistrust in the minds of the people.

We could not doubt it was so, for we were no sooner landed than a great crowd collected, and in it were priests and lawyers and Pharisees, and many other well-dressed and overbearing strangers. Nathaniel-bar-Tholmai said some of them were Sadducees and had probably been sent up from Jerusalem, for the High Priests there were also Sadducees; and some were councillors from the court of Herod the Tetrarch, who was our ruler in Galilee.

These all approached The Master with what seemed to us like studied cunning. For they gathered the people close about him and said, "Master, you do such great things that we wonder if you are not in truth the messiah. You can satisfy us at once if you will. . . Give us a sign ! Work for us, now and here, some great wonder such as Moses did, and Elijah." And all the people waited eagerly to see if he would do it. But those crafty leaders knew that he would not, for they had asked him many times and he had always refused.

And I myself was greatly puzzled by this whole matter — so little at that time did I understand him.

Had they not had signs enough in the wonders he had wrought among them ? — the incurable cured, the blind given sight, devils cast out, the dead restored to life. What greater signs of his power could any man need ? And why, if they still really doubted him, would he not work for them some overpowering wonder which should convince them once for all ?

I doubt if Simon and the others understood it any better than I did at that time. But I will set down here something that Simon told me later on, since it casts a light upon what was puzzling me then.

He said that The Master told them one day how, when he first came to a full understanding of the work God required of him, he was so overwhelmed by the thought of it all that he went away into the wilderness all by himself to think it all out, and was there many days.

He understood that he was to have powers such as no man had ever had, but that they were to be used only for the furtherance of God's work. And he had to think deeply how to use them.

He could, if he chose, use them to make himself master of the whole world, for he could call upon all the forces of heaven and none could stand against them.

But he knew that force could never win men's hearts to God. It could only bring about lip-service, pretence, a forced submission through fear, whereas what God wanted was the willing devotion of loving hearts.

And The Master told them that the temptation to put these wonderful powers to the test was so strong upon him that he had to fight against it as though fighting for his life.

The use of them would make the whole matter so simple and so easy. . . But what God wanted was not easy though it might be simple — just the drawing of men's hearts to Him in trust and love. And the use of all the outside forces in the world could not do that.

And when Simon told me all that, I understood why he always refused to work wonders and give signs simply to satisfy men who doubted him. It would have been giving way to the very temptations he had fought and conquered in the wilderness.

But all that only came to me later, and, as I have said, at the time I could not understand why The Master not only refused but was stirred to anger by such requests.

I had seen him angry before, in Jerusalem, and, as then,

I knew — by the tight clenching of his hands as they hung down at his sides, and the way he drew himself up till he seemed to look down upon them all — how deeply he was stirred. Perhaps (I think now as I write) he felt himself fighting again the temptings of the wilderness.

He looked round the circle of cunning faces boldly and contemptuously. They could not but see that he saw through them and their tricky ways.

Then he said — quietly, but in that deep strong voice which went to one's heart — "It is a wicked and adulterous generation that craves a sign . . . no sign shall be given it . . . save the sign of the prophet Jonah . . . Nineve will rise at the judgement and will condemn this generation. For when Jonah preached, Nineve did repent . . . and here is one greater than Jonah."

And he spoke harshly to them, "Woe, woe, woe to you — Pharisees, Scribes — all of you ! Hypocrites ! — Vipers !" and he turned and went back to the boat.

He bade the boatman go away up to the north end of the lake again, and as we passed slowly along our own coasts his face was very sad. For it was a beautiful little country, lying sleepily under its hills behind which the evening sun glowed like gold. And it was home . . . but it did not want him.

I thought again of his own saying about a prophet in his own country.

CHAPTER XXXII

THE NEXT day we went on into the neighbourhood of Caesarea Philippi, where Herod Philip, the Tetrarch, lived. These Itureans were not of our race though long ago that country had belonged to us. Now they were idolaters and loose-livers, but at all events they did not persecute The Master with the venomous cunning of the leaders of our own people. And so here again he could go on quietly with the teaching of his special followers.

But his face was often troubled, and I am sure it was the thought of his rejection by his own that weighed upon him.

I remember very clearly one thing that happened there.

He had been speaking very earnestly with his twelve, and they were following behind him, full of what he had been saying to them, when suddenly he turned and faced them, and asked abruptly, "Who do the people say that I am ?" And he looked questioningly round at them till one by one they spoke.

"Some say you are John the Baptiser come back from the dead," said Thomas.

"Some say Elijah," said Philip.

"And some Jeremiah or one of the other prophets," said Bar-Tholmai.

"And who do you say that I am ?" he asked.

For a moment they hesitated. Then Simon burst out, "You are the Christ, the son of the living God, the High and Holy One."

And at that the shadow passed from The Master's face and it was calm and full of peace again.

"You are a blessed man, Simon, son of Jonas," he said.

[173]

"It was surely my Father in heaven that revealed this to you. You shall be called Peter." (Now that word with us means 'a rock'.) "On this rock I will build, and Hell itself shall be powerless against it. I will give you the keys of the Reign of Heaven. Whatever you bind on earth shall be bound in heaven, and whatever you loose on earth shall be loosed in heaven."

And to them all he said, "But for the present tell no man these things," and we went on again filled with wonder, for we were all full of the desire to proclaim him everywhere as the messiah, the Promised One, the Deliverer.

It was, I think, at about this time that I perceived — or so it seemed to me — a change in the look on The Master's face. You see, I had got into the way of watching it as one watches the sky for the weather, and everything about him was so dear to me that I noticed the very smallest change in him.

I had watched him radiant and full of deep, earnest joy as, in the early days, he taught the people and healed their sick.

I had seen him indignant as he drove the traders out of the Temple in Jerusalem, and then full of wroth at the High Priests in the Sanhedrin. I had seen him hurt and angry at the venom of the Pharisees in our own country. And I had seen him full of sadness when he felt that his own people did not want him.

But now — I had never seen him quite like this. His face was calm and high — as it always was save when he was stirred to anger. But now it was at times unwontedly grave, as though the burden of his thought was almost too heavy for him. There was upon it a new set look — a look of brave determination, as of one facing, open-eyed but without fear, some great and perhaps perilous adventure — and a far-away look in his eyes which always saw so much more than any other man's. And I wondered.

He was walking in front with his special ones when we behind saw him suddenly turn on Simon with strange hot words.

"Get behind me, you Satan ! You are a stumbling-block to me. Your outlook is not God's but man's," he flamed. And Simon shrank back before his lightning glance and stumbled along behind, with a shamefaced look at the others — like a boy who has been caught in a fault and whipped.

Then The Master turned and went on again and they gathered close about as he spoke, but Simon was quieter than usual and went on under a cloud.

Later on, when they were discussing things among themselves, Philip happened to fall behind and I edged up to him and whispered, "Whatever was it, Philip ?"

And in a whisper he told me that The Master had been telling them strange, upsetting things — that in the founding of his New Kingdom they would have to face many and dire troubles — loss, and persecution, and even death, and that he himself would be the first to be killed. And at that, Simon had caught hold of his robe and said hotly, "God forbid, Master ! that shall certainly *not* happen. We will fight to the death and lay down our lives for you." And then The Master had turned on him as we had seen.

"What does it all mean, Philip ?" I asked, in great perplexity.

"We don't know, Esli," and he shook his head depressedly. "We don't know . . . but it is all very different from what we've been looking for," and I think he was quite as much puzzled as I was.

Then The Master stopped and stood facing the rest of us who had been following behind. And he said some strange deep words to us all which have remained in my mind because they went to my heart.

"If any man wishes to follow me, let him deny himself, and take up his cross and so follow me. . ."

That gave me, and, I am sure, most of us, a chill down the back, for the cross was the most accursed death one could die, and the Romans made great use of it. What did he mean ? Were we all doomed to the cross if we tried to follow his teaching ? It was a terrible thought.

"For whoever wants to save his life will lose it," he went on, "and whoever loses his life for my sake will save it. . . . What profit is it for a man to gain the whole world and to forfeit his soul? What could a man offer in exchange for his soul?"

Those sayings of his rang in my mind and heart and I have never forgotten them.

I could not fathom all their meaning at that time, but I did feel that they pointed in some way to greater and deeper things than we had been expecting, and it seemed to me that if such thoughts were ruling in his mind it was no wonder that his face wore a strange new look.

We journeyed quietly on, day after day, till we were quite near to Hermon again, and everywhere here the people flocked to listen to his teaching and he healed many of their sick. They were not of our nation, and I doubted if they really understood much of what he spoke about — since even our own people did not. But they received him gladly, they listened quietly, and there was none of the venomous opposition which had wearied him so in our own country.

One evening he went off alone, with Simon and James and John, over the hills which looked so small with the great white mountain towering above them. They were away all night, and when they came back in the morning it was quite clear to all of us that something out of the usual had befallen them up there. There was a wondering, uplifted look in their eyes as though they had seen something strange — but good, for they bore themselves with a new sense of power and assurance.

But they said nothing, and no questioning brought us any enlightenment. It was not until very long afterwards that we heard that, up in the mountain there, they had with their own eyes seen The Master talking with two men in glistening white robes, whom they believed to be Moses and Elijah. And then a dazzling white cloud had enveloped them, and in it a deep quiet voice had said to them, "This is my Son,

[176]

the Beloved. Listen to him !" — and they knew it was the voice of God.

We, at the time, knew nothing of this, for they had been forbidden by The Master to speak of it. But it is no wonder that the effect of it was visible to us all in their faces and their bearing.

While we awaited their return we fell on trouble. For there came upon us a number of Sadducees from the court of the Tetrarch, and began to question and argue with The Master's followers. They had probably been set to this by the priests and Pharisees in our own country, for they acted in just the same way. And those of us who were there had not the wisdom and understanding to answer them as The Master would have done.

We were becoming upset and angry when, to make matters worse, there came along a man dragging with him a boy of most pitiful and terrifying aspect. His father said he had been deaf and dumb and possessed of an unusually evil spirit from his birth. And truly he looked it. He was more like a wild beast than a boy, as he foamed and bit and fought, and made hideous noises though he could not speak.

The father begged The Master's followers to heal him. And they, remembering how they had had that power when they went on their teaching-journey, commanded the devil to come out of the boy. But their words had no effect. The devil inside the boy went into still greater paroxysms of fury, and flung him to and fro till it did not seem possible he could live.

Andrew and Philip and the rest, when they found themselves powerless, were sorely taken aback, and the Sadducees began to jeer at them, and some of the crowd did the same, and all was uproar and confusion.

Then suddenly, when things were at their worst and we would all have been glad to get away, a small boy on the edge of the crowd cried — "The Rabbi !" — and when we turned we saw with joy The Master coming down the hill with Simon and James and John. And a silence fell — even the possessed one was quiet for a moment. For there was something about the four who were approaching us which made them look like men of another world compared with all the rest of us.

It was not that their bodily aspect was changed — except their faces, but those were as we had never seen them before.

What had happened to them up there we did not then know — though, as I have said, we learned it long afterwards. But such was their appearance that that whole crowd fell silent and waited excitedly.

"What is your dispute with them ?" asked The Master, in that voice that went through one, and never had I seen him look so commanding, so lofty and fearless, so much more than any man I had ever seen or even imagined. There was that in his face and eyes which made even those arrogant strangers shrink and feel small and mean.

Before the venomous ones could find their tongues, the father of the possessed one, dropping his boy, ran up to The Master, and fell on his knees.

"Teacher !" he cried in hot despair, "See this my son. He has a dumb devil. It throws him about. He foams and gnashes his teeth. He is wasting away with it. I brought him to your people and asked them to cure him but they cannot."

"O you faithless ones !" said The Master. "How long must I still be with you ? How long have I to bear with you ? . . . Bring him to me."

They brought the boy and he fell at The Master's feet, foaming and writhing, his eyes turned up till only the whites could be seen.

"How long has he been like this ?" The Master asked of the father.

"Since his birth. Many a time it has thrown him into the fire and into the water to destroy him. If you can do anything, do help us — do have pity on us !"

" 'If you can !' . . . Anything can be done for one who believes."

"I do believe," the father cried, in agony lest he should miss this wonderful chance. "Help thou my unbelief !"

The Master looked down on him kindly for a moment, then looking down on the tortured boy, he said sternly, "Spirit, come out of him and never enter him again !" And after flinging the boy about and dashing him up and down on the ground, the evil spirit shrieked and came out of him, and the boy lay like one dead.

"He is dead," said the onlookers, greatly exercised by it all.

But The Master bent down and took the boy's lax hand, and lifted him up, and he stood gazing dazedly about him.

"Remember ! — it is God gives him back to you," said The Master to the father, who was sobbing and gasping so that he could not speak. And the crowd fell back before The Master, full of amazement, as he turned and went.

From there we turned back and came down towards the lake again, and always, The Master, on in front with his followers, was talking with them with deep earnestness, and their faces were often puzzled and disturbed, and at times of a night, when he had gone apart, they argued hotly among themselves.

That some great happening lay ahead of us they were all agreed. But what and when they knew not, and each had his own ideas.

We were all, I think, beginning at last to doubt if our great hopes of seeing an end of the Romans and the re-establishment of our nation were what The Master intended. But hope dies hard, and we still clung to a vague belief that in some way or other it would come to pass.

I gathered very little of what passed between them and The Master as they walked, but I could see from their faces that they found some of his teaching difficult to comprehend and disturbing.

We journeyed quietly along the hills bordering the great marshes, and he seemed desirous of avoiding even the villages. Often of a night we slept under the stars, and more than once we were without food, for that country is but sparsely peopled and I could not get even bread. But we none of us suffered. If we were hungry we had plenty of more importance to occupy our thoughts.

Even when we crossed the Jordan and were in our own country, The Master still kept to the hill-paths, as though he no longer desired to have the multitudes flocking to him. And that puzzled me much, for, before, he had always welcomed them.

Now, looking back, and with fuller knowledge, I think I understand.

I think now that he had sorrowfully made up his mind that the venomous and widespread opposition of the priests and Pharisees, and the way they had succeeded in poisoning the minds of the people against him, would prevent his teaching winning them as he had hoped. His time was short, though we did not know it, and he had decided to devote himself to the training of his followers in the New Way so that they should be able to carry it on when he was gone.

We came down into Kaphar-Nahum from the hills almost unnoticed, and he went first to the house where his mother was living and stopped there for a long time talking with her.

She came to the door with him at last, and it seemed to me that she looked even whiter and more anxious than the last time I saw her. She clung to him and kissed him as lingeringly as though she never expected to see him again — which, indeed, I am sure was always in her mind; and then he went on into the town, to the house where he might hope to find quiet. For at his own home the others were not of his mind and would not understand him, and I think he was weary of wranglings and disputings.

As we came along the side of the hills his followers had been arguing as to which of them was the greatest — a rather foolish matter, it seemed to me.

But the three who had been with him that day on the hill

under Hermon were still uplifted by whatever it was that they had seen up there. They would say nothing about it, as they had been expressly so commanded. And the mystery this made of it, and their own deep feeling about it, rather provoked the rest.

The Master had evidently heard them, for no sooner had he sat down than he asked, "What was it you were disputing about?" and waited, but got no answer, for, in the light of those calm searching eyes of his, the matter seemed suddenly of little consequence.

"If any of you wants to be first," he said, and we knew that he understood and disapproved of it all, "he must make himself last of all and the servant of all."

Just then, a little girl, Miriam, a baby almost, the daughter of a neighbour, having heard that he was in the house, came pushing her way through to get to him. And I, not wishing him to be interrupted, took hold of her to keep her back. But he caught sight of her, as she struggled silently but with much determination to get through, and with a smile of welcome he held out his hands to her — an invitation no child could ever resist.

She broke away from me and ran to him with a little cry of delight, and he took her up in his arms and set her on his knee.

Then, looking quietly round at us, he said, "I tell you truly, unless you become like little children you will never get into the Kingdom at all. Whoever humbles himself like this little child he is the greatest in the Kingdom of Heaven."

We all gazed at him wonderingly at such a strange saying. Little Miriam, from her perch on his knee, stared round the circle of bearded faces, and then turned away from them and looked up into the gentle face above her, and put up her hand and stroked it. He kissed the wandering little hand as it passed his lips, and went on — "Whoever receives a little child like this in my name receives me, and whoever receives me receives Him who sent me. . . But whoever is a hindrance to one of these little ones who believes in me, better for him to have a great mill-stone hung about his neck and be sunk in the deep sea."

John broke in, "Master, we saw a man casting out devils in your name, but we stopped him because he is not a follower of ours."

"Do not stop him," said The Master, "he who is not against you is for you."

And then he went back to where John had interrupted him —

"Woe to the world for hindrances! Hindrances have to come, but — woe to the man by whom any hindrance comes!"

And he went on to say that it was better to cut off a hand or a foot, or tear out an eye, if these things were hindrances to us.

He also spoke about the duty of forgiving one another, and this time it was Simon who broke in — "How often are we to forgive, Master? Up to seven times?"

And The Master looked at him with a twinkle in his eyes and said, "Seven times? . . . I say seventy times seven." And he told us a story of a servant who owed his master ten thousand talents, and when he could not pay and begged for mercy his master forgave him. But as the servant went out he met a fellow-servant who owed him a hundred pence, and he took him by the throat and bade him pay his debt, and when he could not, the other had him thrown into prison. But their master, when he heard of it, was wroth and took the hard-hearted one and gave him over to the torturers.

These sayings of his impressed me so much that I got Matthew to let me copy them out from the record he made each night of the things that had struck him most during the day. And I often wish I had done more of this, but others have done it better, so nothing is lost.

CHAPTER XXXIII

WE STAYED several days in Kaphar-Nahum and I had the joy of seeing Ruth each day.

She was very eager to hear all about our journey and had endless questions to ask. She wanted to know all about Tyre, and Sidon, and was especially interested in hearing that we had come back by the way of Hermon and the great marsh-lands.

"Hermon I have known all my life," she said. "I used to sit and watch him all day long and he was always wonderful. But, oh Esli — think ! — if we had never come down to the Lake, and you ! And to be able to walk ! . . . It has all been very wonderful and I am very grateful. . . Are you going away again ?"

"It depends on The Master. I follow him."

My father's greeting was a sneering,

"Well, has your carpenter made all your fortunes yet ?"

And I answered him quietly that they were still in the making but that we had had a great journey and were all the better for it.

He would, I think, have liked to hear more about it, but his carping mind would have got no good from anything I could tell him. And as regards myself he had no reason for fault-finding since I was costing him nothing.

The time of the Great Feast was close upon us — the Feast of Tabernacles, which commemorated the passage of our people through the Wilderness, in the beginning before we had become a nation.

It was a time of general rejoicing, and multitudes gathered

at Jerusalem and for seven days lived out in the open in little booths made of branches.

I wondered much if The Master would go up to it, and hoped, and yet rather feared for his sake. And one day I asked Simon, and he said, "We none of us know, Esli. He has not said. I rather doubt it, for his people were at him again the other day, and this time they were urging him to go. They said that if he is the messiah, he ought to declare himself so, and do some great wonder that would make all the world believe in him. They were very set on it."

"And what did he say?"

"He put them off and told them to go themselves. We can't make out what he intends to do."

But a few days later, when all the rest had gone, The Master said we were to go and we started that night.

Again, as of late, he evidently wished to court no notice. We avoided all but the smaller villages, and we walked much by night, and arrived at Jerusalem in the evening of the third day.

Instead of going to Bethany, to his friends, Lazarus and Martha and Mary, as we had done before, he led us round to the Mount of the Olive Orchard, and there we built our little shelters and only went into the city in the daytime. I can only think that he did not go to Bethany because he did not want his friends there to suffer in any way in case he had trouble with the authorities in the city. For it would be just like him to think like that.

On the morrow he went with his followers into the city, but the streets were so crowded that I got separated from the rest. As I was pushing along, trying to find them again, I came suddenly face to face with the youth named John, whom I had met at Nazaret with those friends of The Master who lived in the house where he used to live as a carpenter — that wonderfully beautiful woman Zerah, and the man Azor who had been The Master's partner.

"Ho, Esli!" he cried, with glad welcome in his face. "I *am* glad to see you," and then, dropping his voice, he asked eagerly, "Is he here ? . . . Everybody's wanting to know."

I nodded. "They are all not far away. I got parted from them in the crowd — in the Temple most likely. He always goes there," and he turned with me and we pushed on together.

"Everybody's been wondering if he'll be here," he said, as we elbowed through the throng. "My mother is hoping he would not come, for Caiaphas and the rest are very bitter against him. Do you understand it all, Esli ?"

"No, I don't. . . I sometimes think I see bits of what he means, but some of it is very puzzling."

"I could tell you what he told us about himself . . . but we can't talk here. . . Come up to our house some night. My mother will be glad to see you. Ask for the house of Mary, the widow of Sala-ben-Mattatha. It's up yonder."

I promised, but I was not able to get there, for which I was sorry.

We made our way into the Temple at last, and found The Master sitting in one of the courts and speaking quietly to a great crowd that had gathered round him. They were all listening intently, their eyes fixed upon him, their faces alight.

Most of them were hearkening to his telling about his New Way with keen interest. But, near us, on the fringe of the crowd, were others who listened, indeed, and very intently, but only, I was sure, in the hope of catching something they could turn against him.

At some of the things he said they whispered to one another.

I heard one say, "What authority has he to say such things ? He is not a Rabbi. . ."

"No — a carpenter ! — from Nazaret !" . . . said another.

"But how does he come to speak like that ?" . . .

"He has a devil. He misleads the people."

"It should be put a stop to."

The Master's eyes, as I have said before, missed nothing. He had seen John and me come in, though we were right

[185]

at the back of the crowd. And he saw and understood the looks of these unfriendly ones about us.

As though in answer to their mutterings and the thoughts that prompted them, he said, "You know me, do you ? You know where I come from and all about me ? . . . But I have not come of myself. I am sent, and sent by Him who is real. . . You do not know Him, but I know Him because I have come from Him.

"That which I teach you is not of myself but of Him that sent me. He that speaks of himself seeks his own glory, but he that seeks the glory of the One who sent him, that man is true. . .

"Did not Moses give you the Law ? — And yet none of you honestly obeys the Law; else, why do you want to kill me ?"

And one of those near us cried out, "You are mad. Who wants to kill you ?"

"Stop judging by outward appearances," said The Master. "Be just !"

Young John drove his elbow into my side, and I saw that a number of men in dark robes had gathered about us.

"Temple-guards," he whispered, and there was fear in his face — not for himself, I knew, but for The Master.

They hovered about and listened, and some of the murmurers seemed to be urging them to do something. But whatever they had come for they did not do it, and presently they went away.

And when the crowd began to disperse we heard what they said to one another and they seemed of very various minds.

"This is the man they want to kill, isn't it ?" said one, "Yet here he is speaking as boldly as ever."

"Can they have discovered that he really is the Christ ?" said another.

"Nay, we know where this man comes from. But when the Christ does come no one will know where he comes from."

"He is a good man anyway. All he says is good and all he does is good."

"Then why do the priests want to kill him?"

"His teaching is good, but he doesn't think as they think; and as for me, I don't know what to think."

Each day he went up to the Temple and spoke to the people, and each day we feared the priests would lay hands on him, and we were thankful each night when we were all safely back in our little shelters on Olivet.

CHAPTER XXXIV

IT WAS on one of these days that I saw what I shall never forget. The free life everyone led during the Great Feast — sleeping in those little shelters made of branches, and the gaiety and feasting and general high spirits brought trouble at times.

The priests and their party had done their utmost to belittle The Master in the eyes of the people. They had tried to find something in his teaching whereby they might drag him before their Council. Everyone knew it. The people wondered, and we all feared.

As he sat talking to the crowd in his usual place that day, there came bustling along a number of the priests' party, dragging with them a woman — young and comely, but dishevelled and weeping, and overwhelmed with shame and distress.

"Here, Master!" they cried, dropping her in front of him. "Look at this! An adulteress! . . . Taken in the very act!" . . . and the woman hid her face and shook with her silent sobbing.

"Moses in the Law commanded us to stone such creatures. But what do you say?" they asked with spiteful urgency.

Moses had certainly so commanded in the Law, but that Law had long since been allowed to fall into disuse — or there would have been over-many stonings.

They knew that The Master's pity for all who had fallen on trouble, and his desire to help them, had won to him many hearts. They hoped, perhaps, that by forgiving this woman he would show that the Law of Moses had no weight with him.

If he did not forgive her he must condemn her, and then

they could say to the people that his tender-heartedness was only pretence.

Something like that, it seemed to me, was in their minds, and I wondered much what The Master would do.

But he, without even looking at them, or at her, simply leaned forward in his seat and seemed to be scanning the floor. They went on clamouring for an answer. He seemed not even to hear them.

Then, quietly, he put down his hand towards the ground, with the long first finger pointing downwards; and to me, who knew every movement of his hands so well, it spoke as plainly as if it had really uttered words.

The clamour around him stopped, every eye was fixed on that long white finger.

In a silence which made the held-in breathings of the clamourers and the stifled sobs of the woman sound rude and out of place, he traced some words in the dust.

What those words were I do not know. I was too far off to see. Nor have I ever been able to find out. For he wiped them out almost instantly and then the clamour broke out again.

Then The Master straightened up for a moment, and as he looked slowly round the circle of malicious faces, his eyes seemed to pierce them through and through, so that they shrank before him.

"He that is without taint of this class of sin among you," he said weightily, "let him first cast a stone at her !" — and he bent and wrote again upon the ground and paid no further heed to them.

My heart leaped with joy, for at his words the straining faces around him reddened with confusion; and first, one at the back, an elderly man with a white beard, slipped away, and then another, and another, till there was not one of them left.

Then The Master looked at the sobbing woman on the ground, and asked gently, "Where are they ?   Has no one condemned you ?"

She looked up at him, her eyes all swollen with weeping, and what she saw in his eyes I am certain she would never forget.

"No one, sir," she stammered.

"Neither do I. Go ! — and never sin again !"

She groped blindly with her hand for the hem of his robe, and kissed it, and then veiled her face and crept away.

When I told all that to Ruth, she put her head against my shoulder as we sat on the shore, and I think she had a little cry. But presently she looked up and said, "He is surely the best and dearest man that ever lived."

All the time, at Jerusalem, all those in authority, priests, scribes, Pharisees, and the rest, never ceased their efforts to poison the minds of the people against The Master. All the weight of their own influence, which had until now been all powerful, was brought to bear against him, and they employed hosts of underlings to spread ill-reports and harmful stories to discredit him.

And so the people knew not what to think. They found his teaching good though often very puzzling, and the great and kindly things he had done commended him greatly to them. And yet their leaders, whom they had been taught to look up to and trust, were dead against him and all that he said and did.

I heard it all as I passed through the crowded streets. And The Master and the others heard it, but, to all appearances, it disturbed him not at all.

Each day he went up into the Temple, calm and untroubled, and sat and talked to the people, earnestly and lovingly and full of eagerness for their welfare. But, if to the crowd he seemed wholly and hopefully set on winning them to his New Way of looking at things, I, who had for so long watched and loved and known him better than most, saw at times, and almost always now of a night, a sadness in his face which was not natural to him.

As we returned to Olivet he always stood for a time on the top of the rise and looked back at the city, humming like a mighty hive, and all aglow from the great golden candle-sticks in the courtyard of the Temple, a wonderful sight to the rest of us, but to him only a cause for sorrow.

Then, when he had broken bread and eaten a mouthful or two in our little camp, he would go apart and spend the night alone — in prayer, the others said.

In the morning he would be his own high self again, and would go up to the Temple, full of hope and courage, while the crowds buzzed about him — for him, against him, but for the most part puzzled, and waiting to see what would happen.

And, usually, of a morning it was the doubts one heard most of, for the enemy had been busy sowing his tares during the night.

"They say he does his wonders with the help of the devil."

"He companies with the lowest, with publicans and harlots."

"He has no care for the Sabbath and he eats with common hands."

"No, he can't be messiah, for he's really only a carpenter from Nazaret. Messiah will come from no one knows whence."

That was what one heard of a morning.

But of an evening, as they loitered back to their booths, it was —

"Whatever they say, he is a good man."

"We never heard teaching such as this before. It's better than the old hard Law."

"His words are good but sometimes I can't make out what he means."

"If he has a devil, as they say, I wish there were more like him."

"If he's what they say, why don't they stop him ? Perhaps he *is* messiah after all, and they know it and are afraid of him."

And so it went on day after day. But every day, while he sat talking to the people, there gathered on the outside of the crowd more and more of the priests' people, hovering like hawks, listening, coming and going as though they carried reports — perhaps to the High Priests themselves. And we, his followers, were kept in a state of great anxiety, fearing that at any moment they might lay hands on him and drag him off to prison, or worse.

Once, just about the last day of the Feast, it seemed as if the end had come.

Possibly they feared that after the Feast he would go off into the country again, and that unless they made good their cause against him at once they might lose him. For on that day they gathered about him in such numbers that there was little room for anyone else. And they found fault with everything he said, and did their best to provoke him into saying things that would give them a hold on him.

I shall never forget that day. He was sitting in the court where the great golden candlesticks stood, and night and day during the Feast shed their light over the city. They were fifteen times the height of a man, and the wicks of their four great lamps were made from the cast-off clothes of the priests — so young John told me.

And to me it seemed strange, and not very befitting, to see stately priests and high and mighty Pharisees dancing round them like so many children. It was the custom however. There were many things allowed during the Great Feast that were not done at other times.

Looking up at the great lamps above him, The Master said to the crowd around him — "I am the Light of the World. He who follows me will not walk in darkness, but will enjoy the light of life."

That started the priests hurling taunts and questions at him, to all of which he replied with unruffled calm, while they grew more and more angry and insolent. It made me think of a valiant shepherd surrounded by a pack of wolves.

He spoke to them of his Father, and they asked who and where his father was; and he told them that they knew neither him nor his Father, for if they had recognised him they would know who his Father was.

When they asked angrily, "Who are you then ?" he said quietly, "In the first place, I am what I am telling you. But why should I talk with you at all ? I have many a judgement to pass on you."

He told them that if they really became his followers they would understand the truth, and the truth would make for their freedom.

That started them on a great wrangle about being children of Abraham and therefore free — never slaves to anyone.

He told them that they were all slaves to sin and children of the devil. They said he was a Samaritan and was himself possessed of a devil. He told them that if they would only hold to what he said they should never see death.

Then something that he said, which I did not understand, about his having lived before Abraham, provoked them to such fury that they ran to a heap of stones, left there by the builders, and made as though they would stone him to death.

We all rushed in front of him, but he quietly waved us back, and drawing himself up to his full height he just stood and looked at them.

Perhaps some of them remembered his words of the day before — about the one who was without sin casting the first stone. I know not, but their hands fell, and he turned and walked quietly away without another look at them.

It was on the Sabbath after this that we passed a man sitting by the roadside and were told that he had been blind since the day he was born.

It was, I think, Simon who asked The Master who was to blame for that — the man, or his parents ? For among us there was a common belief that a calamity such as that was the result of sin in someone.

The Master told him that no one was to blame, but since the man was so afflicted God's good-will towards him should be made plain.

N [193]

He went up to the man, and picking up a bit of clay from the ground, he wetted it and smeared it on the closed eyes; and bade him go and wash his eyes in the pool of Siloam, which lay just outside the wall of the city. He went off, groping his way as he always had done, and we went on into the court of the Temple.

And then we saw something of what followed. But some of it I heard from young John, who knew everybody about there, and as he was of a very enquiring nature, and always wanting to see for himself all that was going on, he had ways of his own of getting into places we would never have dreamed of attempting.

Presently we saw the man who had been blind being dragged by the arms by some priests through the outer court breathless with the unusual pace he was forced to, but still more with amazement at this his first sight of the wonder of the Temple itself. He had never seen anything, and to see, as one of the very first things, those mighty pillars and domes and colonnades almost overwhelmed him.

They were met by some of the higher priests and Pharisees who asked what it was all about.

A dozen different voices told them, and they turned to the man himself and bade him tell his own story.

"And who was it did this thing for you?" they asked, when he had told them.

"It was the man they call Jesus."

"But that man is not from God. He does not even keep the Sabbath."

But some among them said, "How can he do such wonders if he is a sinner?" and they were not of one mind.

They asked the man, "What have you to say about him for opening your eyes?"

"I say he is a prophet," said the man boldly.

Then they said they did not believe that he really had been born blind.

"Well, if you won't believe me, send for my parents and ask them. They should know," said he stoutly.

When his parents had been brought they asked them harshly,

"Is this your son ? And do you tell us he was born blind ? How is it that he can see now ?"

And they answered warily, "This is our son, and he was born blind, as all the neighbours know. But how he can see today, we do not know, nor do we know who opened his eyes. Ask himself. He is of age. He can speak for himself."

For, you see, the priests had decreed that anyone who acknowledged The Master as messiah should be denied the synagogue, and they were afraid.

So they turned again to the man and said, "Now give God the praise for this. This man Jesus we know quite well, and we tell you he is a sinner."

But the man was a sturdy fellow and he had had enough of them. They had never done anything for him in his darkness, and now when the light had been vouchsafed to him in this marvellous fashion, they did nothing but cavil at it.

He said, "I do not know if he be a sinner. But I know this — that once I was blind, and now I see."

"What did he do to you ?" they asked again. "How did he open your eyes ?"

"I've told you that already," he said, becoming impatient with their mulishness, "and you do not believe me. Why do you want to hear it all again ? Do you want to become his disciples ?"

Then they lost their tempers and shouted at him, "You are his disciple. We are disciples of Moses. We know God spoke to Moses, but this fellow — we don't even know where he comes from."

"Well now," he flung back at them, "this is truly astonishing. You do not know where he comes from and yet he has opened my eyes ! God, we know, does not listen to sinners. He listens to those who are devout and obey His will. Never, since the world began, has anyone opened a blind man's eyes. . . If this man were not from God he could do nothing."

At that, they fell upon him, crying, "So you would teach us — you ! — born in the depth of depravity" — and they thrust him out of the Temple court and bade him never enter it again.

The Master saw them at it, and rising, he went quietly out after the man, and we followed him.

Overtaking him, he asked him gently,

"You believe in the Son of Man ?"

The man stopped, startled. He recognised the voice that had bidden him go wash his eyes in Siloam. He stood gazing worshipfully into the face of the man who had given him his sight.

His mind and eyes had been full of the bitter faces of the priests and Pharisees, and now — ah, here was a face that did him good just to look at !

All the faces he had ever seen in his life, in this last wonderful half-hour, had been distorted either with amazement or disbelief or anger. He had got a bad idea of the human face.

But here was something of another texture entirely — the very opposite of all those others — a lofty serenity that soothed him, a loving-kindliness that drew him as nothing had ever drawn him in his life before.

And this was "the sinner" who had given him his sight !

"Who is the Son of Man, sir ?" he stammered. "Tell me, that I may believe in him !"

"You have seen him. He is talking to you."

Seen him ! That, one could see, touched him to the quick. First, he had only heard him. Now he heard and saw.

"Lord, I do believe !" he cried, and fell on his knees and worshipped him. And from that time he was one of The Master's most devoted followers.

CHAPTER XXXV

WE LEFT our little camp very early next day. The mountains beyond the river looked like a great frowning wall, but as we climbed the shoulder of Olivet the sun came silently up behind them and made the dome of the Temple blaze like fire, and the houses and walls below rise out of their shadows, and it was a wonderful and beautiful sight.

The Master stood looking at it and his face was sad. He had striven to the uttermost to bring it to his Way, and it had rejected him. We stood in silence behind him, feeling somewhat of what he felt, but still with but small understanding.

He turned at last and went on, but stopped and stood again, as a fold of the hill showed us Bethany, lying in its hollow among its olive and almond and oak trees, and just beginning to get the sun.

He looked longingly at it, as though he would dearly have liked to go down and greet his friends there. And then — since it might only bring trouble upon them if he did — with a sigh he turned and set his face resolutely to the north.

We were a larger company now. For though the priests and Pharisees would have none of him, and were desirous only of getting rid of him in any way they could, there were some even of them, and still more among the people, who had been convinced by his teaching and had risked everything to follow him.

There were many fine men among them — Stephanos of Pamphilia, Barnabas of Cyprus, Lucilius of Antioch, and many others.

Lucilius had great medical knowledge and so was deeply

interested in all The Master's healings. He was also a
ready writer and made almost as many notes of his sayings
as did Levi — whom they had begun to call Matthew.

These all were a great cheer to him, though, indeed, they
were few compared with what he had hoped for. And I
am quite sure they understood no more than we did what
was the nature of the Kingdom which we all believed to be
so close at hand. He told us so continually of its nearness,
and we believed it because he was the greatest and most
wonderful man any of us had ever seen, and we reverenced
and loved him.

We journeyed by easy stages in the soft Autumn weather,
through Ephraim and Samaria, into our own country of
Galilee, and came over the western shoulder of Tabor to the
hills above our own lake.

And all The Master's heart and time on the way were
given to the special instruction of those who had cast in their
lot with him.

Sometimes he would speak to us all, as we lay resting about
him, and at other times he would gather his special twelve
around him and talk with them in a way that left its effect
even on their faces.

I knew them all so well, through being so much in their
company, that the gradual change in them impressed itself
upon me.

As The Master's face, though calm and gracious as ever,
seemed to me to be graver than it had been, and even
shadowed at times, so also the faces and bearing of the twelve
showed plainly that their minds were exercised with matters
of deep import.

And always, in all of them — and in the rest of us — I
could perceive a feeling of puzzlement and perplexity which
grew and grew.

For myself, I felt very much as I used to do when swim-
ming in the lake, when the morning mist was still thick
upon it and the early sun was trying to shine through —
bewildered, not quite knowing where I was getting to, yet

full of joy and hope. But I often heard the twelve in vehement discussion of things The Master had said, which they could not understand.

We all knew that he was set on introducing a new way of life, and it was, we were sure, a happier way than that of the old Law.

We still clung to the belief that he would establish an earthly Kingdom, free from Rome. And what a wonderful Kingdom that would be to live in — a Kingdom ruled by such a Master, with all his gracious wisdom, and his wide, new, joyous views of life, and his mighty powers !

That was, indeed, something to hope for, and live for, and, if needs be, to suffer for.

More than once he foretold troubles, both for himself and for all who tried to follow him. But we were so uplifted with our hopes that they outweighed the possible troubles. What could any troubles do against him ? And how could we expect to found such a Kingdom without raising trouble, and suffering for it ?

In all of them I noticed changes. Simon was at times touchy and restless. John and James were often heavy with thought. But the greatest change was in Judas of Kerioth. He had always been rather aloof among us, thinking his own thoughts, hoping his own hopes — a keen, dark, rather gloomy man. But now his face was full of life and his eyes were keen and even gleaming at times. He seemed very confident that all our great hopes would very soon be realised.

We kept to the hill-paths above Tiberias and Magdala, and only came down when we reached Kaphar-Nahum. And there, as he had done after our former journey, The Master, instead of going to the house of Simon's wife's mother, went straight to the place where his own mother was living.

She was sitting in a corner of the courtyard, and when we came in it seemed to me that she had often sat there waiting for just this thing to happen — waiting, waiting, with anxious face and expectant eyes, for him to come back to her. That was what I thought I saw in her face as we turned into the courtyard.

She sat quite still for a moment, as though doubting her eyes. Then she rose quickly and came running to him more swiftly than I had thought possible for her. But love puts wings to longing feet.

She fell on his breast and folded him tight in her arms, as though she would never let him go again, and so they stood in a long and loving embrace.

We all dispersed to our various homes or temporary lodgings. This, we knew, was to be a short rest before undertaking some greater journey which The Master contemplated. He would meet his special followers from time to time to continue his teachings; meanwhile, those of us who had families or friends were to see all we could of them before we set off again.

And little any of us thought where that next journey was to take us, or how and where it would end !

It was a great joy to Ruth and me to be together again. She wanted to know everything that had happened since I saw her last, and, as far as I could tell her, all that The Master had said. And we passed many happy hours sitting on the sandy shore, or up on the hillside looking out over the lake, while I told her.

But each day I went along to Kaphar-Nahum to see if I could be of any service, and very often Ruth went with me.

The Master was living quite quietly with his mother and doing nothing to provoke the authorities. Each day he went almost unobserved up the nearest hill, and there his followers gathered round him and he sat and talked with them, and if any sick were brought to him he healed them.

His mother, I am sure, believed that her hopes had been realised at last, and that he had done with his strange wanderings and had come to settle down with her.

That is what I read in her face, which had lost its careworn, anxious look, and was very sweet and comely. And her eyes had a joy-light in them which I had never seen there before.

When the others went up the hill with The Master, Ruth and I would follow, and so we heard much of what he was teaching. But a great deal of it was beyond us, and we puzzled over many of his sayings and wondered what they meant. And her finer womanly mind and heart got closer to his meaning than I did.

"Can you imagine him driving out the Romans and setting himself up as a King, Esli ?" she asked, one night when we were going home along the shore. "I can't. . . He is not like that. . ."

"What does it all mean then ?"

"Oh, I do not know. That is beyond me. . . But I am sure it is not that."

"All the others believe in the Kingdom he is going to set up. You should hear them talk when he is not there. Why, I heard them disputing, one day, as to which of them would have the highest places in the New Kingdom."

"And how did they settle it ?" she asked dryly.

"I don't know that they did settle it. But Simon and James and John seem to think they have the first claim. You see, he takes them with him sometimes when he doesn't take the others. But one day he heard them — " and I told her how he had taken little Miriam on his knee and had said that unless we became like little children we should not be in his Kingdom at all.

"I wonder . . ." she said softly.

"Wonder what ?"

"What he really means by his Kingdom."

But our eyes were not yet opened to the understanding of it.

My father and Ruth's mother were just as before. They deemed The Master mad, and me the same for casting in my lot with him instead of settling down and earning my living like other men.

That Simon and Andrew, and James and John and so

many others were doing the same perplexed them greatly, for they had always held these old acquaintances and customers in esteem. But they could make nothing of it, and they set us all down as mad as one another.

"Unless," said my father, "your carpenter is secretly working up to some great end of his own. If that's the case — " he eyed me keenly, as though to fathom anything I might be trying to hide from him — "you may not be such fools as we all think you are. . . If he only knew how to use those powers of his. . . But if he's not careful the priests will put a stop to him before he gets there. They are very hot against him still."

One day when I went up to the house at Kaphar-Nahum to see if I could be of any use, I found The Master sitting in a shady corner of the courtyard with his mother, talking quietly together.

And in answer to my question, he said, "Yes, I have a message for you, Esli. I have a great desire to see my good friends of Nazaret, before we go journeying again. I cannot go to them. Will you go and ask Zerah and Azor-ben-Azor if they can come up here for a day or two? My mother will be glad to welcome them."

"I would welcome the whole world if I had room," said his mother eagerly, "if it would only keep you here with me."

"Ah — if only the world would come!" he said wistfully. "But as it will not I must seek it."

"I will go at once," I said, rejoicing in the opportunity of serving him.

"Nay — it is a long day's journey. Go home and tell your people and little Ruth, or they will be anxious about you. Then start early tomorrow. It will be a wonderful walk over the hills," and there was a great longing in his voice.

CHAPTER XXXVI

I WAS on my way before the sun was up next day, and from our own hillside I watched him come soaring up above the mountains of Decapolis on the other side of the lake, which was completely hidden by the thick white morning mist.

It would be quite a journey, as The Master had said — close on twenty miles from our house — and I knew I would enjoy every step of it.

But, as I came round the shoulder of The Horns, when I had gone less than halfway, I saw coming towards me down the long hill-road a procession of five little asses, on one of which a woman was riding, with a man and a boy walking alongside.

And as we drew near to one another I saw that they were Old Peleg's asses, and that the man was Simon, The Master's cousin, and the boy was young John from Jerusalem, and the woman was Zerah, to whom I was on my way with The Master's message.

"I am on my way to Nazaret with a message from The Master," I said, when I had greeted them.

And I thought again, as I gazed up at Zerah, that she was surely the most beautiful woman the world had ever seen.

"A message ?" she asked, and her great dark eyes had stars in them as she looked eagerly down at me. — "A message for — ?"

"For you and Azor-ben-Azor," and the lovely face lit up as though a beam of rosy evening sunlight had fallen on it — or as though a golden lamp had been lit inside her.

"Yes ? — Tell me !"

"He greatly desires to see you both again before he starts on his next journey, and I was to tell you that his mother would make you both very welcome."

"How like him ! . . . I am glad. . . For I too desired greatly to see him again. Simon told us he was at Kaphar-Nahum, so we came at once."

"But where is Azor ?"

"Ah !" she said, with a little wrinkle of the brow. "We hope he is following us. You see, just as we were starting, the house of our neighbour Naggai showed signs of falling at last . . ."

"Ought to have fallen years ago," growled Simon.

"Everybody's been expecting it to fall — except Naggai, and he's a fool," said young John.

"And Naggai and his wife and Damaris were inside, so Azor told us to go on, as Simon was waiting for us, and he said he would follow as soon as he could," said Zerah.

"He will come then without my going to fetch him ?" I asked.

"He will surely come."

"Then I will go back with you," and I put my hand on the little ass's neck and walked along beside her.

And as we went she asked endless questions about The Master's journeyings, and how the people received him, and about his followers.

She did not ask about his teaching, for I was sure she understood more of what it all meant than did any of the rest of us.

She was very keen to hear all I could tell her about Simon and James and John — and the rest, but mostly about those three, when I told her that they seemed to be his special friends.

We had much talk, but at last we fell silent, for I had something I much wished to ask her and was wondering if I should.

More than once I felt her looking down enquiringly at

me, and I knew she was wondering at my silence. And presently, the others being on in front, she slipped down from her beast and walked beside me.

"One gets stiff with riding when one is not used to it," she said, and it was a joy to me to see her walking, so graceful was her carriage and so light and buoyant her step.

I screwed up my courage and asked her, "Zerah, what exactly does he mean by his Kingdom? Will he turn out Rome and make himself King here?"

"No, Esli. He wants something very much bigger than that."

"What then?"

"He wants to win the hearts and minds of men — of all men everywhere — to his Father."

"His Father?"

"Yes. You surely know by this time who and what he is?" and she looked searchingly at me.

"I know that he is the most wonderful man that ever was. . . We believe," I said hesitatingly, "that he is the son of . . . Jah. But we none of us understand it."

"Yes," she said, as one who knew, "he is the son of the High and Holy One. He is truly the Son of God."

I would have believed anything she told me, and so would any man who looked into her radiant face and great starry eyes; for, as I have said, she spoke as one who knew, absolutely and certainly, without any shadow of doubt.

It was too great a matter for me to comprehend but she brought it nearer to me than it had ever been.

"Do you understand it all yourself, Zerah?" I asked wonderingly.

"No. It is much too great and wonderful for any of us to understand. But I know him so well and love him so very dearly, and so I believe what he has told me himself."

"He is the Son of Jah," I puzzled over it. "But . . . was he then not the son of Joseph-ben-Heli, the carpenter? . . .

I know his mother there in Kaphar-Nahum. She is very sweet but often rather sad. I think she fears for him . . . How *can* he be the Son of Jah ?"

"I can't explain it all," she said softly. "There are many strange stories told about it. But . . . believe me, Esli, our dear friend Jesus is the Son of Jah. He is the Christ, the messiah, the Promised One."

"I would believe anything you told me, Zerah," I said stoutly. "But I can't say I understand it."

"It is better to believe and to trust even than to understand," she said, in a tone that thrilled me as The Master's so often did.

We came at last to where the road dips down towards the lake, and Simon went along it with his little asses while we took the higher path along the hillside.

And before long I saw in the distance what I had expected.

"There he is," I said; and Zerah, her face ablaze with eagerness, quickened her pace towards a distant hillside which looked as though its green slopes had suddenly blossomed out into many-coloured flowers.

The Master's back was towards us as he sat facing the crowd, and we crept quietly up and sat down on the outside. But he turned almost instantly, and there was a look of great joy in his eyes when he saw Zerah there.

When he had finished speaking, he came straight to us and gave her and John warm welcome, and to me a word of thanks.

"And Azor ?" he asked, and Zerah told him.

He nodded understandingly. "Azor would do his duty, no matter what it cost him."

Then, talking very earnestly together, they went down the hill towards the town, and John and I followed behind.

And every now and again, at something The Master said to her, Zerah would glance quickly up into his face with, it seemed to me, a startled look, and I wondered what he was telling her. And when we reached the house, and The

Master's mother came running with outstretched hands to welcome Zerah, it was Zerah's face that was the graver.

I saw Zerah and young John among the crowd listening to The Master the next day. And the day after that they went back to Nazaret, for Azor had never come and they feared some ill had befallen him.

It was very soon after this that The Master began sending out a number of his chosen followers to different parts of the country, in much the same way as he had before sent out the twelve.

He gave them very similar and clear instructions and certain powers of healing. But now they were not only to tell the people of his teaching, they were to tell them also that The Reign of God was near, and that he himself was coming close behind these his fore-runners.

And this cheered us greatly and raised our spirits high, for — in spite of what Zerah had said to me — it really looked as though he had at last decided to rouse the country and set up his promised Kingdom; and that belief was strong in all of us.

In all he sent out about seventy of these messengers — men like Stephanos, and Barnabas, and Lucilius, all men whom he had proved and could trust; and the rest of us were all impatient to follow them as soon as possible.

But The Master had his own plans, and no impatience of ours or anyone else's might interfere with them.

I was at the house in Kaphar-Nahum one day, hoping to pick up some word that would enlighten me as to when we would be starting, when a number of the opposition — priests, and Pharisees, and Sadducees from Herod's court, came bustling in and demanded to see The Master.

His mother came to the door with him, but when he saw the mob of crafty faces he bade her go back into the house, and he himself strode out of the court and down the road outside.

They hastened after him and told him, with more appearance of concern for his welfare than they had ever shown before, "Teacher, you would do well to get away from here, for Herod is planning to kill you, as he killed The Baptiser."

The Master just looked at them quietly, and then, in such a tone of contempt as I had never imagined possible to him, he said, "Go tell that fox that I am casting out devils and working cures today and tomorrow, and on the third day I complete my work. But I must go my own way, today and tomorrow and the next day. For it cannot be that a prophet perish out of Jerusalem."

I did not know what he meant by those last words, but the earlier ones made me hope that we were to start within a very few days now, and I went home on light feet to tell Ruth.

BOOK IV — THE GREAT ADVENTURE

CHAPTER XXXVII

OF OUR START ON THE GREAT ADVENTURE

IT WAS more than three days before we received the good news that we were to start on the morrow. And our hearts and faces showed that we believed that great happenings lay just in front of us.

The Master's own face confirmed our hopes. We had often seen it shadowed by the carping opposition of the authorities, and latterly by the indifference of many of the people.

They were willing enough to accept any benefits he could confer on them, and they listened to his teaching, for it was always fresh and bright and attractive. But when it came to practising it in their daily lives, then they stopped short. They were afraid to break openly with the priests and the old laws which had served their fathers and in which they had been brought up. And the priests were all opposed to this New Way, which had in it no place for them unless they broke with the old, and they poisoned the minds of the people against The Master in every way they could think of.

I was, of course, very young still and had no great understanding of matters, but I felt that if I had been The Master I would certainly have given it all up in despair and left the people to go their own way.

And so the calm high confidence of his face and bearing at this time made me sure that things were not so bad as they seemed to me, and that he had his own good reason to believe that better fortune lay ahead of us.

His eyes were bright with a great hope. The very sight of them filled us with hope too, though our understanding of him was so small.

The only sad and anxious face I saw was his mother's, when he bade her farewell. For always, when he left her, she feared she would never see him again.

Though the mass of the people in our crowded little plain were proving themselves so set in their own old ways, and so loth to change them even for the better, we were still a goodly number who started off for the South that morning, in the clear crisp air that filled one with joy just to be alive. And all our hearts were high with hope as we followed our great leader.

At every village the people came running out to see us pass, and some would have joined us — seeing how many we were, and believing that this must really be the beginning of the triumphal march of messiah to the setting up of his Kingdom, of which they had so lately been told.

But The Master wanted none he could not fully trust. And to all who came he said plainly that the journey we were bound on would be full of perils. He even went the length of speaking again of possible crosses, and the word struck chill on many of our hearts and turned back any who had wanted to join him simply for their own benefit.

As we climbed the road which leads to the Great Plain, The Master stood awhile looking back over our own country, with the lake gleaming like silver between the green shoulders of the hills.

And his face was sad again now, for in spite of all that he had done for them his own had come short of what he had hoped from them.

He sighed as he gazed over the beautiful little land, thick with villages and towns and people, all needing him so badly yet not willing to receive him, and from his lips came words which showed how deeply he was feeling it — words which those of us who heard them could not forget, though they were barely more than whispered. "Woe to you,

Khorazin ! Woe to you, Bethsaida !" (my own little village where Ruth was). "Had the wonders performed in
you been done in Tyre and Sidon they would long ago have
been sitting penitent in sackcloth and ashes. It will be more
bearable for Tyre and Sidon at the judgement than for you.

"And you, Kaphar-Nahum ! . . . Exalted to heaven ?
No, you will sink to hades !" Then, with one long last
look, he turned and led us forward again.

From the shoulder of Tabor we saw the wonder of the
Great Plain with its innumerable streams, and very far
away the bold head of Carmel dark against the evening sky.

We were joined before nightfall by Simon and Andrew,
who had been sent on in advance and had arranged for our
accommodation in and about a good-sized village this side
of En-dor.

The next day we crossed the Plain, under Little Hermon
and Gilboa, and climbed the hills beyond which lay Samaria.

We were hoping to stop that night at En-Gannîm, but
before we got there James and John-ben-Zabdai, who had
gone on to arrange things, met us with the word that the
villagers would have nothing to do with us, because we were
bound for Jerusalem.

They were so hot and angry at the reception they had had
that they begged The Master to call down fire from heaven
to make an end of the place — as Elijah did on Carmel
yonder, when he slew the priests of Baal. And most of us,
I think, were of the same mind, for we were tired with
the day's journey and we felt this rebuff keenly.

But The Master just looked at them quietly and said,
"You do not know what you are saying. I am come to
save men, not to destroy them," and he turned and led us
away along the hillside till we came to Gilboa at the foot
of the mountain, and there we were able to get some food
and to camp for the night.

Next day, keeping along the side of Gilboa and so still in
our own country, we came down into the valley of Beth-

shean, which leads straight to the Great River — the Jordan.

As we came down towards a village, there stood across the path, barring our road, no less than ten lepers — pitiful objects, all sores and rags, crying as the custom demanded, "Unclean! Unclean!"

They must have heard that the Great Teacher and Healer was coming, and so had gathered together to beg his help. For as we drew nearer they began to cry, "Jesus — Master, have pity on us!"

No one ever appealed to him in vain. He went right up to them, while we all held back, and said, "Go and show yourselves to the priests!" — And even as they turned to go they felt the new life in them and knew that they were cured.

We followed them towards the village, and presently met one of them coming back. He came to The Master and fell at his feet in his gratitude, and gave thanks to God. And we knew by his speech that he was a Samaritan.

"Were not all the ten cleansed?" said The Master. "Has only this foreigner returned to give thanks for his cleansing? What of the other nine?"

But the other nine came not and we were ashamed for them, for they were our countrymen and they made but a poor show compared with this stranger.

I could not but hope that he came possibly from En-Gannîm, and that he would go home and tell them there that he had been cured by The Great Teacher whom they had turned away from their doors the day before.

"Get up!" said The Master gently, to the man at his feet, and lifted him with his hand. "Go your way! Your faith has made you well."

We crossed the river by the ford and went on into Perea — the wild country to which all men fled when their own people cast them out. It was here that Abner came with the remnants of Ishbosheth's army after the fight at Gilboa — and King David when he fled from Absalom.

And day by day as we journeyed, The Master healed all

who came asking his help, and taught those who were with him, and those who came flocking about him at every place where we stopped.

But here also, those in authority, even in the villages, did all they could to oppose him and to belittle his teaching, though they could not belittle the kindly deeds he was always doing, and many had reason to bless the men of En-Gannîm for turning him aside into Perea.

Some of the many stories he told in his teaching have remained with me. Two I specially liked, and often went over them again in my own mind.

One was about a traveller who was set upon by thieves and left for dead by the road-side. And a priest came along and saw him lying there, but instead of helping him crossed to the other side and went on. And then a Levite came, and stood looking down at him, and went on also. Then a Samaritan — a foreigner, whom the wounded man would have despised and would have had no dealings with, saw him and had pity on him. He asked no questions as to who he was or how he came there. He just saw his need and did everything he could for him.

It was a smart lawyer, I remember, who drew that story from him. He asked The Master how he could make sure of eternal life. And when The Master asked him what the Law taught, he answered correctly that we were to love God with our whole heart, soul, strength, and mind — and our neighbours as ourselves.

"Right !" said The Master. "Do that and you will live."

Then the lawyer, feeling rather foolish before the crowd, to justify himself asked, "But who is my neighbour ?" — and The Master told the story to make that clear to him and the rest of us.

The other story was of a younger son who persuaded his father to give him his share of the family money. And when he got it he went off into a distant country, fell into bad company, and spent it all in riotous living.

Then he fell into want so dire that he had to hire himself

out to tend swine. His former companions only laughed at him, and to keep himself from starving he had to eat the pigs' food. Then in his misery he thought of his father and the comfortable home he had left, and he determined to go back and beg him to take him in again even as a servant.

And he went timidly, for he had behaved badly. But, while he was still a long way off, his father came running to meet him — as though he had always been hoping, and on the look-out, for him. And the old man took him to his heart again and did everything he could to show him how welcome he was.

But his elder brother was angry at the fuss his father made over the scapegrace. And as to that, most of us felt the same. But the thing that remained most outstanding in my mind was the old father's unbreakable love for his son, which no ill-behaviour on the boy's part could destroy.

Of all that I could remember of The Master's sayings, those two stories were the ones that Ruth loved most, when, long afterwards, we used to talk over these days.

CHAPTER XXXVIII

So WE journeyed on through that country that was almost unknown to most of us — fording innumerable merry little streams which rushed down through the hills that came crowding close up to the river on that side. Often of a night we had to camp out and manage as best we could for food, but no one suffered. And in the places where his messengers had been, The Master was welcomed gladly, and the messengers' accounts of how the people had received them cheered him greatly.

But it was only the common people in whom he could find any joy. For here, as everywhere, the authorities made trouble whenever they could, and time after time it was on the matter of the observance of the Sabbath, about which his ideas were so very different from theirs.

In spite of the fact that the priests at Jerusalem had forbidden him to enter the synagogues, he always went to them on the Sabbath in the country towns. It was curious that almost always he found there someone who needed his help.

Indeed it seemed to us as though at times the sufferer had been brought there simply to see if The Master would heal him and so give the priests occasion against him, for he never hesitated to do so and they knew it.

Then the priests would denounce him as a Sabbath-breaker and make the most of it.

The Law of the Sabbath had become with us a very grievous burden. The things we were forbidden to do were indeed more than the things we might do.

It was forbidden to wear a shoe with nails in it, for that was a burden. No fire might be lighted and no food cooked.

No sick man might send for a physician, nor even seek to alleviate his own pain. If you had a false tooth you must not wear it — it would be a burden. You must not write two letters of the alphabet. You must not walk on the grass — that was akin to threshing, and threshing was forbidden.

The Sabbath was ringed round with endless such forbiddings, and a breaker of the Sabbath was regarded as not much better than a murderer.

But always when they challenged him as a Sabbath-breaker, The Master would eye them quietly and ask some such simple question as — "Does anyone of you hesitate to take his ox or his ass to the water on the Sabbath ?" — or — "If any of you has an animal that falls into a pit on the Sabbath, will you not lift it out to save its life ?" . . . though, indeed, in this last case the stricter and more stiff-necked held that the proper thing to do was to push a piece of wood under it, and give it food, and leave it there till the following day.

"Well then," he would say, "surely it cannot be wrong to heal a man on the Sabbath !" — and he always did so and left them to make the best of it.

He told them plainly that they had got things twisted round the wrong way — that the Sabbath was made for man's good — for his rest and enjoyment, not man made to be squeezed into the narrow rigid mould which was what they had made the Sabbath into.

It was as we rested that The Master usually spoke to us and to any of the country-people who came to listen to him. As we walked we talked much among ourselves, discussing the meanings of the strange things he said at times, and always wondering and hoping as to what lay in front of us.

We were still all very much in the dark about it all, and The Master's words very often puzzled us, and sometimes started in our minds fears of we knew not what.

I remember one day Mary of Magdala striding up alongside me and asking, in a whisper almost, if I understood it all — where we were going, and what was going to happen.

She was a very handsome woman, with black hair and great dark eyes, and I had only seen one other woman who carried herself better than she did, and walked with that same long free stride — and that was Zerah of Nazaret.

Mary was as devoted to The Master as Zerah herself, for he had done very great things for her. He had changed her whole life from darkness to light. But her understanding of him was almost as nothing compared with Zerah's.

"Esli," she whispered, as we walked, "do you understand it all ? Are we going to conquer the world, or are we all going to our deaths ? . . . The things he says at times frighten me . . . The priests, I know, would make an end of him. But surely, with the wonderful powers he has . . . What do you think about it all ?"

"We are all puzzled, Mary . . . except perhaps Zerah and Azor up at Nazaret. I think they understand more than the rest of us. You see they grew up with him — "

"You know them ?"

"I have met them several times. They made me think of The Master. They are very like him in some ways."

"I wish I had known them. . . Is she very beautiful ?"

"Very beautiful, and very wonderful. She is different from anyone I have ever seen, and that, I think, is because she understands The Master better than anyone else, better even than Azor, and Azor was more than a brother to him."

"Better than his mother ?"

"Yes, his mother does not understand him any better than we do, I think. And she is full of fears for him. . . But even Zerah says it is better to trust and believe in him than to understand. She says some things are beyond our understanding. And I am sure he is."

She sighed and presently said, "I envy you, Esli. You can do so much for him."

"It is not much he will let me do, Mary. But he knows I would give my life for him."

"I would give seven lives for him, if I had them. He has

[217]

done so much for me and there is so little I can do for him . . . I wonder what the end is to be. . . The Kingdom, surely," she said as though thinking aloud, "for if it is not that it is the end of us all. . . And with his wonderful powers . . . it is unthinkable. . . Yes — the Kingdom !"

None of us, I am sure, had got much further than that. Simon, I know, had not, for I often spoke with him, and he said that he and James and John were often very puzzled at The Master's sayings and did not know what to think. And if they did not I am quite sure none of the others did.

Of all our company, Judas of Kerioth, with whom I had never got very friendly, seemed the least puzzled. He was still very reserved and aloof, but he seemed to know — or to be satisfied in his own mind as to what was going to happen. His dark keen face was alive and his gloomy eyes were bright with anticipation.

I did not know him well enough to ask him myself, but I asked Simon about him, and he said, "He is quite certain we are on our way to proclaim the Kingdom, and that a leader with such powers can certainly carry it through."

"But sometimes," he said presently, "The Master says things which puzzle the rest of us till we don't know what to think."

CHAPTER XXXIX

WE CROSSED the river by the ford at Betharabah, within sight of the Great Salt Sea, under which lie Sodom and Gomorrah; and turning our backs on Nebo and Pisgah, and the dark mountains of Moab, we followed the road up a stream till we came to Bethany. And to be at Bethany again was almost like getting home, so quiet and friendly were its groves and vineyards.

To The Master it was always a joy to be with those very dear friends of his, and Lazarus and Martha and Mary could not do enough to show how glad they were to have him there.

His face, when he was with them, lost some of its soberness; for, of late, it had at times been grave and even sad. I put that down to the stiff-necked opposition of the priests and their party, and the wonder was that he could suffer their unceasing venom as calmly as he did. For they never missed an opportunity of thwarting him and belittling him to the people, and it must have been very hard to bear.

But in that quiet, friendly household he felt himself at home, and it was a joy to see him there.

Martha, the elder of the sisters, was an excellent housewife, and nothing was too good for The Master when he came. She let me help her at times in little ways, but her eager desire to do him honour would have had everyone in the house as bustlingly active as herself.

That first night, when she was busy getting supper ready for him, her sister Mary had been so drawn by what The Master was telling Lazarus that she sat herself down on the floor at his feet to listen.

And Martha, seeing her there, put her head into the room and cried, "Master, is it no matter that she leaves me to do everything alone ? Tell her to come and give me a hand."

But The Master smiled at her and said, "Martha, Martha ! Mary has chosen the best dish and she is not to be dragged away from it !"

And Martha enjoyed the joke; and so, to keep her in good humour, I set my mind to recalling some of the other quaint things I had heard him say . . . such as — the man who carefully strained his wine so that no gnat should get into the cup, and then swallowed a camel, humps and all. . . And the man who thought he could take a splinter out of his friend's eye, though he had a plank in his own. . . And the man who made a great point of polishing the outside of his cup or dish, which men could see, but left the inside dirty.

And I remembered too his enjoyment of the answer of that woman on the coast near Tyre — that the little dogs under the table might be allowed to pick up the children's crumbs.

"Yes — that would please him," she laughed. "He loves all the beasts, especially the little ones. And once he had a little dog of his own which he was very fond of." And by the time I had finished, the meal was ready.

I suppose the priests kept themselves well informed as to The Master's movements. For as soon as we went up into the Temple next day, a great body of them gathered round him as though they had been waiting for him.

It was the Feast of Dedication, always a time of great rejoicing. The Temple was sumptuously decorated, and Solomon's Porch, where The Master was standing, was bright in the winter sunshine. The priests and Pharisees were in their most gorgeous raiment, and he stood there in their midst in his simple white robe — the very opposite of all they represented but looking like a King among them.

This Feast commemorated one of the fleeting bright intervals in our nation's generally gloomy history. These leaders of the people were very full of it, and some of them even seemed eager to learn the truth about The Master and his intentions. But with men like that you never could tell what might be behind their outward show.

"How long are you going to keep us in suspense ?" they demanded. "If you are the Christ — The Promised One — tell us plainly !"

We waited breathlessly for his answer.

If he had fallen in with their ideas I believe they might have thrown in their lot with him and helped him to proclaim the Kingdom we had all so long hoped for. They seemed ready to do so; but, as I have said, with men like that . . . For, on the other hand, they might simply be trying to trap him once more, as they had tried so often before.

If they would accept him as messiah, he could, with their help, undoubtedly set the whole country aflame. For he had done wonders which no other man had ever done. And, backed by them, the people would flock to him, and if things went well the golden age would come again, and their own positions would be assured and even strengthened.

How little we any of us understood him yet — and they still less !

But he understood them.

Since those days I have had much time to think over all that happened, and it seems to me now that that was one of the times in The Master's life when things were in the balance — not in his mind, which was set on a purpose too mighty for any of us to understand, but in theirs, which were set on lower things.

For I am as certain as I sit here writing this record, that as soon as they saw that they could not use him to serve their own ends, they decided to get rid of him as speedily as possible.

They waited intently for his answer, and we waited. Everything depended on it.

They pressed close about him in their rich festive garments, and he stood there in his simple white robes looking taller and statelier than any of them.

He gazed round, gravely and calmly, at their dark, eager faces, and never, it seemed to me, had he looked more like all that he claimed to be.

Then he said quietly, "I have told you and you do not believe. The deeds I do in the name of my Father they testify to me, but you do not believe because you do not belong to my flock . . ."

And he said much more on that head — that like a good shepherd he was ready to give his life for his sheep — that thieves might try to get into the fold over the wall — that if they had listened to him they would have been safe in his keeping — that in all that he did he was following his Father's orders — and he ended by saying, "I and my Father are one — "

At which they cried out furiously, and ran, as once before, to a pile of stones, and prepared to stone him.

He stood quietly, without a trace of fear in him — and waited.

One well-flung stone would have ended him. But it was not flung. Possibly they remembered again his words when they wanted to stone the woman, the last time he was there.

"I have shown you many a good deed of God," he said gently. "For which of them would you stone me?"

"We mean to stone you, not for any good deed, but for blasphemy. You are only a man and you make yourself God," cried one of the priests.

"Is it not written in your Law — 'I said you are gods'?" said The Master.

"If the Law said they were gods, to whom the word of God came — can you say to me, whom the Father consecrated and sent into the world, 'You are blaspheming,' because I said 'I am God's son'? If I am doing the deeds of my Father, believe them though you will not believe me, that you may learn that the Father is in me and I am in the Father."

They had dropped their stones while he was speaking. Now they surged at him as if to lay hands on him.

His grave deep eyes swept searchingly round the close circle of angry faces, then he turned and walked quietly away and no man lifted a hand to stop him.

He went out of the city by the East Gate and took the road over the Mount of Olives, and we followed, depressed and wondering.

What *did* it all mean ? How and when would he declare himself and fulfil all our hopes ? So many chances offered, it seemed to us, and he let them all pass.

On the shoulder of the hill, where the road turns down to Bethany, he stopped, as he always did, and stood for a while gazing, sadly and wistfully, at the great shining city.

I could not but think of his own story of the beautiful dish, well-cleaned outside but foul within.

We were all much disturbed in our minds as to what would happen next. The others were feeling, just as I was, that the priests were so bitter against him that his life was in danger now each time he went into the city. Twice he had barely escaped. The next time might bring the end. So our hearts were full of fears.

It was a mighty relief to us all when, next morning, he said,

"The time is not yet ripe. We will leave this country and return whence we came," and with lightened hearts we followed him down the valley and crossed the Jordan, and came to the other Bethany where John the Baptiser began his teaching and had spent most of his time.

Here The Master was safe from the priests, and yet not too far from Jerusalem for any to come to him if their desire was strong enough. And here we stopped many days.

CHAPTER XL

OUR STAY in Bethany-beyond-Jordan was in some ways a rest and relief to us all. But the whereabouts of The Master could no more be hidden than could that of the sun. Wherever he was, there people flocked to see and hear him.

Many came from Jerusalem, just as they had done to The Baptiser, and among these at times came companies of the Pharisees and lawyers trying, as always, under the guise of a desire to seek his advice, to trap him into statements which they could twist to his discredit.

I remember a number of them coming one day and asking his views on divorce — a dangerous subject in a country where The Baptiser had been murdered but a short while before, for his outspoken condemnation of the shameless life led by "that fox" Herod, the Tetrarch. Machaerus, where John was done to death, was indeed but a short day's journey from where we were living.

But The Master, with the penetrating wisdom which was always his, referred them back to God's original law on the matter, which, he said, should carry more weight with them than the law of Moses or any other man, and he denounced all breakers of that law as strongly as John had done.

But so loose and tangled were our general ideas on this matter that even his closest followers questioned his saying, and he had to argue it out at length with them.

As always, he gave himself without stint to all who came to him, but he also gave much time and care to bringing his chosen ones to a clearer understanding of himself, as God's

[224]

good message to the world, and of all that it would involve for both him and them.

And yet . . . and yet — how very little we understood! I can see it now, but at that time our hearts were still as full as ever of the hope of a coming triumph and the founding of an earthly kingdom. And when he spoke of dangers and death we took that as a necessary part of the mighty adventure on which we were bound.

A rumour got round that The Master was about to leave that part of the country, and one day, when he was deep in earnest talk with his special followers, a number of women came up, leading and carrying their children, hoping to get him to give them his blessing before he left.

Simon and the rest were annoyed at their importunity, as they wandered round behind them, begging this one and that to ask The Master. Indeed they grew so angry at last that they brusquely told them to be off, they were interfering with weightier matters.

The Master noticed the disturbance, and when he learned what was the matter, said gently, "Let them come to me. The Realm of Heaven belongs to such as these. I tell you, no one who will not submit to the Reign of God like a little child will ever get into it at all."

And he took the children up into his arms and kissed them, and gave them his blessing. And they, young as many of them were, seemed to feel his great love for them. For they clung to him, and laughed up into his eyes, and stroked his face with their eager little hands, and could hardly be drawn away from him.

I was on the outside of the throng but saw and heard it all. I heard a sob just behind me, and turned and saw that it was Mary of Magdala. Her great dark eyes were brimmed with tears, and as they ran down her cheeks she tried to smile.

"How he loves them!" she said in a whisper, " — all little, innocent, helpless things. And how they all love him! . . . He is like a father to them all."

P   [225]

That same day there came in haste another who had heard the rumour that he was going. He was a young man of the neighbourhood, very wealthy and very comely, and he had come often to listen to The Master's teaching.

He knelt before him and asked eagerly, "Good Teacher, what must I do to gain eternal life ?"

And The Master said, "Why call me 'good' ? You know the commandments — do not kill, do not commit adultery, do not steal, do not bear false witness, honour your father and mother."

"Teacher," said the young man earnestly, "I have observed all these commands from my youth."

The Master looked at him wistfully, and one could see that he was drawn to him.

But with, I suppose, that peculiar deep insight of his into the very hearts of men, he must have seen that there was still something between the young man and his hope.

He said, "There is one thing you lack. — Go and sell all you have and give the money to the poor ! Then come, take up your cross, and follow me !"

But at that, the young man's face fell. He gazed up at The Master in dismay. . . Sell all he had — houses, vineyards, sheep, cattle, everything ! — and take up a *cross !* . . . It was too much to ask of any man. He bowed his head despairingly and went slowly and sadly away.

The Master stood looking after him, his face full of longing and regret.

"Children," he said to those about him, "it is easier for a camel to get through a needle's eye than for a rich man to get into the Realm of God."

"Then who can be saved ?" asked one.

"It may be impossible for men, but with God anything is possible."

"Well, we have left our all and followed you," broke out Simon. "Now what are we to get ?"

"No one who has left his home and his friends and his dear ones and all that he had, for my sake, but shall get a hundred times as much in this world — together with persecutions; and in the world to come life eternal. . . When the Son of Man shall sit on the throne of his glory, you who have followed me shall also sit on twelve thrones to govern the twelve tribes of Israel."

That is one of The Master's sayings which remained very clearly in my mind, and I have often pondered it long and deeply.

For his twelve special followers were but recently fishermen, a tax-gatherer, a follower of Judas of Gamala, and so on — good men but, until they came to know him, in no way distinguished above their fellows.

But especially I have wondered because Judas of Kerioth was one of the twelve to whom a throne was promised. And we all know now that, within a short span of days, Judas fell away and played the traitor to his Master.

And from all this I believe I am right in thinking that at this time Judas had no such thought in his heart. For, had it been so, surely The Master, with his wonderful insight into men's hearts and minds, would have known it.

No — I believe Judas was at that time still a true man, like all the rest, but I think, from his manner, that, perhaps more vehemently than any of us, he looked for the founding of an earthly kingdom. And it was only at the last, when he saw all his hopes crumbling to nothing, that he did what he did in hopes of forcing The Master to show his power and do what he so longed for.

How very little even the best of us understood !

CHAPTER XLI

THERE came one day an urgent message from the other Bethany — from Martha, saying that her brother Lazarus was grievously ill.

We knew how very dear Lazarus and his sisters were to The Master. We knew also that it might be as much as his life was worth for him to cross the Jordan again. But we knew also that no thought for his own safety would stop him going.

Our fears for him were therefore stilled somewhat when he said quietly, "This illness is not to end in death. . . The end of it is the glory of God."

We did not understand but were glad that he did not need to go.

Two days later he said, "Let us go into Judea again." At which we cried out, reminding him how the Jews had tried to stone him the last time he was there. Why would he risk his life again ?

He answered that till his work was done he could go in safety. And then he surprised us all, for no other messenger had come, by saying, "Our friend Lazarus has fallen asleep. I am going to waken him."

It was, I think, Lucilius who said quickly, "If he has fallen asleep he will get better."

"Lazarus is dead," said The Master gravely. "For your sakes I am glad that I was not there. Come — let us go to him !"

"Let us go too then," said Thomas. "We can but die with him," and we set off for the Fords in the lowest of spirits.

That was a doleful journey. We had all liked Lazarus and his sisters. And he was dead, and they would be mourning him. What else might await us we hardly dared to think.

We reached Bethany before sunset, but while still a long way off we could hear the sound of the wailers, and when we came within sight of the house we saw it surrounded by a great crowd of people, come out from the city to show their respect for the dead, for the family was held in high esteem there.

The Master had no wish to go among them; and while we stood there waiting, a woman robed all in black came hurrying towards us. Her face was white and sad.

It was Martha, to whom someone had carried word that their friend had come at last.

"Lord," she said, with a touch of wondering reproach in her voice, "had you been here my brother would not have died. . . But now . . . well, I know God will grant you whatever you ask of him. . ."

"Your brother will rise again, Martha."

"I know he will rise at the resurrection — on the last day," she said resignedly.

"I myself am resurrection and life," said The Master. "He who believes in me will live even if he dies. And no one who lives and believes in me will ever die. You believe that ?"

"Yes, Lord, I do believe you are the Christ, the Son of God, who was to come into the world," and with that she covered her face with her veil to hide her tears, and went away back to the house.

She must have told her sister that The Master had come, for Mary came running out, followed by a number of friends who had been mourning inside with her.

She fell on her knees at The Master's feet with almost the same words as her sister's. It had no doubt been the one thought in both their minds since their brother died.

"Lord, if you had been here, he had not died," and those who had come with her broke out into wailings again.

The Master's face was grave and troubled.

"Where have you laid him?" he asked, and those with her cried, "Come and see, sir," and led him to the tomb in the side of the hill, with a great boulder closing it. And as he went the tears rolled down his cheeks — the first time any of us had seen him so moved.

"Take away the stone," he said quietly.

But at that Martha interposed hastily. "Lord . . . he has been dead four days . . . he will be rotting . . ."

"Did I not tell you?" he said to her very gently. "If you will only believe you shall see the glory of God."

Then some of them put their shoulders to the stone and pushed it aside, and we all stood straining to see and hear.

Standing there in his white robes, in the golden glow of the sunset, he was a wonderful sight. More than ever he was like one from another world. None who saw him then will ever forget.

Raising his right arm and looking confidently up towards heaven, he said, "Father, I thank Thee for listening to me!"

And then, gazing steadfastly at the dark mouth of the cave, he said, in a voice the like of which I never heard from him or any other — "Lazarus! . . . Come forth!"

And we all fell back in amazement when, instant on the word, Lazarus came out from the tomb, still wearing the linen bandages of the dead, but otherwise just as we had known him.

"Untie him!" said The Master gently, and it was Martha and Mary who ran to their brother, before any of the rest recovered their wits.

And as Lazarus knelt at The Master's feet, they two fell on their knees beside him, and The Master laid his hands upon them and blessed them, and then bade Martha get her brother something to eat.

The great crowd of mourners and others stood for a while in amazement, and then their tongues were loosed and buzzed freely, and they began to disperse, and some hurried off to the city.

The Master turned and led us away round the shoulder of the Mount of Olives, and on over the northern hills into the wilderness.

That great wonder remains in my mind as though it happened but yesterday. For though I had heard from the others of The Master's power to call men back from the dead . . . to see it with one's own eyes . . . that was indeed something to remember till one's own time came, and meanwhile to be ever filled with the wonder and the joy of it.

CHAPTER XLII

WE WENT on and on till we began to hope that The Master was going right back home, to suffer the smaller evil of the authorities there rather than the malignity of the Sanhedrin at Jerusalem.

But we came at last to where a steep cone-shaped hill rose out of the plain, and perched on its top, a little town. It was far enough from the regular routes to be quite secluded and far enough from Jerusalem to be safe. And there The Master said we would stop for a time.

While it was still quite early next morning, I was wandering about the place in great content. For, no matter where one looked, the view was wonderful — on the one side into the valley of Jordan, with the green heights of Gilead beyond, and the dark mountains of Moab to the south; and on the other side, through gaps in the mountains of Ephraim, long stretches of plain which I knew must run right down to the Western Sea.

As I sat there in the morning sun I saw, afar off like a speck on the road, a traveller coming towards the town. And presently I saw it was a man on a beast and he was coming at speed.

At the foot of the hill he dismounted and climbed slowly, with his arm on his beast's neck. And when he drew near I saw that it was the young fellow, John, the friend of Zerah and Azor of Nazaret, whom I had met there and again in Jerusalem.

He waved his hand when he saw me, and came panting up.

"Is he here, Esli ?" he asked anxiously.

"The Master ? Yes, he is here."

"I've come to warn him. . . Urge him, all of you, not to go into Jerusalem again. They mean to kill him. The whole city was talking last night about Lazarus, and everyone was saying that Jesus is without doubt messiah and they will make him King. Joseph Caiaphas and the rest are mad with anger. You see, they cannot deny that raising of Lazarus, nor belittle it, for everyone knows he had been dead four days, so there's no question of a trance as Caiaphas tries to make out. He summoned the Sanhedrin last night and they were at it till early this morning. We live just beside him, you know, up on the Mount, and Nicodemus came in to tell us about it. He believes in The Master, but — well, he's not yet been able to bring himself to saying so openly."

"What was it he told you ?"

"Caiaphas put it plainly to them that if The Master came into the city again there would certainly be a rising and rioting; and if there was, Rome would make an end of them all. If they could make an end of The Master that would stop the trouble. He said it was better that one man should die than that the whole nation should perish. Those were his very words, Nicodemus said."

"I'm quite sure The Master has no such idea, John. But what his idea is I don't understand, and I don't believe any of the others do either. Do you ?"

"No. I know it's not anything like that, but what it is I don't know. I asked him once if he was going to drive the Romans out, and he said there were worse things than the Romans to drive out. But it doesn't matter what is in his mind, their minds are made up to kill him."

"You'd better come and tell him about it yourself, John — if we can find him. I've not seen him yet this morning. He was tired to death last night. We had walked far — and then there was Lazarus . . ."

We found The Master at last, sitting in the sunshine with

his back against the wall, and gazing restfully out over the Jordan valley and the mountains beyond.

And by his side were bread and honey which the woman of the house had given him, with some goats' milk to drink.

He welcomed John with a smile, and said, "You must have started early, my son. Have you eaten yet this morning?"

"No, sir. My mother told me to seek you at once, and I started before it was light. I'd have been here sooner but I had to find out where you had gone."

"You must be hungry," and he broke the bread, and holding it a moment in his hand, as though asking a blessing on it, he gave John half and pushed the honey and the milk towards him.

He looked up with a smiling enquiry at me but I told him I had already eaten. I was sorry that I had.

Their simple meal did not take long. While they ate, The Master spoke only of the happy days he and John had spent in Nazaret with their dear friends, Zerah and Azor-ben-Azor.

"Tell them, John, when you see them, that I bear them always in my heart. . . It is not likely that I shall see them again."

And when they had finished, he said quietly, "Now — your ill-news, my son? — though, truly, it is but what I look for."

And John told him what he had told me.

The Master's face was quite undisturbed as he thanked John, and told him to bear his thanks to his mother also.

"I will come again, sir," said John, "if I get other news. Will you be here?"

"Yes, we remain here till the time comes, and then — as God wills."

Then Simon and some of the others came up and we went away. And presently Simon and Andrew came upon us and must hear all that John had to tell, and their faces were troubled and anxious when they heard.

Simon nodded his great shaggy head and said, "He is greater than them all. . . It stands to reason. One who can bring back the dead when they've been four days buried is not going to be beaten by a pack of venomous priests . . . All the same, I wish it was all clearer to me. And I wish he would keep away from the city, but I doubt if he will."

CHAPTER XLIII

WE STAYED on in the little town on the hill-top for many days, and were well content.

Most of The Master's time was given to long and earnest talks with his special followers, and the rest he spent alone, sitting as a rule in some secluded place, gazing out over the mountains and the plains, and thinking his own deep thoughts. His face in those days was calm and strong, but now there was on it nearly always a touch of wistful sadness. Sometimes he sat far into the night under the great close stars, which were very wonderful up there and lifted one right out of one's self.

It was a very gracious and restful time for us all. I often looked back on it afterwards, and wished . . . But there — his way was not ours and our hearts were very blind.

The only communication we had with the outside world was through young John Marcus, who came out at least once each week on that beautiful white beast of his — it was really his mother's, brought for her from Persia by her husband, Sala-ben-Mattatha, before he died, and she was very proud of it.

He very early brought us word that Caiaphas had issued an order that anyone who knew where The Master was, was to reveal it at once. And he urged us all, with all the strength that was in him, to do our utmost to dissuade him from going anywhere near the city.

"For," he said gloomily, "we have known Joseph Caiaphas all our lives and he can be a bitter and unscrupulous enemy. He is full of fear for his own position, which he thinks The Master endangers. . . If he could have him killed secretly in the dark, he would rejoice."

"Is there any danger of you being followed, John ?" I asked.

"I take good care of that. Each time I come a different way and always start out in the wrong direction."

"Good lad !" said Simon. "I wish there were more like you over yonder."

"There are many, and they are all waiting eagerly for The Master to proclaim his Kingdom. When will it be, Simon ?"

But Simon only shook his head.

THE TIME came at last when, from our hill-top, we saw in the distance, on both sides of the river, the first thin streams of pilgrims making their way to Jerusalem for the Passover.

And then one day The Master said, gravely but resolutely, "Come — it is time for us to go too !"

Remembering young John's warnings, they did their utmost to persuade him not to go.

But to all they could say he answered simply, "My time is come. I must do what I came to do. It is God's will." And then and there he started.

We were all dismayed at thought of what it would surely mean. But when we saw him walking quietly on by himself we could do nothing but follow.

It was Thomas again who said hopelessly, "We can only go and die with him, for they will surely kill him." And, with heavy hearts and reluctant feet, we went down the hill after him.

Something about the lonely white figure in front of us struck a new note in my thought and heart. He seemed, in some way which I could not understand, different from what I had ever known him.

And suddenly, as he looked from side to side, observing as he always did everything he passed, I caught in his face a new look, and my mind flew back to the eagle I had once fought outside the woods of Safed.

That was it. There was in his face something that reminded me of that great King of Birds — a high, command-ing look, unflinching, steadfast, a look of conscious power, of invincible determination. But in him there was none of the eagle's fierce craving. His face was perfectly calm and untroubled, touched with sadness, as I have said, but it was the face of a King.

As he strode on in front there, he looked to me taller than usual, and his firm light step and the grace and dignity of his carriage were a joy to watch.

He led the way down into the bare rock-valley by which a stream ran down to the Jordan. And presently he sat down on a boulder and beckoned us to gather round him.

And then he told us once more what we were to be pre-pared for in Jerusalem.

Simply and quietly, he said that he expected to be be-trayed into the hands of the priests and Pharisees who were seeking his life — that they would mock him, scourge him, crucify him . . . at which word our hearts became like water, such awful shame and suffering attaches to the cross in the minds of our race.

He said also that after three days he would come back from the dead — as Lazarus had done — and would be with us again.

We did not know what to make of it all. It was all so different from what we had been hoping and looking for.

It did not seem possible that he really meant that he was deliberately going to suffer all that — he who had powers such as no other man had ever possessed, even the power over death itself.

And he was so perfectly calm about it. His face indeed was very grave, but it was quite untroubled, without a trace of doubt or fear, and the stars in his eyes shone with so bright a hope that it did not seem possible that anything could quench it.

We were all quite bewildered by it. Simon showed it very plainly. He sat gazing at The Master with wide eyes and bated breath, and now and again an angry shake of the head. Judas's black brows knitted tight, and his startled eyes snapped and blinked as he searched The Master's face fitfully, trying, perhaps, to reconcile his words with his own great hopes. But we were all the same. We could not understand.

How blind of heart we all were you will see by a strange thing that came about when we had started on our way again.

James and John-ben-Zabdai went up to him and broke out eagerly. "Master, we want you to do whatever we ask of you !" — which truly seemed much to ask.

But The Master held them very dear, so he smiled at them as though they were children, and said, "I must first know what it is you want me to do."

"Give us seats, one at your right hand and one at your left hand, in your glory," they said vehemently.

At that The Master's face went grave again. He looked at them with a touch of regret and said quietly, "You do not know what you are asking. . . Can you drink the cup that I have to drink ?"

"We can !"

"You shall indeed drink the cup that I have to drink, but it is not for me to grant seats at my right hand or my left. These are for whom they have been destined," and he went on again in front, full of thought. But the others were bitter against the brothers, and I thought they had good reason.

The matter had been weighing on The Master, I think. For he turned again and when we came up, he said,

"You know the rulers of the Gentiles lord it over them, but it is not so with you. Whoever wants to be great among you must be your servant. Whoever wants to be first must be your slave. . . The Son of Man himself has not come to be served but to serve . . . and to give his life as a ransom for many."

We loved him very dearly. We believed he was, as he told us, the son of the Most High and Holy One, for he lived, and taught, and did mighty works, such as no man ever had done. But we did not understand him.

CHAPTER XLIV

WE WERE glad to get out of that bare hot valley into the wide river-plain where, right in front of us, lay the town of Jericho, very green and fragrant-looking, amid its palms and olives and sycamore-trees.

It was a very wealthy place. There was great traffic through it with all the country on the other side of the river, and in it were many officials for the collection of the dues on the goods that streamed in and out.

When we joined the great road there were many others journeying the same way, and they recognised The Master at once, as, indeed, they could hardly fail to do. For no one could look at him without knowing that he was some-one unusual.

And yet the difference between him and other men was not that of the wealthy Pharisees, who impressed the com-moner folk by their haughty manners and sumptuous attire. His white robe was of the simplest, but his bearing was so quietly dignified and gracious, his face so calm and lofty, that he looked a King among them all. And the crowds drew towards him, delighting to be of his company.

As we passed into the town under the sycamores, whose spreading branches overhung the road, he stopped suddenly, and looking up into one of the trees, called out,

"Zacchaeus, come down at once, I must stop at your house today," and to our astonishment, a short stout man came scrambling down out of the tree, and ran to The Master and bowed before him, and made him welcome to his house.

How The Master knew even his name we did not know, unless he had passed that way before and had heard about him. For, according to the sour talk of those about us, Zacchaeus was only too well known over all that district as an overbearing servant of Rome, although he was a Jew, and a harsh and unscrupulous exacter of dues, whereby he had become wealthy at the expense of his brethren. And this was the man The Master had chosen to honour out of all the men of Jericho ! We were as surprised as our neighbours.

But there was at heart something better in the man, and The Master evidently knew it and that he could draw it out.

For so overcome was Zacchaeus with joy at The Master's graciousness that, before they even reached his house, he stopped, and there, in the road, so that all could hear him, he promised to give half of all he had to the poor, and to restore four-fold any money he had wrongfully exacted from anyone. At which The Master rejoiced, and gave him his blessing.

While at Jericho he restored the sight of another blind man, a beggar named Bar-Timaeus. All his life he had sat by the roadside begging, and everybody knew him. When they saw him following The Master and seeing like anybody else, but greatly amazed at all that he saw, all the people held The Master in great awe and reverence.

I have always thought that he found peculiar pleasure in giving sight to the blind. For he himself rejoiced in all the beautiful things he found everywhere, and his own wonderful, searching eyes missed nothing by day or by night.

We stopped that night in Jericho, for the next day's journey would be an arduous one.

From Jericho to Jerusalem it is one long continuous climb up a steep rocky gorge, infested at ordinary times with robbers, but safe to us because of our numbers. We were glad, indeed, though very weary, when we came at last up into the open again and caught sight of the great shining city.

We passed along the side of the Mount of Olives and

turned down into Bethany, where Lazarus and his sisters came running out to greet us and gave us very joyous welcome.

Lazarus himself looked well and strong; better, it seemed to me, than when I had first seen him. But, except to The Master, he was reserved and somewhat aloof. For the curious still came out from Jerusalem to see the man who had been dead for four days and was now as full of life as ever, and their questions which he could not answer were a trial to him.

The following day was the Sabbath, and we were all glad of the rest. But in the evening Martha prepared a great supper for The Master and some of their friends, and as once before, she was over-stressed with work and allowed me to help her.

Her sister Mary helped too, but lingered longer and longer in the outer room, and this time Martha made no complaint.

She was, in fact, as I could well perceive, much troubled in spirit, and had little to say. But at last she whispered to me, "Esli, my heart is heavy for him. They will kill him if they can, and they have no scruples."

"We are all full of fears for him," I said, "but we cannot stop him. . . What he is going to do we do not know, but whatever it is he will do it. . . He knows they want to kill him. He has told us so, and much besides that is beyond us."

"They have even been plotting to kill my brother," she said protestingly.

"To kill Lazarus ? . . . But why, Martha ?" I asked, in much surprise.

"Because he's a living proof of The Master's power and they can't gainsay it. The people believe in The Master more and more. They hold that one who can bring a man back from the dead can do anything he wishes. . . And Joseph Caiaphas and his lot know there is not room in the world for him and them. And they're right as to that," she said vehemently. "I wish The Master would make an end of them all."

Mary passed swiftly through to her own room and then back again, carrying something hidden in her robe.

"Now, what is it ?" said Martha, looking after her.

And then, as a sudden marvellous fragrance filled all the house, she gasped, "Ah — what has she done ? . . . Her spikenard ! . . . Her very greatest treasure !" and peering anxiously through into the other room — "She has broken the vase and poured it over his feet ! . . . What a thing ! . . . It was worth a fortune ! . . . But . . . yes — after all," she said more thoughtfully, "he gave us back our brother."

From the other room we heard exclamations and murmurs. And then The Master's voice, clear and compelling, and with a note of joy in it, "Let her alone ! Let her keep what she has left for the day of my burial. You have the poor always with you, but you have not always me."

CHAPTER XLV

THE NEXT day, to our grievous anxiety, The Master said quietly that he must go into the city. He set off by the lower road and we followed him in silence and with much fear and misgiving.

He stopped on the slope of the hill and stood looking down on a little hamlet below, and then told Simon and John to go down there and bring up to him an ass and a foal which were tied up to the back of one of the houses.

And when they had brought them they spread some garments on the foal, and The Master mounted it and rode on up the hill at a foot-pace.

There were many pilgrims on the road, and when they saw who it was they shouted with joy, for all who came up for the Feast that year had been wondering if the Great Teacher would be there and had been hoping for it.

They came from the country places. Many of them had listened to his strange new teaching. Some of them may have been healed of their ills. They knew that he had called back to life those who had been dead.

They were as pleased as children. They pulled off their outer robes and spread them on the ground, and tore down branches, for the little foal to walk on. They welcomed The Master with snatches of song from the great Hallel which was sung at the Feasts — Hosannas and Blesseds. They greeted him as the Son of David, as the King of Israel.

At the time we saw in it only the rather childish joy of the simple country people. We were rather surprised at it, but the feeling of the others caught us and we joined in the singing and shouting.

[245]

I had a passing misgiving as to how those in the city would take it — if indeed it lasted till we got there. And I am sure that was in the mind of some of the others also. For they looked puzzled and anxious.

Judas, I know, watched it at first with a look of sour contempt on his dark face, as though it were all just childish nonsense. But presently some other idea seized him, and to my surprise he sang and shouted more vehemently than any, and he did his utmost to get them to keep it up right into the city. I never could understand that man.

Afterwards . . . when all our eyes and hearts were opened, we saw more meaning in that strange little likeness to a triumphal procession, and we thought we fathomed something of Judas's curious behaviour.

Some Pharisees, who had to draw to one side to let us pass, called out to The Master to check the people.

He replied to them, "If they were quiet the very stones would shout."

The road up to Olivet lay through fields and vineyards and under shady trees. Then, as we climbed the shoulder of the hill, the great city lay before us all aglow in the morning sunshine, white and wonderful, the mighty dome of the Temple shining like gold — a sight that almost took away one's breath.

And there The Master stopped and sat gazing at it all — behind us, the peaceful smiling country-side — in front, the great shining city, teeming like an ant-heap and buzzing already like an angry hive.

To our surprise, as he sat there looking across at the city, some strange feeling overpowered him; tears rolled down his face, and he spoke strange sad words as though he foresaw some terrible doom hanging over it.

"The time is coming for you," he said, speaking to the great city as though it were a living thing, "when your enemies will throw up a wall round you, and besiege you on every side, and raze you to the ground and your children within you, and will not leave one stone upon another —

and all because you would not understand when God was visiting you."

It sounded very woful, but we understood it no more than the city would have done — then. Afterwards . . . ah, to our bitter sorrow some of us lived to see those direful words of his fulfilled to the very last letter.

He rode on. Many of those camped outside the walls, when they heard the shouting and singing, pulled down branches also and came to join us. And so we came into the city, led and followed by shouting crowds, and greeted by further crowds in the streets and on the house-tops.

The whole city was in a state of excitement and alarm. Those inside cried, "Who is this ?" and our followers shouted back, "This is Jesus, the Prophet of Nazaret." But Judas, with all his might kept shouting, "The Son of David ! The King of Israel !"

At the foot of The Mount The Master alighted, and we went on up into The Temple.

I have often wondered what became of that little foal, which, the first time it was ever ridden, bore so wonderful a rider into the city. I did hear afterwards that one of The Master's wealthy but secret followers bought it and kept it all its life in great honour, and I like to think that was so.

As we went up into The Temple I saw The Master's face darken with anger, as the clamour of the marketing met us — the hoarse voices of the money-changers and the lowing of the cattle.

He had cleansed it once before, but it was as bad as ever, and with a stern sad face he did as he had done before — drove out the sheep and cattle and those who tended them — threw down the tables of the money-changers — drove all the trespassers out, as one drives hens out of a garden.

They cursed and threatened him as before, but his flaming white anger overbore them. They were in the wrong and knew it, and he did not stay his hand till the place was clear of them all.

Then the people came flocking round him and he sat and

taught them, and through the courts and corridors the little singing-boys were still shouting the words they had picked up from the crowd, "Hosanna to the Son of David !" to one of their Temple tunes.

Some priests came up and asked him angrily, "Do you hear what they are saying ?"

And The Master said, "Yes — have you never read, 'Out of the mouths of babes and sucklings Thou hast brought praise to perfection,'" and they went away scowling and muttering.

All day he sat there talking with great earnestness to the people, but it was obviously not safe to stop the night in the city. The dark narrow streets were full of opportunities for violence, and young John Marcus vehemently asserted that Caiaphas and his party would stick at nothing to get rid of The Master.

So when night fell we went quietly out, and took the way round the wall and across the valley to the Olive Orchard on the little hill, and we slept there under the trees.

The Master could well have gone to Lazarus in Bethany, but I have thought that, since he had learned of the priests' bitterness against his friends there, he thought it best to keep away. His first thought was always for others.

CHAPTER XLVI

HOW LIKE A KING HE WAS

THE MASTER rose very early next morning and went quietly up into the Temple, before the crowds were astir or the dealers and money-changers had set out their wares.

I would like to put down here, as well as I can, my recollection of how he looked as he slowly paced the long colonnade in the early morning sunshine — to and fro, to and fro, talking with quiet earnestness to his followers.

But it is not easy, for his face and his bearing were such as, I am sure, were never seen in any man before.

Perhaps my thought of him then is heightened somewhat by my later knowledge, but indeed the gracious white figure that passed in and out of the sunshine behind the wonderful marble columns seemed to me exactly my idea of a great and noble King.

I had never seen a King, and those I had heard of were neither great nor noble; but the original idea of a King was, I suppose, that, as in the case of Saul and David and Solomon, he was deemed the very best man of his time for such high position. And that was what The Master looked, every bit of him.

His face, these days, was calm and high as I had always known it, but it no longer had in it the radiant joy of living which I had loved in him from the first moment my eyes opened on it.

It was grave and determined — something of the majestic look of the eagle in it without the eagle's ferocity — it was set bravely to face the opposition which beset him now at every turn.

His eyes were steadfast and fearless. The stars in them

glowed with tenderness and sympathy when the sick were brought to him for healing, but they kindled and flashed when the priests came baiting him.

Now and again that morning some of the polluters of the Temple, traders or money-changers, would come up into the court to see if the ground was clear for them. And when they saw him there they slunk away again, growling and cursing.

Then, when they heard he was there, the people came flocking in and crowded close about him and he spoke to them, simply and earnestly, but with mighty urgency, of his New Way and of the peril they were in if they refused it.

As they hung upon his words, their eyes fixed intently on his face, in a silence that told its own tale of touched hearts and stirred consciences, there broke in upon us a stir and a rustle, and a body of the Temple great ones came pushing haughtily through the throng. They were so gorgeously arrayed that the common folk fell back to make way for them, and they stood confronting The Master.

Their faces were full of anger and disdain. The eagle in his eyes looked out at them as calmly as though they had been so many harmless gaudy peacocks.

"Tell us now — you fellow," broke out their leader, in a rude angry voice, "What authority have you for going on in this way? And who gave you this authority?"

And all the people waited, breathless, to hear what he would say. For these were the all-powerful ones, and none ever dared to gainsay them. They could put a man out of the Temple. They could put a man outside the Law, and make an outcast of him.

The Master looked very straightly at them, and said quietly, "Well, I will ask you a question, and if you answer me, then I will tell you what authority I have for acting as I do. . . Where did the baptism of John come from? From heaven or from men?"

They looked at one another. They whispered to one another as their minds quested to and fro. For, as every man there well knew, they had made searching enquiry into John's teaching and had acknowledged him as the prophet of the messiah.

If they now said, "From heaven," The Master would ask, "Then why do you doubt me, since it was of me that John spoke ?"

If they said, "From men," the people would have ripped off their gaudy robes and chased them for their lives, for everyone knew John was a prophet.

"Answer me !" said The Master boldly.

"We cannot tell," they said, and a murmur of derision ran through the eager crowd.

"No more will I tell you what authority I have for acting as I do," said The Master, and they went away scowling and muttering, while he turned quietly again to his talk with the people.

That encounter cheered us greatly. It proved him more than a match for the priests with all their cleverness. It might be the beginning of all that we hoped for.

He turned again to the crowd and continued his teaching, driving home his points with little stories whose meaning was evident, and the stories themselves such as would often be recalled and passed on to others.

Some of the priests who had lingered to hear his talk shot vicious looks at him as the points pricked them. Both they and the people caught his meaning, but there was nothing they could turn against him. The people listened spellbound and admired his boldness. The priests were bursting with venom.

We spent that night again in the Olive Orchard on the hill. And it was barely light next morning when young John Marcus came in haste seeking The Master.

He was full of fears for him. He said the authorities had been sitting in Council nearly all night, and from the very plain hints given to him and his mother by some of their friends, The Master's life was in very great peril. He begged and urged him to go right away beyond the High Priest's reach, and we all joined him in his pleas.

But The Master smiled gravely at us, as though we were just so many children begging for something which could not possibly be granted.

"I must do my Father's will while it is day," he said weightily. "The night will come all too soon. . . Let us go down into the city !" And as we passed through a narrow street, I saw Simon slip into a little shop, and he came out with a short sword in a leather sheath, which he slung by a cord under his robe.

The Master was hardly seated in his usual place when another body of richly dressed ones came hastening to him, not the ones he had put to confusion the day before, but bound on the same errand.

"Rabbi," they said, so earnestly that, for a moment, I half believed in them, "we know you are true and teach God's way in truth, and fear no man. . . Tell us then what you think of this — is it lawful to give tribute to Cæsar, or is it not ?"

Then I, and I think all who heard them — and a great crowd had gathered round — saw what they were at, and we all waited anxiously. For, if he said it *was* lawful, they would tell all the people that he sided with Rome and so could not be the Promised Deliverer. And if he said it was *not* lawful they would tell Rome that he taught the people sedition.

But we might have known him by this time.

He looked at them — through them — with the eagle look in his eyes, and said — quietly, but with such an edge to his voice that it bit the deeper — "Hypocrites ! Why do you tempt me ? . . . Show me the tribute money," and one of them stepped outside to a money-changer and came back with one of the detested Roman coins and handed it to him.

He stood for a moment turning it over and over and looking at the Roman Emperor's head on it. It was the only time I ever saw money of any kind in his hands.

"Whose likeness is this ?" he asked, looking keenly at them, no longer at the coin.

"Cæsar's."

"Very well then — give back to Cæsar what belongs to Cæsar . . . and give to God the things that are God's !"

A murmur of recognition of his wisdom ran through the crowd, and the others went away, sullen and bitter at being so confuted and put to scorn.

But there was no peace for him now. The authorities would not let him alone. They were bent on catching him tripping, and all the evil cleverness they possessed was set to that end.

Twice more that day they came with subtle questions — once as to whose wife in heaven would be a woman who had — according to old custom — been married to seven brothers in succession. To that he answered that in heaven there was no marrying, all were as the angels, children of God, and no more subject to death.

Then another, a learned lawyer, asked which was the greatest commandment of all.

And he told him it was the one which bade them love God with their whole heart and soul and mind — but that there was another equal to it, and that was that they must love their neighbours as themselves.

Then he turned to the crowd and denounced all these high-placed ones, who would not accept his New Way themselves and were trying so hard to keep others out of it.

It was a terrible set of "Woes" he uttered against the Scribes and Pharisees — and the by-names he called them — hypocrites, impious, irreligious, whited sepulchres, vipers, serpents, murderers; no words seemed strong enough to describe them. And, much as they deserved it, we, his followers, were terrified by it all, for it could but make his enemies hate him still more, and they were powerful.

But at the end his voice softened, and his eyes were soft and bright with tears and he said, almost to himself,

"O Jerusalem, Jerusalem — how often I would fain have

[253]

gathered your children as a hen gathers her brood under her wings ! . . . But you would not. . . Your house is left unto you desolate. . . "

(I never forgot those words. For I have lived to see them fulfilled to the last letter.)

He rose. The teaching was over for that day — and though we did not know it, it was his last visit to the Temple.

The crowd dispersed in silence, full of awe at his words, so different from what he usually gave them.

As we were leaving, we had to pass the Court of the Women, where stood the great money-chests with their mouths like trumpets, into which all comers dropped their contributions, and The Master paused for a moment to watch.

He saw the wealthy ones throwing in their gifts with pride — the larger the gift, the greater the show. Then a comely young widow came, all in black and poorly clad, with a child on her arm and another holding on to her robe, and she dropped in two small coins worth, in all, less than half a farthing.

He looked very graciously upon her and said, "She has given more than all the rest; for they have given out of their abundance, and she, out of her neediness, has given her all."

And I think the woman heard, for she held her head high and went bravely on her way.

As we went down the great marble steps, Simon and some of the rest of us, to whom the Temple was always a marvel, were full of admiration of the huge columns, and the great doors, overlaid with gold and Corinthian brass and hung with bunches of golden grapes as large as a man, and the mighty blocks of polished stone, twelve times as long as a man and five times as high.

But The Master's face was very sorrowful as he listened to our babblings, and he silenced and amazed us when he said gravely, "Ay — it is very wonderful. . . But — I tell you truly — not one stone of it all will be left upon another, without being torn down," and we followed him, full of wonder and grief at that strange saying.

(That also I have lived to see fulfilled — to the very fullest, and in circumstances I dare not let my mind dwell upon.)

I do not think another word was said by any of us till we were back at our little camp in the Olive Orchard. Then some of them ventured to ask when that time would be, and he spoke long and earnestly and very solemnly about it, and about the sufferings those would have to undergo who remained true to him. But he held out great hopes for those who did remain faithful.

And then, once again, and in words that we could not misunderstand, he laid our hearts in the dust by saying that those who hated him so in Jerusalem would certainly kill him within the next few days.

It seemed impossible to us — incredible. We sat, in silence and uttermost bewilderment, looking across at the great shining city which the setting sun was filling with golden mist. But the shadows were creeping up the walls and our hearts too were dark with fear and dismay.

CHAPTER XLVII

THE NEXT day, to our very great relief, The Master never went near the city. Instead, he went off by himself onto the hills overlooking Bethany and did not return till the sun was setting.

And when he came back his face was calm and untroubled, as it always was after one of his days or nights alone on the hill-tops. We almost dared to hope that he might have decided to lead us back to our remote little village on the hill where we had rested before, or to some other safe place in the desert.

But there was a great sadness in his eyes, and a tenderness in his voice and manner, greater even, I now think, than ever I had known in him before, gentle and loving as he always was to all who sought him.

Again, the next morning, he gave no sign of going into the city, and as it was the day before the Passover, and as preparations for keeping the Feast had to be made, some of them asked him where he would like to eat it.

He bade Simon and John-ben-Zabdai go down into the city, and near the Mount they would find young John Marcus who would show them the way to his mother's house. He would be on the look-out for them by the fountain. There they would make ready, and he and the others would follow later.

"Tonight, Master?" Simon asked in surprise. For the actual Passover was not until the next day.

"Yes, tonight," he said gently. "Tomorrow is in God's hands."

And they went, wondering.

He spent most of that day alone again, but towards evening he came down to the ten who were left, and they went down into the valley, which was full of shadows, and so into the city.

And presently the rest of our company dispersed, some to the city and some to Bethany, wherever they had arranged for lodging, and I was left alone in our little camp to wait till The Master should return.

And as I sat and saw the sun go down, and the shadow of the great city crept further and further over the country below me, my spirits sank too and my heart was full of fears and darkness.

The time seemed very long. I began to imagine all possible evils. . . They had sat too long and the gates had been closed. . . The priests had seized the opportunity and had taken him. . . They would make an end of him. . . Perhaps he was already dead. . . Those dark, narrow streets. . . One thrust of a sword or dagger by an unseen hand. . . I believed that overbearing High Priest, Caiaphas, capable of anything to gain his own ends.

I was in the lowest depths of fear until I saw in the moonlight a little company come up out of the valley and up the hill, and even at that distance I knew the tall white figure in front of them, and my heart leaped with joy. The Master had come back safe.

I was lying among the bushes in the shadow of an olive-tree, and they passed above without seeing me. There was no talk among them as they went on towards our camp, slowly and heavily, it seemed to me, as though their minds were burdened.

I was getting up to go after them when another figure came stealthily up the hill and nearly fell over me, for it was trying to keep in the shadows also.

It stopped short and then dropped flat alongside me. It was young John Marcus and he seemed to have nothing on but a coverlet flung round his inner vest.

"It is you, Esli ?" he panted. He was obviously much disturbed and excited. "Where have they gone ?"

"Up towards our camp. I am thankful The Master is safe back."

"O, why won't he go away ? Can't all of you get him to go ? . . . They will kill him, Esli," he said with a sob.

"They have done their best to get him to go, John. But he will not. . . I can't understand it. Whenever he clashes with those others he always beats them, and yet he has said plainly, and more than once, that they will kill him in the end. And if they do . . . well, that is the end of everything."

"And he could get away now if he would. O, why won't he go ?" he said passionately though in a whisper.

"It is all beyond me. But truly, John, he seems to have made up his mind that he must die. And that is very strange, for he can do wonders that no man ever did. . . Why did you follow them ?"

"Listen !" he whispered. "I was in my little room alongside the one in which they were supping. They had been a long time and I could hear The Master's voice as he spoke to them.

"Then at last the door opened and I thought they were going. And I was full of fears for him, for Joseph Caiaphas and the others have been meeting almost day and night of late, and I knew they were plotting against him.

"I wanted to see if they got safely away. But only one man came out and went quietly down the stairs, and as he passed the window the moonlight showed me that it was the one they call Judas — the one from Kerioth. I knew him by the shape of his head.

"He stood in the archway at the foot of the stairs and seemed undecided which way to go. There were only two ways he could go — down into the city, or up towards the Mount. And when I saw him turn towards the Mount, all my fears came on top of me and I slipped down the stairs to see where he went. . . And, Esli, he crept along in the shadows till he got to the house of Caiaphas and he went in there. . ."

"But what could he possibly want there ?" I asked, startled by John's story and his evident great fear.

"I don't know. But I know that that's where all the plotting against The Master is going on; and so I watched till he should come out, to see what he would do next. It was a long time before anyone came out, and then it was not he. It was Joseph Caiaphas himself . . . and where do you think *he* went, Esli ? . . . He went straight across to the Palace where the Procurator is living. . . What do you make of that now ?"

"I don't know what to make of it all," I said, all my fears on top of me just as his were.

"I must see what they're doing up there," he said, getting up restlessly — as was his way. He always wanted to see all that was going on. "If I can get hold of Simon or John I'll tell them. Perhaps they can persuade him to go."

He slipped away among the shadows, and I waited there in great fear, for I knew that nothing anyone could say would change the mind of The Master; though why he should be willing to risk his life in this way was quite beyond me.

The city lay dark and silent below me, and as the time passed I began to hope that our fears might be groundless.

Then a stab of fear shot through me, as a spark of light pricked the lower darkness of the city wall. Then another and another, till they were many, and I caught the glint of steel below them and knew that they were armed men with torches, and they were coming towards the hill.

I sprang up, with my heart in my mouth, and sped away to warn the others.

They were sleeping but were up in a moment when they heard me.

"Where is The Master ?" I panted. "They are coming !"

"He went into the Garden yonder," said Andrew, as they

crowded to the side of the hill, and when I ran off towards the Garden they all came running after me.

As we got to the gate we saw The Master coming quietly towards it, and with him Simon and James and John. And through the trees below we saw the glare of the torches and heard the noise of those who carried them.

They came out from the trees straight towards the Garden, and in front of them was Judas of Kerioth.

The Master walked quietly to meet them. His face was as I had never seen it — white in the moonlight as though carved in marble; set tight, indeed, but not hard like that of a carving — bravely calm and composed. And his eyes seemed very large and bright, and there was not a sign of fear in them, only a great sadness.

Judas went straight up to him and kissed him on the cheek with a "Hail, Rabbi !"

Then our eyes were opened to his treachery and our blood boiled, and not one of us but would have liked to strike him dead.

"Judas !" — The Master looked sorrowfully at him. "Do you betray the Son of Man with a kiss ?"

The miserable fellow clung to his shoulders for a moment and gazed up into his face — hungrily ? — expectantly ? — I do not know — nor what he saw there, but he suddenly loosed his hold and fell back among the crowd.

To them The Master said quietly, "Whom are you seeking ?"

"Jesus the Nazarene," said one.

"I am he."

And at that — at finding themselves suddenly face to face with one of whose more than human powers they had heard so much — they fell back before him, and in the confusion some even fell over one another.

"Whom seek ye ?" The Master asked again.

And again one replied, "Jesus the Nazarene."

"I told you that I am he. If then it is me you seek, let these others go away."

Our hearts were filled with despair. We saw that he was set on giving himself up to them. Why — we could not tell.

But, against that armed mob, and his determination, we were powerless.

Simon, indeed, in his usual headlong way, pulled out that short sword of his and struck at the man nearest him, and cut off his ear.

It was a foolish and useless thing to do, yet very natural. For we were all feeling as Simon did — full of rage and fury, and the more so that we were helpless.

I saw The Master stop Simon, and touch the man's bleeding head with his hand. And then I felt rising within me that wild fury from which I had thought myself freed forever. The old thunders and lightnings began whirling in my head. I wanted to rend and tear, and I knew that I must not. I flung myself down flat. . . I dug my fingers into the earth. . . I bit savagely. . .

When the fit passed and I came to myself again, I was alone. The leaves above me rustled and whispered. There was no other sound. Below me, across the valley, the city lay dark and silent.

But that was where they would have taken him and I must go and find out what they had done with him.

I felt utterly bereft and emptied of life — helpless, hopeless, nothing left. For he who had given me life, and had been very life to me, was in the hands of his enemies and they were cruel and heartless and would do him to death.

"Alone ! . . . I craved someone to touch, someone to speak to, as never in my life before.

Martha, Mary, Lazarus — the friends he had loved — they were but just over the hill there. . . I hungered for them, or for anyone who had loved him as we had and would understand.

I got up on to my feet to go to them. But I could not. My Master was somewhere down there in the silent city. My feet carried me stumbling down the hill and up out of the valley to the great grim walls.

The moon had gone, and I stumbled along in the darkness till I came to a portal — the one, I thought, out of which the torches had come.

I hammered on it with my fists, but no one came.

I went on to the gate, but it was shut and would not open till dawn. So I dropped down with my back to the wall and waited; and worn out and utterly spent, I fell asleep.

CHAPTER XLVIII

WHEN I awoke, the people from outside were pouring through the gate, and when I joined the throng the narrow streets were already so packed that it was hardly possible to move.

Everyone was talking, everybody was eager to know what was really going on. But to get even within sight of the Mount, which was everyone's desire, one would have had to walk upon the heads of the people. I wormed my way through till I could not move another step.

Disjointed word of what was happening up there was passed along at times and was hastily seized and discussed.

"He's before Pilate. . . Caiaphas took him himself, they say."

"Last night, somewhere outside. No — no trouble, he made no fight for it."

"They'll end him now. He's upset them too much."

"Why should they want to end him ? He's a good man and has done no harm."

"He's a wonder. But, all the same, they hate him and they'll end him."

"Ay, he touched Old Annas's pocket when he cleared that scum out of the Temple. They're bad ones to cross, up there."

A woman beside me began to sob quietly.

"He healed my little one," she jerked. . . "I'll never forget his face. . . Why should they want to kill a good man ?"

"He's a good man, but he's all for new ways and they're all for the old — "

"His ways are good ways —"

"Maybe, but there's not room for both, and the old ways are in the high places."

It was a weary time, and sickening. The sun smote us rudely. One could hardly breathe in the narrow, packed street. Everybody was panting and sweating. The air was thick with the smell of human bodies — so much more sickly than the clean smell of beasts. If we had not been so jammed together some of the women would have fallen.

"Pilate's sent him over to Herod."

And presently — "He's back again. Herod won't have him."

Then, from beyond there, we heard harsh shouts — yells as of savage beasts — "Bar-Abbas ! . . . Bar-Abbas ! . . . Bar-Abbas !"

"What's that ? Why are they shouting for Bar-Abbas ?"

But we were too far off to learn what it meant.

Then, in a fiercer shout than ever, a word we all knew and all that it implied, and it sent a cold shiver down all our backs, a stab of horror into all our hearts — "Crucify ! . . . Crucify ! . . . Crucify !"

"Oh . . . No ! No ! No ! . . . Oh, why ?" screamed the woman near me, and then the life went out of her face and she sank down like an empty sack against her neighbours.

"They are scourging him."

Then a long and weary wait.

And then the masses in front came suddenly rolling back on us, and we were thrust along not knowing where we were going or why — knowing only that unless we went we would be crushed to death and trampled on.

We were thrust at last through an arched gateway, struggling and panting, thankful to get through alive and whole, for the pressure there had been frightful.

We were torn and dishevelled, but, once through the gate, we struggled free and scattered into the open, and most of us sank down onto the ground to recover ourselves.

The grim old gateway continued to belch its gasping crowds. There seemed no end to them.

And then suddenly — splashes of light against the sombre gateway and the seething crowds — brass helmets and breastplates, spears and swords, flashing as they came out into the sunshine, the tramp of heavy, mailed feet — a cohort of Roman soldiers, burly, hard-faced men who made our people look weak and puny, and scattered them like chaff.

And in the midst of them, one bearing as best he could a heavy beam and staggering beneath it.

For a moment my brain stood still, too dazed to work — my heart seemed to stop, and then beat on with a fury that choked me. . . It could not be ! . . . It could not be ! . . . His face as of one dead, but stained with the leaden marks of bruises and patches of filth — his eyes sunk almost out of sight in the depths of his suffering — a mock crown of twisted thorn pressed hard on his head, the blood from it still dripping down his brow — his white robe all soiled, and and bloody on the back and shoulders. . .

The Master ! . . . It could not be ! . . .

My brain stopped. My heart shrivelled into nothing . . . The Master !

Then I saw that the dead-white face was calm and un-daunted still. The eyes in their dark hollows shone brave and steadfast as ever. And, though he stumbled beneath his load, I knew that it was only because his tortured body could stand no more — that his valiant spirit was unbroken.

Some of the baser sort hurled stones at him. They jeered when he fell. They tried to hit him with sticks between the soldiers.

It takes long to tell, but I saw it all at a glance. I saw too that there were others with crosses behind him. But my thought was only for him.

Then my heart, which had died, came furiously back to life. My brain, which had stopped, boiled and whirled. The thunders and lightnings stormed within me.

I rushed blindly towards him — to get to him — to help him — to comfort him — I do not know what. But he was there — the one I loved and reverenced more than anything on earth — he was there, and in most desperate case, and I must get to him.

A burly soldier shot out an arm to stop me. I struggled wildly to get through. Beyond the mailed arm the eyes I loved, strained, bruised, bloodshot, looked full into mine and they were alight with love and pity.

He knew me. He knew what I wanted. I believe he said my name. . .

Then a crash on my head from behind and everything passed from me.

When I came to myself it was all dark about me. The earth heaved and shook. From somewhere beyond I heard a sound as of falling walls or houses.

I was dazed and dull, and bruised in every part of my body.

Cautiously I felt myself all over. There was a lump the size of an egg on the back of my head. But my limbs seemed unbroken though very stiff and sore.

I must have been trampled on by innumerable feet. It was morning when I was struck down. I must have lain there all through the day, since it was now night. I felt weak and broken, as the recollection of it all came back on me.

There were people passing me in the dark, going towards the city. They were mostly silent — hastening as though in fear. Some muttered a word now and again. And some beat their breasts and groaned.

I tried to think. They had taken him up that way — where all the people seemed coming from. I must go and see what they had done with him.

I was sick and dizzy when I got onto my feet. It seemed to be growing lighter, but — extraordinary thing — the new day was coming up in the west. The sky was growing lighter there every minute — something evidently wrong with my head still.

Then one came running swiftly, bent double almost, as though in fear of being seen. He was muttering to himself like one demented.

He almost ran into me, and I saw that it was Judas of Kerioth.

In my dazed state I forgot for the moment how I had last seen him. I thought only that here was one who would know.

"Where is he, Judas ?" I cried. "What have they done to him ?"

He straightened up for a moment and glared at me with bedevilment in his eyes.

Then he gripped my shoulders with hands like claws, and shook me to and fro as if I were a sack.

"He is dead. . . He is dead. . . They have killed him," he panted hotly in my face — "And I never meant that. . . I never meant it. . . The devils ! . . . I am in hell . . . in hell . . ." — he flung me from him, and as I lay sprawling, I still heard his despairing "in hell . . . in hell," as he sped away towards the city.

Dead ! . . . The Master dead ! . . . Everything ended ! . . . It seemed impossible, incredible. His powers had seemed unlimited. How could he possibly be dead ?

I must go and see for myself. Judas was obviously mad.

I went on painfully towards the place from which the people were coming in increasing numbers. On in front on a mound there was still a crowd, and as I drew near I saw just above their heads three low crosses, and my heart sank again.

I was limping on, with bated breath, stumbling, because my eyes were fixed on those grim crosses in front, when they lighted on two who were coming slowly towards me, a man and a woman. The man was John-ben-Zabdai and the woman was The Master's mother.

Her face was partly hidden by a fold of her robe, but it

was white as death, and she was sobbing heart-brokenly. She was leaning heavily on John's arm and seemed scarce able to walk, and his hand was laid comfortingly on hers and his face was bent towards her. They passed me close but did not see me.

I pushed on through the thinning crowd till I could see. And when I saw I sank down on the ground and all the savour of life went out of me.

The Master ! . . . The noblest and dearest and best of men ! . . . Fuller of grace and truth and all goodness and love for his fellows than any man ever had been !

And I had loved him as I had not known it was possible to love any man ! Every bit of him had been sacred and dear to me ! I had reverenced and worshipped him — body, soul, and spirit !

Son of Man ! . . . Son of God ! — his own words came back to me.

And he hung there, in most pitiful case, between two others who were still alive.

He was dead. His body hung slack and motionless. His head had fallen forward on his chest. There was a wound in his side as of a spear-thrust. Dazed and broken as I was, I was thankful that his agony was ended, for the cross is very cruel. The other two still writhed and groaned.

I saw it all, but I could only think brokenly. My heart and my mind were dull and dead.

It was all over . . . the end of everything. All our great hopes — and his — gone — vanished into nothing. No Kingdom . . . nothing !

I felt stripped bare — bare of all but life . . . and there was nothing left to live for.

The Master . . . dead !

I felt as one brought up in a palace and suddenly despoiled and flung out naked to die on a dunghill.

I know not how long I lay there, gazing, dull-eyed and hopeless, at that forlorn figure on its cross — forlorn and pitiful beyond words — and yet, as I looked and looked and

[268]

saw nothing else, there grew within me a strange new sense of the greatness of him.

Perhaps it was the titulus nailed to the beam above his head —

THE KING OF THE JEWS

that set me thinking that way.

For, indeed, his face, calm and high still even in death, and in spite of its mocking crown and its bruisings, was the face of a King. Even in his undoing he was still The Master, and those who lingered there — some soldiers sitting on the ground below him, several women, a few men — they were all quite silent and seemed to feel it as I did.

A group of richly robed ones passed me — of the Temple perhaps, come to see the end of their scheming. But they went heavily and in silence. They had won, but . . .

The sun was low in the west. How and why, my humming head refused to wonder about. But I knew that that darkness into which I woke up could not have been the night.

Into the aching emptiness of my life there came again an overpowering craving for the sight and sound and touch of someone I knew.

The only ones my dull mind could think of were his friends at Bethany. I set off slowly round the North Wall, down into the valley and up the other side, and so came to the road we always used, and got to Martha's house just as the night fell.

They were all broken with despair and grief; Lazarus, deadly pale and very silent; Mary, with her eyes swollen with weeping; Martha the same, but still full of kindly concern for all my bruises, for she anointed them at once with ointments which gave them great relief. And she fed me and got ready a bed for me.

"How did you hear, Martha ?" I asked, as she attended to my bruises.

"We went," she said.

"You went ? . . . You saw it all ?"

"Young John-ben-Matthat came running in at dawn to fetch some very dear friends of The Master who were stopping with his aunt Rachel next door, and we heard. We followed them as soon as we could, but they went quicker than we could."

"We had to go," said Mary softly, understanding my surprise at them having run that risk.

"Our hearts were with The Master," said Martha.

"I know. . . But after what John said . . ."

"Yes, we had to go, priests or no priests," said Lazarus.

"But when we got to the top of the hill we saw the people swarming into the city like ants," said Martha. "We could not get even near to the Gate. Then we heard they were going out by the Damascus Gate and we went round the wall . . . and we saw . . ."

"Oh, it was terrible . . . terrible . . . to see him so," sobbed Mary. "And we could do nothing . . . nothing," and her tears ran down again at thought of it all.

"Are the others here?" I asked, for I had been anxious to know where they had got to.

"Most of them came in last night," said Martha. "They are broken. They don't know what to do or think. And they are troubled about Simon and John-ben-Zabdai. They fear the priests have got them."

I told them how I had met John and The Master's mother, but of Simon I knew nothing.

"His poor mother !" Martha sighed. "It is terrible for her . . . terrible ! It might well kill her too."

"It is terrible for her and for all of us . . . the end of everything. . . The Shepherd is dead and the sheep are scattered," I said gloomily.

Then silent Lazarus spoke.

"It is not the end, Esli. I am sure of that," he said, quietly but with completest conviction.

"How not the end, Lazarus ?" Martha asked, with just a

touch of sharpness in her voice, as though she feared his wits were wandering, and would recall them. "The Master is dead."

"They could kill his body, but that was all, and that was not the best of him. . . And even the dead can come to life again. *He was Life!* . . . You cannot kill Life."

Martha shook her head bewilderedly.

"I don't know what you mean."

"I don't understand it myself," he said, slowly and thoughtfully. "But I feel it. . . This is not the end. We shall see him again."

And Mary, who was sitting on the floor below him, slipped her hand into his as though to thank him for that new and comforting hope.

*

BOOK V — THE CROWNING WONDER

CHAPTER XLIX

OF THE CROWNING WONDER OF THE EMPTY TOMB

IN SPITE of my bruises of mind and body I slept very soundly, for I had been quite worn out with all the doings of that terrible night and day.

The following day was the Sabbath, and when they heard I was there, all The Master's followers who were in Bethany came in, eager for anything I could tell them.

But they had all of them been in the city and then outside it the day before, and some of them had seen more than I had.

They were all anxious for word of Simon and John. Of John I could tell them, but for Simon our fears were great, for we had seen him strike one of the Temple men with his sword, up there in the Olive Orchard, and the others might well have paid him out for it.

We were all quite hopeless as to the future — in the uttermost pit of despair — all our mighty expectations shattered — our leader dead — the hoped-for Kingdom gone.

We talked gloomily of what we would do. All we could do was to go back to our homes, shipwrecked and broken men, and find work again, and live on the memories of these last uplifting months.

Life could never be the same to any of us, for we had known The Master. And his sayings and his doings, and most of all himself, we could none of us ever forget. But always, over all our thought of him, gracious as it could not but be, would rest the shadow of the cross, the tragedy of a mighty hope buried in a tomb.

And we had reason enough to fear for our own safety. Having killed the Shepherd, Caiaphas and his people might deem it well to make an end of the sheep also. We comforted ourselves with the thought that we were after all but a handful of very ignorant men, and they would probably consider us not worth troubling about.

At that time, in our complete undoing, not one of us had a thought of carrying on The Master's work. With his going everything had gone. We were men without a hope.

That was the longest and blackest day of my life.

I WAS wakened very early next morning by an impatient thumping on the outer door, and then the sound of excited voices.

It might be word that Caiaphas was upon us and we must flee. I slipped into my tunic and went out, and found the others round young John Marcus. He was hot and panting and ablaze with excitement.

Lazarus and Mary were listening with sparkling eyes and a great glad light in their faces. Martha had, I think, been questioning him doubtfully.

"He says," she said, turning to me, "that The Master is not in the tomb where they laid him — "

"I have been in it, Esli," said John eagerly, "and he is not there. He has risen, as he said. It can only mean that."

"Unless someone has stolen him from us," said Martha sharply.

"But who would? And why should they?" cried John. "The priests — "

"The priests want him dead. They sealed the tomb last night and set a guard over it, to make sure no one touched it. I saw them. And now — he is not there."

The Master's followers came running in. They had heard John had come and knew it must mean news.

But news such as this they could hardly credit and they regarded him doubtfully.

"Now, listen!" said John, when he had at last got his

S   [273]

breath again. "I followed you all up to the Olive Orchard that night, and I followed them when they took The Master away to Caiaphas's house. I came here to fetch Zerah and Azor, and we were there on Golgotha and . . ." he dropped his voice almost to a whisper ". . . we saw it all. . . It broke Zerah's heart, I think," — at which Mary glanced quickly at him.

"I slept all through the Sabbath. At night Zerah insisted on starting for home. I went with them a bit of the way, and coming back I went round by Joseph's garden, just to see again the place where they had laid The Master.

"The priests were sealing it when I got there. They left some of their people to guard it, and I went on home.

"I did not sleep much that night, and when I heard people passing, before it was light, I ran down to see what was going on, and I was just in time to catch Malchus. He was the man whose ear Simon cut off up there on the hill and The Master healed it. I've known him all my life. . ."

"Do you know where Simon is ?" Andrew asked anxiously.

"He's at our house, up on the Mount. There's room for you all there if you want to be with him."

"And my brother ?" asked James.

"He's at Raguel's house, where he always stops. The Master's mother is there with him."

"What about Malchus, John ?" asked Martha eagerly.

"I caught him by the arm and asked him what was wrong, for he was panting and all in a tremor. And he gasped, 'The Nazarene !' — that's what they called The Master, you know.

"'What about him ?'" I asked, and I shook him to make him sensible.

"'He's not there . . . the tomb is empty. . . We were watching — not one of us asleep. I swear it . . . and the earth shook and there was a great white light, and when we could see again the stone was moved and there was nothing inside.'

"I left him and ran faster than I ever ran in my life. For I remembered how The Master had said he would come back, and more than once he had said something about 'the third day,' and this was the third day.

"I reached the tomb, and it was as Malchus said — the stone rolled aside. I was frightened, but I looked in. It was empty, but full of a very sweet smell of spices from the long linen sheet which lay on the slab.

"While I was sitting there getting my breath, I heard footsteps outside and voices. Then, after a minute, a woman came to the opening and looked in.

"When she saw me she gave a cry and turned and fled, and there were two others with her.

"I ran out and shouted after them that The Master was not there — that he had surely risen as he said. And I remembered that, as you went up with him to the Olive Orchard, he had said that when he came back he would go before you into Galilee. So I called that after them too. But how much they heard, I do not know. They were very frightened. I suppose they took me for a spirit. It was hardly light, you see, and they had expected to find The Master's body there, and instead they found one who shouted after them.

"But it can only mean that The Master really has risen as he said he would" — and John's joyous face showed that he, at all events, had not a doubt about it.

"I knew the women would tell Simon and John at once. So I came on here as fast as I could to tell you all. I was sure you would all have come here."

Most of their faces had changed wonderfully as John told his strange story. They had been dull and hopeless and despairing. They were alight now with new hope, and their eyes, though they were full of amazement, were bright and eager.

But — "Can we go and see the tomb ourselves, John ?" asked Thomas.

"Why not ?" said John, in no way hurt by what might

look like a doubt cast upon his story. He was in too up-lifted a state to feel like that. "There will be many going to see it, once it gets known, and it will be all over the city by mid-day. What Caiaphas will say about it, I don't know," he said hopefully.

"He will say that some of us stole The Master's body so that we could say he was not dead," said Lazarus thought-fully.

"I shouldn't wonder," John nodded. "He will be furious, and he'll say and do anything, for the city is full of talk about it all. They are saying the trial was not according to the law."

"Caiaphas would not let that stand in the way of his purpose," said Lazarus, with quiet bitterness.

"No. But the people are talking about it, and this will make him worse than ever."

"I too would see that empty tomb," said Lazarus. "Not that I doubt for a moment," he added quickly, "but it would be a deep joy to me. That The Master has risen I am certain. For I knew they could not end him so."

"I will take you there, Lazarus," said John, "and all of you. But . . . if we all go together the priests will be onto us."

"We will break up and follow at a distance," said Thomas, who, we all knew, would never be satisfied till he had actually seen for himself. "Let us go." And John jumped up ready to lead the way.

Martha had slipped away into her own part of the house. She came back now with a platter full of thin dry cakes and another of dates.

"We will eat as we go," she said cheerfully. "We've had greater things to think about this morning. And The Master would not have us faint on the road."

So we all helped ourselves and set off, breaking our fast as we went.

John led us over the shoulder of Olivet, and across the ravine, and then round the eastern and northern wall of the city till, between the North Gate and Damascus Gate, we came near to Joseph's garden, and there we broke up into twos and threes, and Lazarus muffled his face in his robe.

There were a number of people about, gazing curiously at the black mouth of the tomb, from which the great round stone had been so mysteriously rolled aside.

There were also here and there priests, keen-faced and determined, moving busily about among the people and speaking very emphatically to whomsoever would listen to them.

"Yes," we heard one say, "they have stolen the body, but we are on their track. We shall find it again. . ." And that was doubtless the story they had all been told to tell.

John whispered to each of the followers to keep him in sight and he would take them to Simon. And he said to me,

"You will come home with me too, Esli ? . . . till you see what the rest are going to do," and I was glad to go with him.

So we said farewell to Lazarus and Martha and Mary, and went on through the gate into the city.

We waited under the arches of the lower storey of a house built up the side of the Mount, and one by one, as they came along, John signalled to the others and bade them go on up the steps to the top room where they had supped with The Master that other night. Then we followed, but turned into a lower room where John's mother greeted us in a state of intensest excitement.

She was a comely woman of middle age and of a most kindly disposition, but at first I was doubtful if she was quite right in her mind.

"What does it all mean, John ?" she cried bewilderedly. ."Are they all crazy ?" and she absolutely gasped with the tumult that was in her.

. "No, Mother. We are none of us crazy. But . . . The Master is not in the tomb where they laid him. He has risen as he said he would."

"I know. . . I know. . . Simon and John have been to the tomb. . . And Mary of Magdala has seen The Master himself and has spoken with him."

"What ?" we both sprang up in overpowering joy and amazement.

"Tell us quick, Mother — tell us all you know," cried John. And she poured it all out as if it was a relief to her to tell it.

"I heard you run out before it was light, and I wondered, so I got up.

"Then, not long after, Mary of Magdala came rushing up the stairs. I just caught sight of her. And in a minute she and Simon came rushing down again.

"Then, after a time, Simon and John-ben-Zabdai came back together, and something had happened to them. For they had both seemed crushed and broken — Simon even more than John, but now they were beside themselves and bursting with joy.

"They came in here and said the tomb was empty, and that that meant that The Master had risen; and truly I thought their wits had gone.

"They were still talking of it and recalling things The Master had said to them beforehand, when Mary came stumbling up the stairs again. When she saw them she turned in here, and from her looks I was quite sure she at all events was out of her mind.

"Her eyes were larger than ever, and shining — oh, like stars. She was like one possessed — but not of evil . . . of something too big for her and all good.

"She dropped onto that seat and looked very steadfastly at us, and said, in the strangest, softest voice I ever heard — 'I have seen the Lord —'

"Simon and John jumped up and cried out together, 'Mary ! . . . You have *seen* him ? Tell us quickly !' and Simon said 'God be praised !'

"And Mary said softly, 'I waited there when you had gone. I could not bear to go. He had been there . . . and

[278]

it was all we had left of him. . . Then I heard someone near me, and through my tears I saw that it was a man. . . I thought he might know something, and I said, 'Sir, if you have carried him elsewhere, tell me and I will remove him.' . . . And then he said, 'Mary !' . . .

"It was his voice. There never was any voice like it. I have heard it in hell, I shall hear it in heaven.

"I cried 'Rabboni !' and fell at his feet and would have kissed them. But he said gently, 'Do not cling to me, Mary ! But go to my brethren and say to them, I am ascending unto the Father — the Father of me and the Father of you, to my God and your God'. . . And when I dared to look up, he was gone. . . I was aflame, and trembling with the wonder and joy of it. And as soon as I could I came here to tell you what he said.

"That," said John's mother, "is what she said, as near as I can remember it, for I was all of a tremble too as she told it all. . . What *does* it all mean ?" and she looked at us with eager eyes which had in them a touch of doubt and fear.

"It means that he has come back to us, as he said he would," said John, and his eyes were sparkling and his face was alight. "We shall have him with us again ! . . . The wonder of it ! . . ."

"Lazarus said he was Life and they could not kill Life," I said, "and he was right. It is very wonderful !"

How that day passed I do not know, for we were all shaken out of our usual minds and turned upside down.

I know we waited in great expectation, wondering what would happen next.

The Master's followers were in that upper room with the doors locked, and in that they were wise. For they were without doubt risking their lives by being there.

CHAPTER L

YOUNG JOHN went out during the day to get any news he could, and came back saying that everyone knew the tomb was empty — the Temple people were furious, and were everywhere spreading the report that The Master's followers had stolen his body in the night, and most rigorous search was being made for them.

Had they known where they were — within a stone's-throw of Caiaphas's own house — they would certainly have seized them and put them on trial.

They, upstairs, spent the day in prayer and fasting — full of wonder but fuller still of joy and exultation, so uplifted, indeed, above all the ordinary concerns of life that they never gave a thought to their bodily needs. This — and more — I learned from Simon next day.

John's mother was troubled, as Martha would have been, at thought of them all so long without food. For none of them could have had time to eat since the previous night — except the small cakes and dates Martha gave us in the early morning, and the day had been a trying one.

So, at last, she sent John up to ask, and at their request we took up to them bread and meat and fish.

There was a strange stillness about the house. Something — we knew not what — impelled us to extremest quietness. We moved about as noiselessly as possible. We spoke only in whispers. The immensity of that day's happenings was upon us and held us in its spell.

If the body of The Master had been lying in that upper room we could not have been more conscious of him. But the spell that was upon us was not one of sorrow, but of joy so overpowering that I think we feared lest anything we did should break it and leave us in darkness and desolation as before.

And, bodily weary as we were, our minds were in such a state that we had no desire to sleep. We all, I think, had the feeling that, being as we were, so close to the very heart of this strange matter, anything might happen at any moment and we must be ready for it.

When, very late that night, we heard hasty footsteps on the stairs, our fears that had been in hiding leaped out and made our hearts sink, for we thought it might be that the priests had learned where our friends were and had come to take them.

We waited, breathless and anxious. But the newcomers were, we thought, not more than two, and they went up quickly, and lightly. We heard them knock gently on the door, and presently it was opened and they went in.

In spite of myself I fell asleep at last on my couch by the table, for I was awakened by the sound of voices, and found Simon leaning in at the door and talking with John.

He looked larger and burlier than ever, as if he had grown bigger in the night.

"Ay," he said, after a moment's hesitation, in reply to some question of John's. "Come with me, if you will. I always like company when it's to my mind."

"Not unless you'd really like us, Simon," said John, but his eagerness showed through.

"Come along. It will do us all good to be out in God's fresh air," and he went on down the stairs, and John and I ran down after him.

It was barely light, but the gates were opened early during the Feast and there were many coming in.

Simon took the path under the south wall and we knew he was going to the Olive Orchard, and that seemed to us the proper place to go to.

He spoke hardly at all — except to say how he hated the city, with its narrow streets, and smells, and lack of air, and the vermin that dwelt there, as he bluntly put it — till we had gone down into the valley and were climbing the side of Olivet.

But when we had got quite away from everybody, it seemed as though the crisp morning filled him like old wine. For he flung up his arms and jerked out bits from the Psalms of David —

> *"Praise ! Praise ! Praise to The Eternal !*
> *Hallelujah ! Thanks be to The Eternal !*
> *Praise to the High and Holy One !"*

and many more.

Maybe he caught a look of wonderment in our faces, for, indeed, we had never seen him like that.

"Ay," he cried, "I am drunk — drunk with the goodness of God to a sinner above most. . ."

Then, falling suddenly to a great calm, he stood still and said, almost in a whisper — "Boys . . . he came to us in that room last night. . . Yes !" as we stared at him in amazement — "He came, though the doors were locked, and he spoke much with us. It was he himself, with his wounded hands and feet. And when we thought it was a spirit he made us handle him, and he ate of our bread and our fish. . . And those two who came in late. He had walked with them to Emmaus, and they came all the way back to tell us. . . It is the Power of God. . . He is with us again ! Do you wonder that I cannot contain myself ? . . . He is with us again and his work will go on ! We shall see his Kingdom after all ! . . . Now, stop you here. I would go on up yonder for a time, and I would be alone."

"He has gone to the Garden," said John, as he looked after him. "That is well !"

We sat waiting for Simon to come back, and as I looked out upon the wonder of the great shining city I felt as Simon did about it. It was full of lurking evils. It had been very cruel to us. And as my mind went back on it all, I recalled my meeting with Judas of Kerioth in that strange darkness three days before, and I told John about it, and said, "I wonder what's become of him."

"He's dead," said John. "He hanged himself that night . . . You know, Esli, I can't understand about him. I never took to him much. He seemed, somehow, to stand apart from the others. . . They say he took money from Caiaphas to tell him where The Master was going that night. . . But, if he was like that, why did The Master ever have him as one of his followers ? For if any man could see into men's hearts it was The Master. . . I can't understand it."

"Nor can I. He always seemed very keen about the Kingdom. But you're quite right, he was different from the others. . . I like Simon the best of them all."

"Yes. . . I like Simon," John said thoughtfully. Then up above us we heard a quiet hail from Simon himself.

But when we came up to him we knew that something had happened to him in there.

It was there The Master had been seized the other night. I thought at first that perhaps Simon had been thinking of it all again and feeling it.

But, as I stared at him, I was sure it was more than that. He had been joyously exultant as we came up the hill, but now he was very quiet. There was a new shy wonder in his eyes, and they shone as I had never seen them before. I had seen them sparkle and even flame at times, but I had never seen them like this.

And his rugged, bearded face had a new look upon it. It was gentler than usual, and yet, in some curious way, it seemed stronger, more quietly determined. There was a finer, loftier look on it, not unlike The Master's. Something had certainly happened to him in there.

He went on without speaking till we were on the crown of the hill and below us in the valley we saw Bethany, sitting among its gray-green olive groves like a bird on its nest.

"We will go to Bethany," said Simon.

As we went down the hill it all came out, in his own impetuous way. When his heart was full he must always share it with others.

"He came to me in there," he said quietly.

"The Master ?" jerked John, standing stock still in his excitement.

"Yes" — and Simon stood facing us, with that gracious new look in his face and eyes. "Three times, that night when he was taken, he bade us watch with him in there, and three times we fell asleep — "

John nodded.

"And that same night, down yonder, three times I — " and then, with sudden remembrance, he checked what he had been going to say, and said to John, "Ay — you were there and you know. But he has forgiven it all. It is all put away. I am his man now forever. . . Praise be to God !" and he led us on down the hill.

Lazarus saw us and came to meet us, and when he saw that look on Simon's face, he asked eagerly, "What is it, Simon ? What has happened ?"

"Call Martha and Mary," said Simon, but they had heard us and were with us in a moment. And their first words were the same, "What is it, Simon ?"

The faces of all three lit up with a look of hopeful expectancy, though the shadow of their loss was still in their eyes.

"We have seen The Master," said Simon, and even his voice, as he said it, seemed new to me. "He has been with us. He has spoken with us. He has eaten with us . . . and not an hour ago, up there in the Garden on Olivet he came to me and talked with me."

Lazarus sank down on a bench. "I knew he would come back," he said. "For he is Life and the Giver of Life."

"God be praised !" said Martha fervently.

And Mary, clasping her hands, cried, "Oh that we might see him once again — if but for a moment !"

And, even as she spoke, the sunlight in the doorway wavered and The Master himself was with us.

We all fell on our knees, and gazed at him, speechless with joy and amazement.

"Peace be with you !" he said gently. "You are very dear to me, for you have loved me more than most. . . You know my will for the world. Carry on my work to the end ! . . . And, remember always — though you may not see me I am near you, nearer than I have ever been, nearer than life, nearer than death, to help you and comfort you. . . Martha, I would taste your bread once more."

Martha jumped up in joyous haste and came back with a plate full of her little unleavened cakes.

The Master took one and broke it, and said, "In the breaking of bread give thanks, and hold me always in remembrance !" — and then he ate of the bread and gave some to each of us.

Then he lifted his wounded hands above us and we bowed our heads to receive his blessing.

"My peace I leave with you, and the blessing of Him who is My Father and your Father !"

And when we dared to raise our heads he was not to be seen. But he was in our hearts forever.

Many others of his friends he visited in those days. And of some of those visitations we heard, but many were treasured in lonely hearts for their joy and consolation in the days of their distress.

That The Master visited his mother I am certain, though I never had any actual word of it. When I asked John about it he said, "Of course ! Could you imagine him not doing so ? But we heard very little about it. . . You see, she is living in great seclusion. I think her heart broke when she saw him there on the cross, and she has never got over it. I am sure he would do all he could to comfort her."

And I was sure of that too, for in all things he was perfect, and the love between him and his mother was what you would have expected, though she understood him as little as the rest of us.

For at that time, in spite of all that had happened, and of all that he had tried so hard to impress upon us, we still had the hope of an earthly kingdom over which in some marvellous way he would rule as Lord and Master.

CHAPTER LI

As soon as the Feast was over, Simon and the rest of us set out at once for our own country. Jerusalem and everything about it — except the friendly little household at Bethany — was abhorrent to us. And The Master had said he would meet us in Galilee.

Only John-ben-Zabdai and The Master's mother remained. They would follow by easy stages as soon as she was fit for the journey.

As we walked I was much in Simon's company, and learned many things from him. I had always liked him more than any of the others, and that morning we had spent together up by the Olive Orchard and at Bethany seemed to have made a new link between us.

One of the things he told me was that The Master had come to them again in that upper room in John's mother's house, when they were all there together, and had impressed upon them once more all that he desired them to do.

The first time he came to them, Thomas, the Twin, had not been there, and when he was told about it he flatly refused to believe it — which was just Thomas all over. He was always for testing and proving things, which is right enough unless it is carried to excess.

But The Master had gently reproved him — had made him feel for himself the wounds in his hands and feet and side, and had told him that to have faith and believe was better than to know.

Simon also told me a thing which touched me deeply.

That night when The Master was arrested, they had all had supper together in that same room. And as they were arranging their places at the table, there had been some dispute on the part of some of them as to where they should sit.

The Master had watched them with sadness in his face, and then he got up quietly, laid aside his upper robes, girded himself with a towel, and set to work, like a slave, washing their feet.

It was that that appealed to me so. How often I had washed his shapely feet and been made happy by his quiet word of thanks !

That lesson — of service to others and not of thought of themselves — was one they would never forget.

Many other things Simon spoke about when we found ourselves alongside one another, for he found in me an eager listener, and he knew that The Master had been the greatest and best and dearest thing in my life.

And through this much talking, in which his heart and mind were opened to me, I came to a still better understanding of the new Simon and a still greater liking for him — and so to some higher comprehension of The Master and his work, and his hopes and wishes.

Many of the others still had hopes of a Kingdom founded on the shaking off of the yoke of Rome. The marvel of The Master's return after his death had encouraged these hopes. For they believed that to one who could conquer Death the conquering of Rome would be a simple matter.

But Simon had at last got beyond all that. He said, "That would be great, Esli. But The Master's aim is very much greater. His Kingdom is to be God's will in the hearts of men all over the world. . ."

"That is what Zerah says. I think she knows his mind better than anyone, Simon. . . And she says that he is, beyond a doubt, the veritable son of The Highest. She does not understand it, but she believes it because he himself told her so."

"When we get back I shall go up there and talk with her. She may know more than any of us. But I, too, believe that

The Master is the son of The Highest. And that is why he was what he was and could do the things he did."

I think he told me most that was in his heart as we walked together during those three days.

Except one thing, and that was a thing no man would be likely to tell about himself. But John Marcus told me that, and much besides, later on.

Loving Simon as I did, it was not easy to believe it of him. But John had been there and heard and saw it all, and it just shows how any man, taken unawares, may be suddenly knocked over by the Devil, just as Ruth and I had been capsized in our boat on the lake that day.

It was on the night The Master was dragged before the High Priest. John had crept in among the Temple guards, and to his surprise Simon had got in also. Some of the High Priest's people taxed Simon with being one of the followers of the Nazarene, as they called The Master. And Simon, taken aback, had denied any knowledge of him, and had even backed up his denial with curses. And, in the thick of all his own trouble, The Master had heard him and turned and looked sorrowfully at him, and Simon had rushed blindly out into the night.

It was that that made Simon stop short and look at John, that day on Olivet, and say, "Ay, you were there and you know. — But it is all forgiven."

And I think The Master and he had talked it all out up there, and it was his mighty sense of The Master's forgiveness that had made such a change in him.

CHAPTER LII

THE GREAT PLAIN was more radiantly beautiful, with its springing crops and many-coloured flowers, and the glint and glimmer of its innumerable streams, than I had ever seen it.

Perhaps there was that within us that opened our hearts and our minds to it all. For we were leaving behind us the terrible and sorrowful things. We were remembering only that The Master was with us again. We were looking hopefully to meeting him in our own country, as he had promised.

We were returning home like conquerors after a great fight. . . And some of us saw, though but dimly as yet, that what lay before us was not what we had so long hoped for but was something infinitely higher and greater.

When at last we climbed round the shoulder of Tabor, and caught sight of our own blue lake, we quickened our steps and were soon at Kaphar-Nahum.

Simon stopped there with his own people. Nathaniel had already struck off across the hills for Cana. Philip and I went on along the white shore of the lake to Bethsaida. He was rejoicing at thought of seeing Zillah and the children again, and I was full of the thought of seeing Ruth.

She saw me coming, as she always did, while we were still a long way off, and came running to meet me. I think — like the father in The Master's story — she was always on the look-out for the return of her wanderer. Her face was alight and her hands outstretched, and she flung her arms round my neck, laughing and crying all at the same time.

Philip greeted her warmly and told her she ran like a gazelle, and then went on.

"I have watched for you every day since you went, my beloved," she panted, as I kissed her again and again. "I knew you would come at last and my heart is glad. But what terrible, terrible things have happened down there !"

"All is well, Ruth — "

"But The Master — "

"He is with us again — "

"Esli !" and she held herself off to stare at me. . . "We heard they had killed him . . . by the cross," she said, with a shudder.

"Yes, all that. But though they killed him they could not hold him. Many of us have seen him. I have eaten with him, so have many others. And he has promised to meet us all here."

"I cannot take it all in, Esli," she faltered. "It is too amazing. Do you understand it all ?"

"No. It is beyond our understanding — or anyone's — except The Master's. But we have seen and we know . . . Zerah would say it is better to believe even than to see."

"I would like to hear all that Zerah can tell us about it all."

"We will go up to Nazaret one day and see them there."

When we came up to the house, my father met us with a dry unpleasant smile and — "So you're back ! And your Wonder-Worker has come to his end — on the cross !"

"He is alive and more wonderful than ever," I said quietly.

"Somebody's lying then."

"The priests are trying to lie it away. But they can't. The Master is with us again. I have eaten with him."

He stared hard at me. "You are all quite mad," he said, and turned away. Ruth's mother said nothing but was evidently of the same mind.

During those first days at home I made myself of some use in fishing. For I found Simon busy in his boat the very next evening and he was glad of my help.

He never could sit long doing nothing, and he said that handling the ropes and nets helped him to think and to wait.

But all the spare time we had — and Ruth's mother saw to it that it was not too much — we spent sitting by the lakeside while I told Ruth all I could of what had happened since we parted.

She shuddered and wept over the story of The Master's sufferings. "How could they ? How could they ?" she sobbed.

And one time she asked me, as was surely natural — "And what will you do now, Esli ?"

"I have been thinking much of that, Ruth," I said. "Simon says The Master will tell us what he wants us to do, and we must wait."

She sighed and said nothing, but I understood.

"We shall soon know. Simon is bursting with the desire to go and tell everybody about The Master, and his New Way, and all the wonder of him."

"Simon is getting old . . . and we are young."

"I cannot hope to do as much as Simon and James and John and the rest, but I must do what I can. . . If I can only even bring some round here to The Master's Way it will be something. And he has done so much for us, you know."

"I never forget," she said softly. "For every step I take I thank him. . . And there is to be no New Kingdom, Esli ?"

"Not as we looked for it — though some of them still hope for it" — and as well as I could, I made clear to her Simon's idea of what The Master wanted of us all and of all the world.

We managed at last with some difficulty to arrange matters so that we could make the journey to Nazaret to see Zerah and Azor.

We started as the sun came up over the eastern mountains, and struck right up into our own hills, by that same path

on which Philip and Nathaniel had met when they set out
to seek one another.

It was a long day's journey. But the sun was bright, the
air was clean and fresh, we had cakes and dates sufficient
for two meals in a bag over my shoulder, we were up above
the world, and we were young and our hearts were full of
hope.

Never had either of us enjoyed a walk so much. For just
to think of my little Ruth as she had been until less than a
year ago, and to see her tripping along by my side with a
step so light and springy that it was almost a dance, was
enough to fill me with great gladness.

We reached Nazaret before sunset, and Zerah and Zoe
and Azor's mother, Miriam, gave us very warm welcome.

But when I asked for Azor, Zerah said, "He is away to
Kaphar-Nahum with Jesus's Mother. She is to live with
John-ben-Zabdai, who brought her here some days ago, but
she wished to spend a few days in her old home first. They
started early this morning, and young John Marcus and his
Roman friend Claudius Flaccus went with them."

Zerah was always bright and happy, but she seemed unusually so now, and that explained itself as soon as our greetings were over.

"Jesus has been here himself," she said — quietly, but with
all the wonder and joy of it very visible in her eyes and face.

Ruth was startled, and gazed at her wide-eyed.

"I was sure he would come to you, Zerah," I said. "All
his friends are still very dear to him; and you, I know, he
held dearest of all. He came to Lazarus and his sisters
when I was there with Simon and John Marcus. It is very
wonderful. It is making new men of us all."

"Yes. . . That is what he came for — to make new men
of us all," she said, in that full sweet voice of hers which put
deeper meaning into words than anyone's except The
Master's.

As we sat in the workshop after supper, with the moonlight bathing the hills and all the countryside in a new

soft tenderness, she told us much about The Master and the gracious simplicity of his life up there in Nazaret.

She always spoke of him as "Jesus," and the tone in which she said his name told more of her love and reverence for him than all the words in the world could have done.

I asked her at last what she thought he would have me do now. "Simon and most of the others," I said, "want to go out and tell everybody about him. But I don't believe I would be much good at that. I followed him and served him as well as I could because he had done so much for Ruth and me, and because I loved him — him himself, you understand. But now . . ."

"It must have been a joy to serve him, Esli — a joy that will abide with you forever. You will never forget it, nor will he."

And, after thinking awhile, she said, "Azor had to face just that same question; and one day when we were up on the hill above Nain, Jesus and Azor and young John and I — it was the day he gave Arni back to his mother when he had been dead — he told us of himself and why his Father, God, had sent him into the world. We were almost beside ourselves with the wonder of it all, and we begged him to let us go with him and give ourselves to his work. And I remember just what he said —

" 'Your work lies to your hand in the home and beyond it. In it you can follow me as truly as if you trod the path I tread. . .' And he said, 'Strive to think of your fellows as our Father thinks of them. You know me and my way of thinking, think of them as you know I would think of them, and do to them as you know I would do. And teach men so !' "

Ruth, on the other side of Zerah, gave a sigh of great relief and content, and put up her arm round Zerah's neck and drew herself up and kissed her.

Zerah smiled understandingly as she bent and kissed her, and said, "You will be very happy, for you both know and love him and will try to serve him."

[294]

CHAPTER LIII

IT WAS almost night when we reached home, for the journey back had been even more joyous than the journey there, and we had dallied so as to prolong it.

Our father and mother had nothing to say to us. They simply let us feel that we were outside the pale and more or less out of our minds.

And when, after we had eaten, I said we were going to marry at once, my father said contemptuously, "And live on fish ?"

"We shall live very well on fish," I said.

Next morning I was setting off for Simon's boat, carrying a net we had been repairing, when Philip overtook me.

I thought he looked at me curiously, and then he asked, "Aren't you going to the hill, Esli ?"

"What hill, Philip ? — and why ?"

He seemed surprised. "Did your father not tell you ? I left Simon's word for you with him last night. The Master has bidden us all meet him at the round hill back of Tiberias this morning — "

I dropped the heavy net and ran back to the house, calling "Ruth ! Ruth !" — and when she looked out I caught her by the hand and explained as we ran.

"Never mind the work," I jerked. "We'll see to that later. . . The Master first."

We caught up with Philip and hastened on, and presently found many others going the same way.

The round hill was well known, for The Master had often sat there and spoken to the people, and when we got there we found a crowd of several hundreds, and all their faces were full of wonder and great expectancy.

[295]

Many were known to us. Philip went on to look for Simon and the others. We sat and waited. Ruth's little hand throbbed and trembled violently in mine.

And suddenly there was a hush and a great silence fell upon us all, a silence so intense that when a pair of sparrows flew past over our heads we could hear the beat of their small wings. For there, up above us, on the little level place where he had so often sat, was The Master himself, talking earnestly with his chosen ones.

Every eye was strained upon him with intensest eagerness. We were witnesses of a wonder beyond nature or human understanding. We scarce dared breathe lest with our next breath he should be no longer there.

He looked as we had known him at his best amongst us, and yet — different. Perhaps my knowledge of all he had passed through coloured my own thought of him, but I know that others felt the same.

Different — changed — but, though I felt it intensely, it is very difficult to convey any idea of it in words.

He looked taller, nobler, more than ever like a King, a Conqueror; and yet it was his own simple, loving, kindly self — with that great something added. To me, it was as though a radiant light burned within him, and shone out from him, and touched with its glow whoever looked at him.

He sat down on the ledge, just as he used to do, and spoke to us. He spoke as a Master of Men, yet as a wise and loving brother to his much-loved brothers and sisters. And that wonderful voice of his, richer and sweeter and fuller than ever, went right to our hearts, and set them leaping, and drew them to him.

And his eyes dwelt lovingly on each one of us in turn; keen as an eagle's they were, but full of tenderest love and the desire for our love in return.

He looked at Ruth and me, and we knew that he was thinking of us and sending us his blessing, and it was the same with everyone.

He told us that the time was almost come when he must

leave us to go back to his Father in heaven who was also our Father. He promised that when he went he would send us a Helper to cheer and comfort us. He warned us that trials would await us, but that those who held true to him would have their reward with him in heaven. But while we were here we were to do our best to follow his teaching — to serve God and our fellows — to do in all things as we believed he would have done. All that we knew of him and his New Way we were to teach to all those about us and in all other places, so that in time all the world should come to know and follow him.

And he promised to be always with us, right to the end.

Then he stood up and lifted his hands to bless us, and as I bowed my head I saw once more the scars of the wounds the nails had made — and everyone else saw them too.

"Peace I leave with you," he said. "My peace I give unto you. Let not your hearts be troubled. Believe in me! Believe in my Father! And we will come and dwell with you."

And when we dared to raise our heads he was gone.

Very quietly, and filled with awe and reverence, the crowd began to disperse. That we had seen and heard would never be forgotten by any one of us, and we went in silence.

As Ruth and I went down the hill, hand in hand, we came suddenly on a man lying prostrate and shaking with sobs. He must have been quite on the outer edge of the crowd.

It was Ruth's startled tightening of her grip on my hand that made me stop.

Then I fell on my knees by the prostrate one and put my arm over his shoulder.

For here was one more marvel. It was my father.

He lifted his head slowly and there was a scared look in his face.

"I thought it was himself!" he gasped. "I have seen him! . . . I have seen him! And I thought it was himself!"

"Perhaps he sent us in his place," I said softly.

"He looked at *me!*" he said, in an awed whisper. "He spoke to *me!* . . . It was himself! . . . I must go and tell Leah!" and he got heavily up onto his feet.

He swayed dizzily as if it had been too much for him.

"We will go together," I said, and took his shaking arm inside my own.

And so, with him between us, we set off home. And every now and again I heard him whisper to himself —

"Himself! . . . Himself! . . . and he spoke to *me!* . . . He looked at *me!*"

Our hearts were full of wonder and awe and thankfulness.

We had been with The Master.

Works by John Oxenham

THE HIDDEN YEARS
THE STORY OF THE BOYHOOD OF JESUS

5s. net.

ILLUSTRATED EDITION. With 14 Coloured Plates
by MARGARET W. TARRANT. 7s. 6d. net.

ANNO DOMINI
THE STORY OF THE MASTER'S WORKING YEARS

6s. net.

THE SPLENDOUR OF THE DAWN
*THE STORY OF THE TIMES WHICH CAME
IMMEDIATELY AFTER THE CRUCIFIXION*

5s. net.

GOD'S CANDLE
With Frontispiece. Crown 8vo.
Paper covers, 2s. 6d. net ; cloth, 4s. net.

*A study of the reaction of certain well-known, yet very little-known
characters to the Crucifixion—the Centurion, Mary Magdalene,
Judas Iscariot, Barabbas.*

CROSS-ROADS
1s. net.

*The story of four strange occasions on which the paths of Dysmas and
The Master crossed one another.*

THE CEDAR BOX
With Frontispiece from a drawing by T. BAINES.
Japon paper, 1s. 6d. net ; cloth gilt, 2s. 6d. net.

*This is a story of the present day woven round the history of a
beautifully worked box, which, tradition states, was made by Christ
when a boy, as a present for His Mother.*

Works by John Oxenham

A SAINT IN THE MAKING

From the Valley of the Singing Blackbird to St. Peter's, Rome

(THE STORY OF THE CURÉ D'ARS)

5s. net.

THE MAN WHO WOULD SAVE THE WORLD

STORY OF A SUPREME ADVENTURE

A story which aims at pointing out the only sure way out of the chaos to which the world is drifting.

Paper covers, 1s. net ; cloth, 4s. 6d. net.

THE WONDER OF LOURDES

WHAT IT IS AND WHAT IT MEANS

With 16 Illustrations.   F'cap 8vo.

Paper covers, 1s. 6d. net ; cloth, 2s. 6d. net.

This work describes the effect of a visit to Lourdes upon the mind of a non-Catholic.

NOVELS

THE HAWK OF COMO

3s. 6d. net.

THE RECOLLECTIONS OF RODERIC FYFE

3s. 6d. net.

MY LADY OF THE MOOR

2s. 6d. net.